BETH CONNOR

Bridge of Blood and Thorns

The Isdralan Chronicles

WOLF GROVE MEDIA
LLC.

For my daughter, whose journey has revealed true strength: overcoming obstacles, embracing who you are, and dreaming boldly. This book reflects the resilience and indomitable spirit you embody. Your courage and grace light the way, sparking inspiration in everyone and everything you touch. May your journey continue to shine.

Contents

The Facade of Power

The icy chill of the marbled floor bit into Durya's bare feet, sending shivers up her spine as she stood naked and exposed in the heart of the grand hall. Here, the air shimmered with an otherworldly light, casting an strange glow over the assembly. A sea of human faces surrounded her—alabaster, olive, and deep browns—each sculpted with the sharp, aristocratic lines of highborn lineage. Their eyes bore into her very soul with a force that threatened to unravel her.

These people, judging, surveyed her with their curiosity. Stares, unwavering, flitted over the bluish-gray tint of her skin, taking in every inch, from her proud stature to the tusks that protruded from her lips.

In the hushed whispers, her ears strained to catch words she could not hear, but the sentiment was clear, "*Why is she here? She doesn't belong.*"

Desperation surged. She tried to speak, to stake her claim, to shout down the doubt that threatened to suffocate her, but no sound emerged.

From the masses, a shadow surfaced. Faceless, foreboding,

it advanced towards her. It's very presence amplifying the gnawing insecurity that had taken root. She longed to scream, to let out a primal roar in defiance but her voice was elusive. Each step the phantom took seemed to taunt with whispers of *fraud* and *imposter* echoing in its stride.

As the silence engulfed her, the utterance of a familiar name broke through: *Edward*.

* * *

In the morning light, the vividness of the dream clung to Durya. The room around her came into focus, but the raw feelings evoked – the scrutiny, the doubt, the challenge to her worth – were etched in her heart.

As the first rays crept into Lady Durya's chamber, the air played through the gaps in the curtains. Even amidst the luxury that surrounded her, there was a weariness. The grandeur of the room seemed to reflect her station more than her spirit.

She rose from the lavish bed, her skin caught the ambient light amplifying its color. The slight protrusion of her tusks from beneath her lips gave her an imposing appearance, but her violet eyes held a glint of vulnerability.

As the door inched open, two young maids entered with practiced caution. Ella, the shorter one, had curly auburn hair sprinkled with freckles, while Liana stood taller, her raven-black hair contrasting against her cream colored skin. Their matching simple dresses, denoted their subservient roles.

"Ella," Lady Durya's voice cut through the air, sharp and icy,

"Where is the pearl comb?"

Ella's eyes widened, "I... I thought I had placed it with the rest, my lady."

"I have it, my Lady,"Liana, eager to deflect attention, intervened as she produced the comb and began attending to Durya's hair.

Durya molded her expression into one of condensation as she observed Ella."There are countless girls who'd give anything to be in your position," she warned. But as she studied Ella's face, something softened. The freckles, the shade of the hair—there was a fleeting resemblance to Kaci. That lingering tenderness led her to add, albeit more gently, "Do be more careful in the future."

Ella gave a nod as she arranged the layers of Durya's dress. The gown showcased exceptional craftsmanship. The style drew attention to curves and a graceful form, qualities revered in human fashion. However, it sat differently on Durya's muscular frame. Her build, inherited from her orcish heritage, emphasized the poor fit of the corset. Ella's fingers trembled as she adjusted the bodice, trying to align it with Durya's awkward shape.

Meanwhile, Liana was meticulous as she wove pearls into Durya's hair. The task was challenging. Noble hairstyles were designed for softer, more pliable strands, not the coarse, thick locks characteristic of orcish lineage. When her hand faltered as she neared Durya's tusks. Durya remarked, "Hesitation does not befit your station, Liana."

Liana lowered her head, chastised, murmuring, "Forgive me, my lady."

With one last look in the ornate mirror, Lady Durya, every bit the ruler, moved to leave the room. Her very aura demanded respect and fear, and she made sure she was both revered and dreaded. The girls exchanged a look, relief in their eyes, their daily dance with the lady having ended, at least for the morning.

When Lady Durya emerged from her chambers. Every detail of her attire was immaculate, from the pearls in her hair to the regal train of the dress that trailed behind.

The grand corridor leading to Her husband, Edward's, chambers was busy with the morning hustle. Courtiers gossiped, and maids and servants darted back and forth. Everyone made way for Lady Durya. She was the epicenter, and the manor's inhabitants orbited around her, some with awe, others with envy.

As she arrived at Edward's room, she was met by two goblin attendants. In Elyndris, goblins were stereotyped as sneaky and untrustworthy. Usually, they were relegated to menial tasks where 'valuable items' were far from reach. This stigma painted them as creatures of deceit and thievery.

The strange guards stood sentinel outside, their green skin standing out and their sharp faces twisted in perpetual sneers. Grig merely nodded, and Grolf managed a curt, "My Lady."

She responded with a nod. She had chosen goblins who weren't fluent in the common tongue to ensure discretion. This decision was a tactical one, a subtle defiance of the court's traditional views.

Their presence in such a high-status position was a topic of whispered debate and hidden scorn. It was believed that Edward's eccentricities had brought them to this unlikely role. However, beneath the surface lay a different truth.

As Durya reached for the massive oak door to enter her husband's chambers, her mind wandered. The whispers and hushed conversations of the courtiers were like a distant hum, but she picked up fragments. "Edward..." "Poor health..." "A year now..." The rumor mill was both a threat and a tool. The longer Edward's condition remained mysterious, the more speculation would grow. She had to stay ahead of it, control it.

A young page, all of about twelve years, ran past her, colliding with a vase. She caught his eye, and he paused, swallowing hard. The fear in his eyes wasn't new to Durya, humans were rarely comfortable around orcs. But she moved on, reminding herself that this, too, was part of the facade.

She reflected on the goblins' quick exchange. Though they spoke little, she knew their loyalty was absolute. At Edward's door, they were more than symbolic - they were a line of defense. These comforts steeled her.

As she entered, Lady Durya's mind wandered, finding itself on the voyage across the Golden Strait. This bustling waterway was an artery for trade and travel and was notorious for its mercurial temperament.

The rhythmic lull of the ocean, and the distant call of the gulls, had been a backdrop to that journey she had both longed for and dreaded. Navigating the strait was a double-edged sword. On one hand, it offered the most direct and expedient route. On the other, it was plagued by unpredictabilities: sudden violent storms that could arise without warning, turning the sea into a tempestuous beast, and the ever-looming threat of pirates lurking in the shadows, ready to pounce on unwary travelers.

She wanted to travel. She had yearned for the warm embrace of her foster parents, the only semblance of family she had ever known. But then, there was Edward, and human like her family. Imperious Edward with his dark moods and darker intentions. Their union was born from political pragmatism; her esteemed social standing was the jewel he wanted in his crown. He had cloaked his greed in matrimonial garb, but beneath the façade, his cruelty thrived, casting its shadow over every shared moment.

Within the ship's confines, she had felt a sense of claustrophobia, trapped not only with a man she loathed but also the unpredictable dangers of the sea. It was here that she had made her resolution. The vial had been discreet, its contents fatal. As she watched the life drain from Edward's eyes, her heart was a battleground of emotions—relief, remorse, and a potent yearning for liberation.

There was no naivety in her actions. Durya had been aware of the magnitude of her decision, knowing that retribution could await her on the horizon. For that fleeting moment, she had felt more free than in all her time under Edward's shadow. She was ready for whatever fate the universe deemed fit for her, even if it was execution.

But the seas, vast and unpredictable, had their own plans. With a violent upheaval, the ship had been consigned to a watery grave, its secrets and sins submerged in the abyss. Durya had emerged, reborn from the wreckage, her actions a solitary anchor in an expanse of emptiness.

She had not planned on surviving, but she did. This trail of events brought her Kaci. Kaci was a beacon of light. The Aelorians, from which she hailed, were known for their reserved demeanor. They had a grace and their society full of ancient traditions and connection to the mystical elements.

But Kaci was none of these things. Her fiery red hair was often untamed, and her freckles danced across her face like constellations. Everything about her spoke of a spirit that deviated from the usual composure of her people. Kaci displayed a brightness and an awkward enthusiasm that was both endearing and unusual.

Beyond Marcus and the ever-loyal Sharn, it was Kaci to whom Durya had extended the hand of friendship. And in a quiet moment, under the bright blue skies of Isdralan, she had whispered to Kaci the dark secrets of that ill-fated voyage. It was a confession that had solidified their bond, as profound and fathomless as the ocean itself. Kaci's laughter, unbridled and infectious, was a balm to Durya's soul. Edward had died by her hand.

Reality snapped her back into the present. Her friend was not here, and she needed to be strong and focused. Durya steeled herself as she entered the room. Like many noble couples of their era, Lady Durya and Edward had maintained separate sleeping chambers. This was a tradition that now resonated with a more somber meaning.

Despite his passing, Lady Durya upheld the illusion of his presence, especially prominent in his personal chamber. His space featured an ornate mirror, an object Edward had cherished. Durya had always been perplexed by his fondness for this mirror, often speculating about his reasons for transporting it to each of their residences.

Also in the room was a grand bed. Upon it lay an intricate arrangement. It was a mannequin crafted to imitate the human form, cloaked in luxurious silks and brocades. It gave an semblance of a resting figure, imitating the nobleman who once occupied the room.

The reason behind Lady Durya's charade was rooted in the harsh realities of her position. As an orc and a woman, she faced the prospect that her authority would be diminished, or worse, outright dismissed in the patriarchal and species-biased society.

The mirror, now an observer of her feigned dialogues with her late husband, was an integral part of the rooms ambiance. In this theater, she crafted the facade of continuing to receive Edward's guidance, a strategic ploy to sustain her influence and command respect in a world reluctant to accept her leadership on its own merits.

When the door latched behind her, the chamber transformed into her stage. Approaching the bed, she paused beside the effigy, her opening act suggesting a communion with the ersatz Edward.

Moments later, she moved to a nearby chair, drawing from her satchel an assortment of scrolls. Clearing her throat, she began, "Regarding the Barony of Larkspire, the annual tariffs shall be increased by a tenth, as per the recommendations of the council. Furthermore, the land disputes between the families of Harrow and Everwick are to be settled no later than the coming fortnight..."

Durya's voice wove through clauses, edicts, and decrees, creating the ambiance of a ruler consulting her sovereign. She'd pause, directing a look towards the faux baron, her eyes narrowing as if deciphering whispered counsel.

This theater continued for over an hour. At intervals, she'd nod or offer a soft murmur of acknowledgment.

Concluding the 'deliberations', Lady Durya placed Edwards' seal where necessary. With her tasks completed, she stood beside the mannequin, whispering words of feigned appreciation for Edward's invaluable 'advice'. This charade was sealed with a gentle touch, a tribute to the illusion she so masterfully upheld.

With a glance toward the bed and the loathed mirror, Lady Durya left. The instant the door swung open, a gaggle of advisors and nobles descended, oblivious to the performance she had just concluded.

"My Lady, what has the Baron decreed regarding the tariffs?" inquired Lord Hensworth, a rotund man with a penchant for fine wines and finer details. His voice, seasoned with a tone of reasonableness and prudence, often marked him as a stabilizing force in the volatile political climate of the court.

"And the matter of the disputed lands? The families await word," added Lady Elara, a young noblewoman with mouse brown hair. She was ambitious, a fresh energy in the court's politics and eager to prove her mettle.

Lady Durya raised a hand, silencing them. "We shall discuss all in the council chamber." The throng cleared a path for her, the sway she held evident in the reverence and wariness with which they treated her.

As they made their way through the grand corridors, Lady Durya's noticed that Sharn was stationed as a guard amongst the ranks of human sentinels. Their eyes connected for a fraction of a second, and his lips curled in a secret smile.

With entourage behind her, she entered the council chamber. It was a vast room with high ceilings and intricate tapestries depicting historic events. There was a large circular table that resided at the center and she moved to its head. To her left sat her brother, Marcus who was raised by the same foster parents.

"My Lords, Ladies," she began. "Lord Edward, in his infinite wisdom, has rendered his judgments on the matters you presented." Her words, carefully chosen, resonated with the unspoken understanding that she was the voice behind the barony. It was a fact that some acknowledged with respect, while others with veiled envy.

With a wave of her hand, she beckoned a scribe forward, ready to disseminate the baron's 'decisions'. The room hung on her every word, a skill with which she used to er advantage, the realm none the wiser to the secret she held so close.

"On the tariffs," she began, her gaze scanning the assembly, "Lord Edward believes it prudent to increase them by a modest five percent. This is to further our barony's prosperity and to ensure the well-being of our subjects." Lord Hensworth, his brow furrowed, gave a slight nod. The decision, while not entirely favorable to his commercial interests, was one he could understand and respect.

Lady Elara leaned forward, her sharp mind analyzing the implications on her family's lands and the broader economic landscape of the barony.

"As for the disputed lands," Lady Durya spoke, "A demarcation team will be sent to make a final assessment. Until then, both families are urged to maintain peace and hold off on any further territorial expansions."

Lord Redmont, a middle-aged man with a well-groomed beard and a sour reputation, interrupted. "My Lady, with all due respect to Baron Edward, wouldn't it be more advantageous to give the lands to the family who offers more to the barony's treasury?"

Lady Durya's icy gaze met his, silencing the undercurrent of murmurs that his question had stirred. "Lord Redmont," her tone was sharp and cutting, "Baron Edward believes in justice and fairness. The barony's treasury will not be swayed by short-term gains at the expense of our people's harmony. Your suggestion is noted, but shall not be entertained."

The room went silent. Lord Redmont's face reddened. No one dared challenge Lady Durya after such a rebuke. The other nobles exchanged glances, some with a sense of relief, others with a renewed awareness of the lady's unwavering commitment to Westerfield. While the title might have read 'Baron Edward,' the real power lay in her hands.

As the discussion progressed, Lady Durya's gaze drifted towards the back of the chamber. Her eyes locked with Sharn's. The half-orc, half-human guard, stood tall, his duty paramount, yet in his face, there was a warmth, a promise of understanding. Their brief connection, a solace amid political storm.

The meeting continued with various matters of the state being discussed, decrees read out, and suggestions made and Lady Durya presided with an air of regal authority. This was her domain, and she ruled with both an iron fist and a keen mind.

At the meetings conclusion, Lady Durya took her leave. Yet, her day was far from over. Status demanded a series of scheduled engagements that ranged from overseeing the preparations of the feast to ensuring the welfare of her subjects.

That evening, she took her place at the head of the grand dining table. With golden candelabras casting shadows on ornate tapestries, the scene was a celebration of wealth and influence. Every dish served was a culinary masterpiece, tantalizing the senses of esteemed guests.

Lord Redmont, however, was not to be outdone in terms of presence. Seated with a strategic view of the entire hall, his eyes darted from one face to another. As a lull in the conversation ensued, he seized his moment, raising his glass.

"To our esteemed Lady Durya," he began with a voice dripping in honeyed insincerity, "How wondrous it is that even one with... orcish blood can appreciate such fine human delicacies."

Murmurs filled the room. The implication was clear: in Lord Redmond's eyes, Lady Durya's heritage made her unfit to rule, regardless of her accomplishments or her union with Edward.

Lady Durya's brother, Marcus, had to restrain himself. He clenched his goblet so hard it threatened to crack. Despite being a hero alongside his sister, Marcus too had felt the sting of human prejudice. They had fought valiantly against the shadows during the rift that had happened last year, but gratitude was short-lived and memories were selective.

"To shared blood and shared battles. May we remember it is unity, not division, that has always been our power." Lady Durya lifted her glass.

The guests toasted, albeit some more enthusiastically than others. As the evening wore on, Lord Redmont's veiled insults became the subject of hushed whispers. While the dinner had been a feast for the senses, a different sort of game was being played in the hall.

Through it all, Lady Durya remained the picture of grace and restraint. Her conversations were deliberate, her laughter measured. Each gesture and comment further solidified her image as a sovereign of the realm.

As the dinner drew to an end and the guests departed, Lady Durya made her way back to her chambers. Two young serving girls, including the redhead with freckles reminiscent of Kaci, awaited her arrival. They proceeded with the ritual of preparing her for bed—undoing the intricate braids, helping her out of her heavy robes, and laying out her nightgown.

Once dressed in her sleeping attire, Lady Durya sat by her vanity as one girl brushed her hair, the rhythmic strokes a soothing end to a long day. The other maid turned down the bed, fluffing pillows and ensuring the sheets were immaculate.

With a curt nod, Lady Durya dismissed the girls for the night. "Rest well," she said, her tone softer toward the redhead.

ONce she was sure they had vacated the room, she approached a mirror set into one corner of her chamber. With a precise press on the frame, it swung open like a door, revealing a concealed passageway. Cool air, tinged with the muskiness of undisturbed stone, wafted through.

With one last scan of the room, she stepped into the passage, pulling the hood of the cloak over her head. The walls of this secret corridor were lined with rough-hewn stone and torches were placed at intervals provided minimal light, creating flickering shadows that danced on the floor.

She navigated the passageway with ease. It branched in various directions, a deliberate design to confuse any who might stumble upon the path. After what felt like an eternity in the tunnels, a thin sliver of moonlight appeared ahead, indicating the exit that opened to a secluded alley within the city.

The Drowned Anchor, nestled by the docks, had always been a refuge for those seeking anonymity amidst the crowd. For Lady Durya, it had its own allure. Tonight, the sounds of laughter and clinking glasses dominated as the warm glow of the lanterns set the mood.

Durya entered the tavern, her hooded cloak concealing the details of her attire. Always keen and observant, she found Sharn seated in a secluded corner. As she approached, he looked up, their eyes meeting with the familiarity of a shared past.

She allowed her hood to fall back slightly, revealing her face. Their hands touched, a fleeting brush that carried the years gone by.

"Do you remember, Sharn?" she began, her voice soft and

nostalgic. "The days in Marshfield, the clatter of wooden swords, and the thrill of our secret duels?"

Sharn chuckled. "Of course. You, so fierce and determined, challenging every boy and standing your ground. Even back then, you possessed the heart of a warrior."

With mischief in her eyes, Lady Durya remarked, "Until Lady Evelyn saw it fit to groom me for a world of ballrooms and ballads. And though I revel in it all, I often yearn for those unfettered days."

As the night matured, their tales flowed, punctuated by stolen glances and unspoken words. Yet, the imminent parting hovered like a shadow over their mirth.

Sharn, his rugged face softened by the candor, brushed her hand with his fingers. "You know, Durya, if you wish to, we can relive those days. The courtyard at dawn, perhaps? Wooden swords in hand? I will go easy on you."

A playful smirk danced on her lips. "Are you suggesting I've lost my touch, Sharn?"

"Wouldn't dream of it," he chuckled, "but maybe, just maybe, I've gotten better."

Their laughter filled the space, casting away her title, even if just for a moment. As she wrapped her cloak around her, preparing to step into the night, she sent Sharn a look, full of promise and shared understanding. Outside, the world lay burdened with its duties and facades, yet within the sequestered tavern near the docks, for a fleeting instant, Baroness Durya Barclay-Conwyn, found herself as just Durya once more.

2

Secrets

Golden rays streamed through the stained glass windows of the courtroom, splattering a kaleidoscope of colors on the marble floors. Sunlit patterns danced and intertwined, creating a radiant backdrop to the hall's proceedings.

At the room's zenith, upon a dais, stood a throne carved with intricate designs. It represented the legacy and history of the barony. Seated on this throne, Durya presided with an elegance that belied her strength. Her demeanor exuded calm and regality, her every gesture calculated.

On either side of the aisle, rows of decorated seats were occupied by the nobility. Each one waited patiently, or impatiently sometimes, for their moment to address the barony. Subjects, from wealthy merchants to humble farmers, all gathered, hoping to have their concerns acknowledged by their leader. The air, though filled with the murmur of whispered conversations, was thick with anticipation.

The grandeur of the court, with its gilded decor, could not mask the simmering unease beneath its surface. Hushed conversations, concealed behind feathered fans, carried more than just idle gossip. Here a giggle, there a sly smirk. The courtiers were adept at their games of subtlety.

In this tapestry of politics and power, many nobles bowed their heads in genuine respect for Lady Durya. Lord Redmont, with his sharp features and meticulously groomed beard, was a magnet for a certain faction. Whenever he spoke, even in whispers, heads would lean in, and eyes would dart in his direction, eager to catch every word. The sway he held was unmistakable.

Durya noted these dynamics, cataloging each glance and whispered word. Yet her poise never wavered. She was calm in the shifting sands, even if the tide turned towards Redmont.

The courtroom's murmurings reached a momentary lull as a lesser noble, Sir Eldric, stood up to address the assembly. Dressed in modest finery, Sir Eldric cleared his throat, but rather than directing his gaze towards the throne where Durya sat, he turned toward Redmont.

"Lord Redmont," he began, a note of undue respect in his voice, "I come before you with a matter of land that borders two estates. There is a boundary dispute."

The room was charged with tension. Nobles exchanged glances, waiting to see how this blatant disregard for protocol would unfold.

Lord Redmont, soaking in the attention, leaned back in his chair, stroking his beard. "Sir Eldric, it is curious that you'd seek my counsel at Lady Durya's court. But continue. I'm intrigued."

Sir Eldric, encouraged by Redmont's response, went on, elaborating on specifics, all the while ignoring the rightful ruler seated only a few feet away.

Throughout the exchange, Durya's expression remained

inscrutable. Her deep-set violet eyes, however, held a glint of icy determination. "Sir Eldric," she interjected in a calm yet firm tone, "While I respect Redmont's insights, remember where you stand. This is my court, and the land you speak of is under my jurisdiction. Direct your concerns to me."

Redmont's smirk faltered, taken aback by her assertiveness. He recovered, turning to Sir Eldric. "Perhaps the good sir recognizes experience over... other qualities," he said, allowing his eyes to linger on Durya's orcish features, making his implication clear.

The courtroom held its collective breath, waiting for Lady Durya's next move.

The stillness in the room was palpable. Durya's gaze, locked onto Sir Eldric, conveyed more than words ever could. It was a simple message: she was not to be trifled with. The lesser noble shifted under her scrutiny, his earlier bravado melting away.

After an eternity, Durya turned her attention back to the matter at hand. "Regarding the land dispute you've brought before us," she began, addressing Sir Eldric directly but loud enough for all to hear, "I suggest a thorough survey be commissioned to establish the rightful boundaries."

She then shifted her gaze to Redmont, her words dripping with subtle sarcasm. "Unless, of course, Lord Redmont has a more... experienced solution to offer?"

Redmont, surprised by her direct challenge and perhaps not expecting such a swift, decisive response, struggled to find words. "A survey... sounds appropriate," he conceded, his voice lacking its earlier confidence.

A ripple of approval spread through the assembly, acknowledging Durya's deft handling of the situation. Regardless of the whispered doubts and political games, Lady Durya was in command.

A sudden hush descended as the grand doors creaked open. All eyes turned towards the entrance as a slight Aelorian woman with unruly auburn hair stepped in. Her attire was unusual, blending elements from many cultures, making her stand out even more in the sea of rigid, courtly dress.

Her wide, green eyes darted around the room, taking in the atmosphere. The woman's gait hesitated, betraying her discomfort. Still, she made her way forward as if she wasn't sure why everyone was staring, but was determined to not let it phase her.

Subtle smiles and suppressed chuckles broke out among the younger members. Meanwhile, the older nobility looked on with disdain. For many, the break in formality was a welcome respite, and the social awkwardness endeared her to them even more.

Still seated, Durya's expression remained neutral, a mask hiding the tempest of emotions swirling within her. The strength in her friend's arrival brought was a breath of fresh air, a reminder of simpler times and genuine connections. Her heart swelled with a warmth and relief that she hadn't felt in months. Amidst the political machinations and veiled threats, an old friend was an anchor, grounding her in something sincere. This was her friend, Kaci.

Durya's heart soared, but she maintained her calm exterior. Only those who knew her well would detect the change in her demeanor, the slight softening of her eyes, and the hint of a smile threatening to break through.

Kaci paused for a moment, glancing from Durya to the faces of the assembly. She then made an awkward attempt at a curtsy, her legs tangling in the unfamiliar layers of her own dress. As she straightened, she cleared her throat and, in a voice laced with nerves, said, "Greetings, Lady and... esteemed audience. May your day be filled with... um, auspicious happenings?"

The room's atmosphere shifted. A wave of stifled giggles rippled through the courtiers. The sight of the graceful Aelorian, flustered and out of her depth, was a source of entertainment they hadn't expected.

Redmont, always quick to seize any opportunity, smirked and leaned over to a fellow noble, whispering just loud enough for those nearby to hear, "Such refined Aelorian grace, don't you think?"

Durya's eyes remained fixed on Kaci, her expression neutral but with an underlying warmth visible only to those who knew her. She addressed the crowd with poise, saying, "Thank you, Kaci, for your unique and heartfelt greeting. We are honored by your presence. Please, take a seat." Then she turned to Redmont and whispered, "Your sarcasm is uncalled for."

Kaci acknowledged Durya's gesture with a smile, then scanned the room for a place to sit. Oblivious to the formalities, or perhaps just choosing to ignore them, she settled herself cross-legged onto the polished marble floor.

Again, chuckles and whispers spread like wildfire. Nobles exchanged amused glances, while several courtiers tried, and failed, to stifle their laughter. Kaci, unfazed, looked around with genuine curiosity, as if wondering why everyone found her choice of seating so entertaining.

Durya offered a faint smile. She had expected nothing less from her eccentric friend. The incident was soon overshadowed by the day's proceedings.

As the sun began its descent, casting a warm amber hue in the courtroom, the matters of the day came to a close. One by one, grievances were heard, disputes settled, and decisions made. Throughout it all, Lady Durya's presence dominated the room. Each judgment she passed, each order she gave, highlighted her undeniable authority.

Redmont sought to test her resolve. However, every sly comment and indirect jibe showcased Durya's ability to rise above. Her decisions further solidified her place as the rightful leader.

Kaci's unexpected, yet heartwarming, presence served as a poignant reminder that Durya wasn't alone. While they might scheme behind closed doors, in this very hall, she had loyal allies.

As the final petitioner left the floor, Lady Durya stood, the motion fluid and regal. The court followed suit, rising in respect. With a nod, she signaled the conclusion of the day's affairs. The echoing footsteps and hushed conversations faded as the attendees vacated the hall, leaving behind the legacy of a day where, once again, Durya had proven her mettle.

* * *

The remnants of dinner lay on the table, a modest fare compared to the previous night's opulence. Bowls of hearty stew, fresh bread, and cups of spiced wine were cleared away, signaling the close of one gathering and starting another, far more secretive.

Durya led a select few through winding corridors, past grand tapestries and silent guards. Behind an unassuming wall panel, she unlocked a hidden door with a key hanging from her waist. They entered a room whose very existence whispered of clandestine meetings and hidden agendas.

The chamber was unlike the rest of the manor. Its walls were plain stone, devoid of any artwork or embellishments. While grand chandeliers graced other rooms, here, the light was provided by an array of candles, their flames casting quivering shadows on the walls, amplifying the room's aura of secrecy.

Mismatched chairs formed a makeshift circle. Their disarray was a testimony to the impromptu nature of such meetings, and the urgency with which they were often called.

Marcus entered just behind his sister. At first glance, the familial resemblance was evident. Like Durya, his skin bore the blue gray tint characteristic of orcs. However, his frame was leaner, with a wiry strength that contrasted his sister's more robust build. His eyes, intense and thoughtful, often bore the far-off look of someone whose mind was engaged in arcane matters. A subtle glow emanated from a pendant around his neck, indicating his magical inclinations.

A goblin named Jeth was next. The goblin's bright eyes darting around as he took in the room. Despite his small stature, he had a cat-like alertness. As he took a seat, he looked small against the large chair, his feet dangling a few inches above the ground. Yet, no one in the room underestimated his capability or influence.

Kaci breezed in, her auburn hair standing out amid the muted colors of the room. Her demeanor was one of perpetual distraction, as if her mind was always engaged with another puzzle. Clutched in her hand was an artifact of some sort, a complex device with moving parts she couldn't put down. Even in such serious settings, Kaci's spirit was undeniable.

Just inside the door, Sharn took his position, standing as an immovable force. His presence was both a reassurance and a warning. His loyalty to Durya was unwavering, and he would ensure that their meeting remained undisturbed, protecting both the secrets and the lives within the chamber.

The room was enveloped in a thick silence for a moment before Durya cleared her throat, initiating the conversation. "We find ourselves on the brink yet again, dear friends. The stability of our realm teeters, and we must act decisively to ensure its future."

Marcus leaned forward, his fingers laced together. "Sister, there's a growing chatter in the city alleys and among the merchant caravans. Whispers about Edward's health. Some even dare to suggest he's been cursed or poisoned. This can breed distrust and panic."

Kaci, lost in the intricate mechanism she held, looked up. "People love their stories, don't they?" she mused before being consumed once again by her artifact.

Durya's eyes darkened, betraying a flash of pain. "Indeed, but such tales are perilous, particularly when they revolve around the health of my husband." She paused for a moment, allowing her words to sink in. Every individual was well aware of the unspoken truth, yet none dared to voice it, even in this secluded sanctum. "We must tread carefully, ensuring that neither panic nor chaos finds its way into our realm because of these unsettling rumors."

Then, with an impatient shuffle in his large chair, Jeth chimed in, his voice raspy with a distinct accent, "Aye, lady. Rumors they be, but not born from thin air. Someone be blowin' these tales into the wind." He paused, looking every bit the spy master he was. "Me spies. They've got ears in every shadow. We find the source of these whisperings, we do."

Durya looked at the goblin, her respect for him clear. "Jeth, do what you must. If someone aims to destabilize our rule, we need to know who."

As the room's atmosphere thickened with concern, Kaci, ever the odd one out, held up a peculiar-looking artifact she'd been toying with. "Do you think this would help?" she quipped with a mischievous grin. "I found it on my last adventure. They said it can tell truths from lies. Or... it might be a fancy paperweight. Honestly, I forgot."

A few chuckles resonated around the chamber, and even Durya allowed a hint of a smile.

Durya leaned forward, her eyes scanning each face in the room with the sharpness of a hawk. "Our discussions about Edward are vital, but there's more we must address. There are whispers from the east, rumors of something stirring in Aeloria. I assume this is why you have come, Kaci. I've heard of a rebellious Aelorian faction forming within our own borders."

Kaci blinked, her expression shifting from serious to bemused. "Oh no, Durya, I just came because I had a dream about missing your lovely orcish scowl!" She said with a playful wink.

Durya raised an eyebrow, the ghost of a smile playing at the edges of her stern lips. "Kaci, your humor remains as sharp as ever," she said with dry amusement. Her gaze, however, quickly reverted to its usual intensity. "But let's not forget the gravity of the matters at hand. Aeloria's situation could have serious implications for us all."

Marcus, his hand gracefully weaving through the air as if conducting an unseen orchestra. "Why not ask to join one of their gatherings?" he suggested, his time among the Aelorians likely shining through his diplomatic acumen. "It would be an opportunity to fortify our alliances under a banner of unity and shared knowledge." His eyes, carried the quiet intensity of one who has seen and learned much, glanced around the room. "And concurrently, we should discreetly reinforce our defenses. Wisdom and strength must walk hand in hand."

Jeth, leaning over the table, almost toppling from his over-sized chair, interjected, "Why wait, when we can act? Me thinks we ought to sneak into their supplies. Thin 'em out a bit. Show 'em we ain't to be trifled with."

As Durya contemplated the contrasting suggestions, Kaci blurted out, "You know, I once met a dragon on the eastern borders. Maybe we could... I don't know, ask it for help? Or at least borrow some of its shiny hoard for bargaining?"

The room fell into a stunned silence before several eyebrows quirked up in disbelief. With a sheepish grin, Kaci added, "Just a thought."

Durya battled between amusement and frustration. She appreciated Kaci's unconventional thinking, a spark of lightness in their often grave discussions. Yet, the absurdity of the idea in the context of their situation was hard to ignore. It was a reminder that Kaci's unique perspective was simultaneously refreshing and exasperating.

"We face multifaceted challenges," Durya began. "We must be strategic and ensure that we use every resource available—though perhaps not dragon hoards this time." Her eyes briefly met Kaci's, a smile softening her stern expression.

"Marcus," she continued, "I want you to reach out to our allies. Arrange meetings, discuss potential collaborations, and ensure they understand the nuances of our current situation."

Marcus nodded, "understood, sister. I will begin immediately."

Turning to the goblin, "Jeth, I want your spies to gather as much information as they can. Who are our enemies? What are their plans? Where do their allegiances lie? But..." she added, "minimal stealing. I don't want unnecessary skirmishes or heightened tensions."

The goblin grumbled, his eyes gleaming. "Aye, aye. Me spies will get ye the information, and just a bit of the shiny stuff."

Durya's lips quirked in a smile. "Thank you all. Together, we'll navigate these waters. Remember, unity is our strength."

She stood at the head of the table making eye contact with each face, every loyal soul who had kept her confidence and stood by her side during the hardest times. "Each of you here has not just shown loyalty to me, but to the entirety of Elyndris," she began. "The truth about Edward... it's a delicate thread holding Westerfield together."

She paused, continuing after drawing a breath. "If the people discovered the truth now, Elanthia could be plunged into utter chaos. We've stood tall against darkness and treachery, from external threats to those lurking within our own walls. I just need a bit more time. Time to stabilize and ensure our kingdom's future. Once Elanthia is on a solid footing, then... then we can address the matter of Edward."

The room echoed with the heavy silence.

After breaking the intense quiet, Kaci interjected with her usual mischief, "Well, I guess for now, we're all just... 'edward-ing' our secrets, right?" She flashed a wide grin, waiting for reactions.

The room was blank-faced for a beat, not quite catching onto Kaci's pun, but the light-hearted attempt was enough to lift the tension. Durya looked at Kaci, a slight, amused smile tugging at the corner of her lips. The mood, though still serious, felt a touch less suffocating.

* * *

After the meeting, Durya's pace was brisk as she navigated the corridors of the castle, guided only by flickering torchlight. She turned a corner and exited the manor into an unused courtyard. Its walls were lined with weapon racks and training equipment and an alcove hidden from prying eyes.

The secluded corner had become Durya's sanctuary. Mossy cobblestones underfoot and creeping ivy shrouding the walls. It felt like a window into Elanthia's ancient past. It was the perfect place to practice combat.

Sharn was already there waiting for her, his broad frame silhouetted against the solitary torch. With a nod, they began. Blades clashed rhythmically, the sound echoing through the room. Each move was precise, each block and parry a testament to their shared history and trust.

"You're hesitating on the thrust, my lady," Sharn said, guiding her stance. Their practice went on, Sharn's coaching interlaced with encouragement and the occasional teasing remark.

After an intense sparring bout, both paused, catching their breath. Sharn's hand reached out, wiping a bead of sweat from Durya's brow. The room became their entire world. A moment passed between them, an acknowledgment of the feelings they dared not speak aloud. Drawn by an invisible force, they leaned in, their lips hovering, mere breaths apart.

The soft rustle of leaves interrupted their moment. Both of them instantly tensed. A shadow shifted near the courtyard's entrance, just beyond the wrought-iron gate. The fleeting glimpse of a figure disappeared as quickly as it came. Someone had seen them.

Panic washed over Durya. The implications of their stolen moment weighed on her. Not just the kiss, but the deceptions she guarded. How could she have been so careless?

"I... I'm sorry," Durya whispered, breaking away from the intense moment. With a swish, she turned, departing the courtyard. After reaching her quarters, she found her serving girls waiting. With a wave of her hand and a strained voice, she dismissed them. "Leave. I will ready myself for bed tonight." The girls exchanged glances but obeyed, leaving the Lady to her solitude.

As Durya settled in, the room's silence amplified each heartbeat, and in the night's void, she was transported back to a chapter of her life she wished she could forget.

Amidst the grandeur of the hall, young Durya felt the weight of a fate she didn't choose. Her father, Duke Maxwell, spoke in an emotionless tone that left no room for objection. "Durya, your marriage to Edward is settled."

Edward, the man who wore arrogance like a second skin, never missed an opportunity to remind her of the "favor" he had done her. "Always remember how lucky you are that I took pity on an orc like you," he'd sneer, a mocking glint in his eyes. His laughter, cold and cruel, echoing the demeaning sentiments he hurled at her day after day.

As the days turned into months, Edward's tyranny intensified. Words turned to blows, blows turned to other unspeakable horrors. The very walls of their home seemed to whisper her pain, though they remained deaf to her silent pleas for relief.

One ill-fated night on their ship, The Golden Gull, driven to the brink and desperate for an escape, Durya turned to a vial of poison she'd kept hidden. It wasn't a decision made lightly, but out of sheer desperation to end her torment. As Edward's breaths became labored and ceased altogether, a storm brewed overhead. The ship, as though bearing witness to her act, was consumed by nature's wrath, casting her adrift and alone.

When she emerged from her memory, there was no remorse for Edward, only for the choices she was forced into. She drew from her past a hardened resolve, using it as armor against the trials of the present.

In the glow of her chamber, Durya sat, surrounded by the rich tapestries and ornate furnishings that bore silent witness to her life's many moments. The day's events played out in her mind like a montage.

Among the myriad of reflections and portraits adorning her chamber, one stood out: that of Edward. The painted eyes seemed to follow her, echoing accusations from the past. His image, which represented a life she had been forced into, now ignited a fire of disgust and anger. As her gaze bore into the canvas, she drew strength from her resentment. For every wrong Edward had done her, for every scar – visible and invisible – she bore, she was now determined to carve out a path of justice and prosperity for the people, whether or not they accepted her.

Yet, amongst these swirling tempests of emotions, a softer, more fragile sentiment stirred. Thoughts of Sharn. He was the one she had truly wanted to marry. She thought of the guarded moments they shared, and the unspoken words between them surfaced. Her heart ached with a yearning, but also with fear. To involve him further, to pull him into her web of shadows, would be to place him in unimaginable danger. The price of her choices was steep, and she couldn't bear to let him pay it.

After she turned away from Edward's portrait, Durya moved

to the balcony, taking in the vast expanse of the city. The twinkling lights from homes in the distance hinted at the lives of her subjects – lives she was sworn to protect. Lives that depended on her strength, wisdom, and sometimes, her secrecy.

Elanthia, her beloved land, had seen its fair share of darkness. Despite the storm of emotions within her, one thing remained crystal clear: her resolve to shield her kingdom, and those she held dear from harm.

In the night's stillness, Durya made a silent vow. She would face any challenge, bear any burden, and pay any price to protect her land and its people. Little did she know how steep those prices would be.

3

Shadows of Allegiance

Lady Durya, looking formidable in her full-blooded orcish heritage, strode alongside Kaci through the bustling courtyard of Westerfield Manor. The morning air was crisp, tinged with the scents of blooming flowers and baked bread from the nearby market. Sunlight dappled through the ancient trees, casting a pattern of light and shadow on the cobbled paths, while the distant murmur of the city stirred beneath the gentle swaying of leaves.

Kaci's presence ignited lightness in Lady Durya's stern demeanor. As of late, the truth she held close nestled in the shadow of her thoughts, unspoken even in this sanctuary. Yet Kaci, ever perceptive, seemed to sense the fears that lingered in Durya's heart.

Raised among humans, Durya had always felt an underlying sense of otherness, her features marking her as different, imposing. Companions of her youth were more companions of circumstance than genuine friendship, their alliances coming from her father, Duke Maxwell's status.

A fleeting memory of Sharn drifted into Lady Durya's

thoughts. Their friendship, formed in the untamed wilds of her childhood, had always been a clandestine affair. Lady Evelyn, Durya's mother, had dismissed Sharn as an unsuitable companion. Being half-orc, half-human — the child of a modest maid and an anonymous father — he fell short of her mother's rigid standards. Ironically, Evelyn often ignored that her own foster daughter, Durya, was of pure orc lineage, a detail that didn't fit her selective perception of nobility.

But Kaci was different. From their first encounter, she stood tall before Lady Durya, her own mysterious powers a swirling cloak around her. There was temptation to leverage those powers for the kingdom's advantage. Durya had learned, however, to curb these exploitative instincts, recognizing the value in genuine connection.

As they ambled through the courtyard, Kaci's words tumbled out in a torrent of raw honesty. "I try to go back to my people, back between adventures. I really do," she confessed. "But growing up, nobody liked me. Why would I return to that?" Her sentiments resonated with Durya, whose own upbringing was marred by isolation and misunderstanding.

Kaci's gaze drifted away, lost in a distant sorrow as she spoke of Arba Vitae. The magnificent tree had been a symbol of the divine, interlinking the realms of magic and nature. Its death signified more than the loss of a sacred symbol; it marked the fading heartbeat of an entire culture. The Aelorian clans still thrived, but the essence, the unity that Arba Vitae had bestowed, had withered with its fall.

Lady Durya listened, her thoughts a labyrinth of strategy, em-pathy, and a relentless pursuit of a stronger Elanthia. Amidst the political chaos and hidden truths, she found an unexpected solace in Kaci's presence, a reminder that even in the darkest of times, the light of genuine friendship could guide one through.

As she continued to walk with Kaci by her side, the usual resolve in Durya's eyes softened. Her friend lit a rare flame of comfort in the cool, calculating expanse of her gaze. Yet, even as a smile threatened to break through her facade, the weight in Kaci's eyes did not escape Durya's notice—a shadow that seemed out of place in the lightness of their reunion.

"Something troubles you," Durya observed, her voice a low thrum that seemed to resonate with the stone underfoot. It was not a question, but a statement—a fact discerned by the subtle language of unspoken words and withheld breaths.

Kaci's response was a weary nod, the corners of her mouth twitching with a truth not yet ready to be born. "You know me, always a storm on the horizon," she said. "But honestly? I just missed you." Her eyes twinkled with a mischief that belied the darkness within.

A rare smile graced Durya's lips. "Then let's find someplace away from prying ears and eyes," she suggested.

Together, they retreated into the manor. Durya led the way to a private room, its door guarded by a silent but stoic goblin. With a curt gesture, she bade the guard leave them.

Inside, the chamber was a secluded sanctuary, its walls lined with shelves brimming with ancient tomes and adorned with the heraldry of the house. It was a library that promised endless journeys within its pages.

Lady Durya relished the rare joy of unrestricted companionship in this hidden haven. The library's seclusion, a world away from the court's watchful eyes, seemed to ignite a spark in Kaci. Her excitement was palpable as she bounced on the balls of her feet, her eyes alight with the thrill of discovery. "Can you believe it? An entire library in your house!" she exclaimed, her voice a melody of wonder and delight. Her animated gestures and infectious grin brought the room to life as she spoke of her adventures through literary worlds, each word painting vibrant strokes of life and enchantment.

"And Earth," Kaci beamed, "it's not like anything in Isdralan or Elanthia. The food, Durya, it's just—there's this thing called 'pizza,' and it's divine. Round like the coin, but more valuable, I'd wager."

Durya listened, her own lips curving in response to Kaci's enthusiasm, though she held back a chuckle. The idea of another world filled with ordinary yet captivating novelties provided a delightful escape from the pressures of governing.

Kaci's eyes danced with mirth as she recounted a joke from her time on Earth. "So, a human told me this: why don't skeletons fight each other? They don't have the guts for it!" She let out a laugh, expecting Durya to join in.

Durya tilted her head, perplexed. "Skeletons are formidable adversaries. I fail to see the humor in their lack of... viscera."

"Oh, it's called a pun, a play on words!" Kaci explained, still chuckling to herself. "It's funny because it's unexpected and... Oh, never mind. Earth humor is *different*."

Yet as their laughter waned, the stark reality of their situation crept back in. Kaci's smile dimmed, a somber note edging her voice as she spoke of a dragon, the edge of the world, and the haunting visage of Arba Vitae. "I thought it was gone," she murmured, "but there it was—or something like it—shimmering behind the dragon's flight."

Durya absorbed the tale with a thoughtful frown, realizing the depth of Kaci's unrest beneath her jovial facade. "Your wanderlust often leads to revelation, Kaci," she acknowledged. "If Arba Vitae lingers, or if its spirit endures, we must understand why and figure what to do."

Kaci nodded. "I had to tell you first," she said, her ancestral duty grounding her sprightly spirit. "Aeloria is splintered, and there are whispers of unrest."

Durya stood, her stature imposing yet reassuring. "We will consult with Marcus. His apprenticeship with Cirden gives him a perspective we need. We'll unravel this mystery together, Kaci. And if danger brews, we'll face it as we always have."

Kaci's smile returned, warmed by Durya's unwavering resolve. "Thanks, Durya. With you, I feel like we could take on a world of skeletons—even if they have the guts for it this time."

Durya offered a genuine smile, her respect for Kaci's resilience mixing with affection. "Then let's ensure we're prepared," she said. "For Aeloria, for Elyndris, for all that hangs in the balance."

In the quiet, she and Kaci sat entwined in the kinship of old friends, speaking of realms beyond and shared hardships. The warmth of the conversation was severed by a discordant clamor that echoed through the corridors, a sound unmistakable and jarring. The castle's alarm, a dire warning that the sanctity of Westerfield had been compromised.

As the reverberating tolls invaded the chamber, a goblin guard burst in. He skidded to a halt, tripping over his own feet, his wide eyes finding Lady Durya.

"My Lady!" he exclaimed, his voice rising over the din of alarms. "An intruder! There has been an attempt—" his eyes darted to Kaci, then back to Lady Durya. "On M'lord."

The peals of the alarm continued to ring out, signaling all within the manor to be on high alert. This was no mere incursion; it was a statement—a challenge to the security that Lady Durya had maintained. With the alarm's call still thundering through the stone, Durya rose. It was a sound she had hoped never to hear, an omen of dark deeds threading through her domain.

The grand council hall was a maelstrom of chaos when Durya and Kaci arrived. The urgent clamor of voices, a discordant symphony of shock and fear, struck them like a physical wave. Among the marble columns and under the high, vaulted ceiling, an almost palpable panic filled the air.

Durya's gaze swept the room, taking in the figures that were represented. First, there was Marcus, her brother, with his scholar's frown. Then Lord Hensworth, red-faced and indignant, spilled his cup of wine in his agitation, droplets splashing on the woven rug like blood. Lady Elara, with eyes wide and an uncharacteristic pallor, seemed to shrink. And Lord Redmont, standing with imperious disdain, his eyes calculating, attempting to veil his hunger for power beneath a guise of concern.

Interrupting their entrance, another goblin guard scuttled forward. The guard was panting, the unusual exertion clear in his posture.

"Lady Durya!" the goblin squeaked, his voice trembling with urgency. "An Aelorian, caught at the Duke's chambers—by sheer luck, the wretch didn't know we'd set up an alarm rune!"

She nodded, and her voice, a clear and resonant command, rose above the din. "Double the guards at the Baron's door. Now!" She pivoted on her heel, her cloak swirling, Kaci a shadow at her side.

Crossing the threshold of the grand council room, Lady Durya and her companions were immediately enveloped in a whirlwind of activity. The cacophony of arguing nobles, frantic gestures, and flustered servants coalesced into a moment of tension. Amidst the chaos, Durya's gaze briefly met Sharn's as he navigated his way through the crowd, their silent exchange speaking volumes in the tumultuous setting.

The outcry was a cacophony of fear and suspicion. Accusations volleyed back and forth, some eyes flitting toward Kaci with unveiled mistrust.

"ENOUGH. I AM THE BARONNESS!" Durya's voice boomed, the words not just spoken but wielded, striking the walls and slicing through the tumult like a blade. She stood there, towering in her presence, her orcish heritage a stark banner of strength amid the sea of human fragility.

Silence fell like a guillotine.

Once the declaration faded, Durya spoke again, her voice now the calm after the storm. "The vigilance of our guards has foiled an assassin. An Aelorian." Her eyes met Kaci's, conveying an unspoken solidarity. "This is not a time for baseless allegations, but for unity and fortitude. We must stand together or fall divided."

In the stillness, Durya's words settled like snow upon the ground, a blanket of truth over the fires of paranoia. She offered a nod to the goblin guard—a silent thanks for his service that transcended the need for words.

The court, now subdued, looked to her, their leader in all but name, as she orchestrated their defense.

The atmosphere thickened with tension as the warning bells continued their relentless toll. Durya observed Kaci, sensing her friend's sudden urge to retreat into the concealing shadows, a natural refuge against the tide of suspicion in her Aelorian blood might invite. Yet, before Kaci could become one with the dimness, Lord Redmont stepped forth, sealing her path. The lord's gaze, sharp and accusing, fixed on Kaci with undisguised contempt, each glint in his eyes a silent challenge, daring her to withdraw and thereby admit a guilt she did not own. Durya's heart clenched at the sight, her protective instincts flaring beside the quiet strength of her friend who, cornered by malice, stood her ground and slid into place beside Lady Durya at the council table, facing the suspicious and startled gazes of the court.

A mix of underlings and guards surrounded the group. The air crackled with a volatile mix of fear, suspicion, and latent aggression.

When Lady Durya spoke, her voice cut through the bedlam with the force of a sword through silk. "Silence!" The command resonated, and the chamber fell quiet, the alarm echoes fading into a background drone. She stood, a pillar of strength, her gaze sweeping over the assembly.

"This assault on our peace shall not divide us," Durya declared, her eyes locking on each face around her, binding them to her will. "We stand united—Even Aelorians among us."

Kaci remained steadfast by Durya's side. Lord Redmont's look of malevolence faltered under Durya's words, and he took his place among the others.

With a stern, resolute look, Lady Durya continued, "The would-be assassin will find no allies here. We are Elanthians and Elyndrans, and we will face this treachery as one."

The grand council room fell into a hushed silence. The reverberations of Durya's declaration, *I AM THE BARONNESS*, echoed in the room. She stood, her imposing figure stark against the tapestries of history, an orc asserting dominion in a human's court, her voice having carved out order from the chaos.

A silent question haunted the back of her mind, a shadow amid the light of her command: Would these people follow her if she didn't have the name Edward Barclay or Maxwell Conwyn, to back her? Her stance was unwavering, a statue of determination, yet within her a sliver of doubt lingered. Only she and a few others knew the truth of Edward's reclusion. The question gnawed at her: Did her right to rule derive from her deeds, from her scars, her mind, her devotion? Or was it propped up by the face of a Duke they revered, now more a myth than a man?

Her eyes, sharp and commanding, swept across the room, reading the shifting expressions—shock, a burgeoning respect, realization. The moment was a crucible, testing the mettle of their faith in her. Durya knew she must stand firm, to embody the trust she sought, to anchor it in the here and now, for Elanthia and for the fragile peace they had all bled to preserve.

A resolve took shape within Durya, as tangible as the sword at her side, its steel a symbol of unyielding strength. The façade they had all upheld, the delicate dance around a truth unspoken, had reached its final bow. She could lead no longer under the guise of a stewardship that was but a memory, could not allow the ghost of Edward to be the tether that bound her people to her.

Her gaze swept the chamber, every eye a witness to the pivotal truth that would test the very fabric of their loyalty. She knew in that moment she must wield honesty as her blade sever the veil of deception with the same precision she would use to parry an enemy's blow.

"In truth," she began, "the Duke, Edward Westerfield, has not drawn breath since before the shadows sought to claim our lands. He hoped that this knowledge be shielded from you, to preserve a continuity of rule until the threat had passed."

A murmur swept through the assembly like a wind through autumn leaves—whispers of confusion, of betrayal. She held up a hand, palm outstretched, commanding silence once more.

"For too long, I have borne this secret, shouldered the burden of a throne that, by birthright, was not mine. Yet, by the right of sacrifice, of blood spilled in defense of this kingdom and its people, I claim not a title, but a duty."

Durya's eyes glinted with the raw power of her lineage, the orcish blood that demanded no throne but took up the mantle of protector by force of will, by deed, by honor.

"This is not the usurpation of a legacy," she declared, "but the forging of a new era. I stand before you as Durya, once child of the Duke of Marshfield, now your Baroness not by the grace of names, but by the will of our people and the strength of my arm. I do not ask for your fealty to the specter of a man long departed but to the living breath and beating heart of Elanthia."

A hush had fallen. The chamber's very stones seemed to listen, awaiting the verdict of hearts and minds laid bare by the stark light of truth. In the silent wake of her declaration, Durya knew the true measure of her rule would not be in the acquiescence of a moment but in the enduring fealty born of respect and shared conviction.

She awaited their response. This would not be spoken not in words, but in the allegiance of those who had once followed a duke, and would now follow the truth of their land.

Chaos erupted like a storm in the council chamber, the immediate, visceral reaction to Durya's confession tearing through the assembled nobles like wildfire. Shouts and protests clashed in the air, the fragile peace shattered by the truth.

Amidst the uproar, Lord Redmont found his moment. His

voice, slick with the oil of treachery, cut through the tumult. "This orc speaks lies! She usurps the barony!" His accusation pointed like a dagger at Durya's heart. "Seize them! They are traitors to the true legacy of Elanthia!"

The room divided as if a blade had split it in two—goblins clambering to Durya's side, their loyalty unshaken, while human guards, swayed by the poison of Redmont's words, rallied to his call. Steel was drawn, and the shimmer of blades reflected the chaos of shifting loyalties.

Durya stood, the surrounding turmoil a crucible forging her resolve. She drew her own sword, its edge a gleaming arc of defiance. Kaci's shadowy form melded into the fray, her movements a dance of survival, while Sharn moved to protect Durya.

The council chamber, once a hallowed hall of discourse, became a battleground. The clang of metal, the grunts of struggle, the shouts of command, all melded into discord. Goblins, fierce and undaunted, clashed with the humans who had turned against their Baroness. The room swirled with the colors of battle—gold and emerald, blood and shadow.

As the conflict surged, Durya found herself back-to-back with Sharn. The tension between them had always been a dance of unspoken words and emotions, but in this moment, it sealed their bond in combat. They fought not just for their lives, but for a future that hung on the edge of a knife.

The battle swayed in the favor of Redmont's men, numbers pressing down on Durya and her loyal defenders. The fight could not be won here, not now. With a heavy heart, Durya signaled the retreat, the goblins responding with agile swiftness covering their withdrawal.

They fought their way through the corridors, a desperate

escape as the walls seemed to close in around them. Kaci and Marcus's spells carved them a path through the chaos, Sharn and the goblins' ferocity holding back the tide of soldiers.

In the end, it didn't matter. Lady Durya was subdued.

Sharn's voice pierced the chaos as human guards restrained her. But. relief washed over Durya at the sight of Kaci, tugging Sharn into a stealthy retreat down a side corridor. Sharn, the ever-stubborn, would never concede defeat, especially not in her case. A tender smile played on her lips, gratitude swelling for her friend's persuasive abilities. Safety for them, above all, was her silent prayer.

Marcus, too, had fallen into the guards' clutches. Durya watched, heart sinking, as they dragged him towards the Manor's sinister depths. The dungeons lurked beneath. A cold comfort, perhaps, that her status as a lady spared her that fate.

The Redmont guards had escorted her back to her chambers, their courtesy a grim reality of her situation. Lady Durya sat alone for what seemed like hours, the silence punctuated only by the distant echoes of the Manor. Her thoughts were a whirlwind, anxiety about her friends' fates gnawing at her.

Eventually, her own ladies arrived — a bittersweet reminder of normalcy in these confined quarters.

Ella, the younger of the two, offered a warm cup of tea with a nervous smile. "To calm your nerves, lady," she said, her voice trembling almost as much as her hands.

"Tsk, control your nerves, child," Lady Durya chided, giving Ella a light flick on the ear. The girl stiffened but managed a nod, then scampered off.

Liana, ever composed, shook her head in mild disapproval as she untangled Lady Durya's hair.

"I suppose you don't know what plans they have for me,"

Durya inquired, seeking any scrap of information.

"No, my lady," Liana responded, her calm demeanor unshaken.

"You are dismissed," Lady Durya sighed, waving a dismissive hand.

As Ella and Liana each gave a small bow, a shadow loomed in the room's corner. Lady Durya's eyes flicked towards it, but she said nothing. Ella, before exiting, whispered something towards the shadow — words too soft for Durya to catch.

Alone now, Durya mulled over her recent outburst to the other nobles about Edward. It had been a reckless move, yet there was an unexplainable lightness in her soul, as if a great burden had been lifted.

The stone walls of her chamber stood cold and indifferent, unlike the warmth Durya had once cultivated within them. She sat alone, her solitude pressing upon her. The hearth in her room, once crackling with life, lay dormant—a mirror to the extinguished presence of Duke Edward, whose death marked her rule.

In the silence, Durya's mind turned inward, tracing the pathways of her choices and the secrets she'd kept. Each one seemed to be a fetter binding her to a fate she had not foreseen. She had stepped into the void left by Edward, animating his shadow to cast continuity over Elanthia. But shadows are fleeting at dusk, and as night fell, so too did the illusion.

As Lady Durya contemplated the situation, her thoughts became muddled, thick and sluggish like a river choked with silt. A haze was creeping at her consciousness, a dulling of her sharp mind. The memory of the shadow lurking in her chamber surfaced, an ominous specter. She recalled the whispered exchange between Ella and that shadowy figure — had it been a mere servant, or someone more sinister?

A sudden chill ran down her spine. The tea — could it have been laced with something? Her suspicions deepened as her body betrayed her. Her limbs felt heavy, her thoughts scattered like leaves in a storm. The realization dawned on her; she had been outmaneuvered.

Her eyelids drooped, fighting against the sedative effects of the tea. In this moment of vulnerability, her mind raced with questions. Who could she trust? What game was being played?

In her mind, she was transported back to those harrowing days following their marriage. The whispers in the corridors, the subtle changes in Edward's demeanor, the tightening grip of control. She remembered the bitter draught she had slipped into his wine that fateful day on the Gull. It was a choice that haunted her, a dark stain on her soul, yet one she had deemed necessary.

Now, Lady Durya realized with a sinking heart, someone had drugged the tea. A fitting, if ironic, fate. Was this retribution? Had Edward returned from the grave to whisper in Redmont's ear? The drowsy haze clouding her thoughts seemed a cruel echo of what she had inflicted on her husband. Did Lord Redmont know of her dark deed? Was this his way of ensnaring her in a web of her own making, a poetic justice for her transgressions?

Her brother Marcus, always her rock, had been caught in the same snare. Their fates, as always, were intertwined. Yet there was a sliver of hope. Kaci and Sharn might have escaped. That faint flicker of possibility held the encroaching darkness at bay.

But the fog claimed her, pulling her down into its murky depths. Even the flicker of hope for Kaci and Sharn's escape dimmed. She found herself adrift in the liminal space between wakefulness and dreams, the drug's potency blurring her reality. Soon, there was nothing left but her faint heartbeat and the suffocating embrace of darkness.

A sharp knock at the door jolted her back to reality. The door swung open, and Lord Redmont stepped into her chambers, his presence an unwelcome anchor in the sea of her disoriented thoughts.

"What did you put in my tea?" Lady Durya's voice was laden with accusation, her attempt to lunge at Lord Redmont hampered by uncooperative limbs. "I am not so easily killed."

Lord Redmont took a step back, his chuckle cold and hollow. "Tea?"

Durya tried to rise, to impose her will, but her strength failed, and she collapsed back to the ground. Lord Redmont, seeing her weakened state, seemed emboldened to reveal his machinations.

He stepped back, his chuckle echoing in the chamber. "You have been subdued, yes, but not by my hand. You underestimate the players in this game. With Edward gone, removing you from the picture required little effort, especially when you did it for me with your confession. Westerfield will never stand behind a fallen leader."

His laugh was devoid of warmth. "You wonder why I stand before you? Power has shifted. I am merely seizing the opportunity presented. As for you, your fate now aligns with a certain faction of Aelorian's ambitions."

Lady Durya's heart raced. The Aelorians Marcus had spoken of — their partnership with Redmont was a dangerous development. "What have you planned?"

Lord Redmont's eyes glinted with cunning. "A convenient alliance. In the chaos of your friend's departure last year, they seek to strengthen their position. And I, to solidify mine. You, Lady Durya, are but a pawn in a much larger game."

Her voice trembled with fury and fear. "And my brother? What of him?"

"Marcus is a different matter. A threat to be neutralized. He will meet his end at dawn," Redmont declared, his tone final.

As he turned to leave, he cast a chilling glance over his shoulder. "Remember, Lady Durya, in the great game of power, the most lethal moves are those unseen and unexpected."

Durya opened her mouth and tried to scream, but there was nothing. She just faded into black.

4

Loss and Confusion

The world came back in fragments. Pieces of light crept through her lashes and painted unfamiliar shapes against the darkness behind her eyes. She woke in her own bed, with no memory of how she got there. Adrift in a sea of confusion, the anchors of her past severed, each moment leading up to her awakening lost in oblivion.

Her first sensation was the coolness of the pillow beneath her cheek, a soft, welcoming surface that contrasted with the fog that swaddled her mind. Awareness crept in like a timid creature, reluctant and halting. She scanned the dim room. The light from a solitary candle was casting long, wavering shadows against the walls.

Her head felt heavy, as if filled with sand, thoughts slipping away before she could grasp them. She tried to lift herself, but her limbs were uncooperative, heavy with a lethargy that seemed born of a long, unnatural sleep. A small, soundless groan escaped her as she propped herself against the carved headboard.

Rich tapestries adorned the room, cascading from ceiling to

floor. Each was a meticulous weave of triumphs and tragedies, epic sagas depicted in vibrant threads, histories of a world she felt she should know as intimately as the heartbeat within her chest. Yet now, each portrayal slipped through her fractured memory like water through clenched fingers.

Above the fireplace hung an imposing portrait of a man. His eyes, dark and piercing, followed her every move, and even in her bewildered state, they instilled an instinctual thread of fear that wove itself into her very bones. The man's visage was proud and stern, a silent declaration of his dominion over all he surveyed. The ornate frame that held his image seemed to cage him as much as it honored him, a boundary between his world and hers.

Command and purpose permeated every corner. This domain was reserved for a powerful individual, and the surroundings made her feel like an outsider.

The portrait drew her gaze again and again. Silent challenge emanated from his eyes. His face, while unfamiliar, evoked a visceral reaction—a tightening in her chest, a quickening of her pulse. She could not remember him, yet her body remembered the fear he invoked, as though his very image could leap from the canvas and command her once more.

She noticed her hands then—wrapped in delicate lace, resting in her lap. They seemed alien to her, large yet soft, like creatures from a story told in whispers. She turned them over, examining the lines on her palms, half expecting them to provide a map back to herself. But there was nothing.

Rising, she approached a mirror that stood against a wall—a slab of reflective glass set in a frame of dark, carved wood. The figure that stared back at her carried a blue-gray complexion with laces and finery that adorned her form. Her wide, searching eyes glinted with a confused shimmer, lost in the mist of amnesia. The mystery was intensified by her distinct cheekbones and strong jaw, giving the impression that she didn't fit in the picture.

As her fingers traced the line of her jaw, they found the protrusion of tusks curving from her mouth, a distinguishing feature. Their solidity provided an odd comfort, a tangible link to a self she could not remember, a grounding point in the disorientating fog that enveloped her mind.

Her gaze lingered on the mirror's reflection, desperate to find recognition amidst the chaos of her fragmented memories. Behind her, the painting loomed, its presence in the glass akin to a silent sentinel observing, evaluating. A shiver of fear gnawed at her, at the sight of her own image. A mysterious and forgotten power shimmered, pulsing beneath her under-standing, suggesting an untapped might she couldn't recall wielding.

The air carried a lingering scent, lavender and something earthy, like rain-soaked soil. It was comforting and yet foreign, triggering a fleeting sense of nostalgia that faded as quickly as it had arrived. She was a ghost haunting her own life.

In the suffocating stillness of her chamber, Durya struggled to stand, her movements hampered as though weighted down by the fog of her forgotten past. She moved, touching the foreign contours of her surroundings. Despite the opulent surroundings and whispers of grandeur, none of it enticed her. None of it brought the spark of recognition she sought.

She picked up a cup, its tea gone cold. The scent it carried was unfamiliar, not a trace of memory hidden within its brewed depths.

Panic bloomed within her, an internal tempest echoing the

ferocity of a sea squall. The more she grappled for a lifeline to her identity, the further it slipped away, much like trying to grasp at smoke. Visions of a turbulent ocean, bolts of lightning against dark clouds, overwhelmed her, but they vanished as quickly as they appeared, leaving no answers, only an abyss of confusion.

The room's quiet was relentless. It was an invisible entity in itself, imposing upon her with unvoiced histories. Only her breaths punctuated the hush, each one a reminder of the life persisting within her, despite feeling so disconnected from the world.

Compelled by some unknown desire, she was drawn again to the mirror. Her reflection showed her unchanged—blue-gray skin, tusks framing her mouth. This time, she delved into her own gaze, seeking to uncover the hidden depths of her being.

A glimmer of something—perhaps a memory—flitted across her consciousness: a powerful gaze, a menacing grin, an outstretched hand amidst the chaos, a voice whispering her name. It was gone as swiftly as it had come, slipping through her grasp, leaving her empty-handed in the quest for her essence. It was there, in her hushed breaths and the shadow of her lost memories, that a soft sound manifested—a whisper at first, like wind caressing the edges of silence.

She leaned in and the sound grew. There was a subtle vibration beneath the glass, a melody of motion and metal. It built in tension, creating an invisible thread pulling at her awareness.

The world stood still for a heartbeat as a subtle click unfurled the hidden truth within the chamber. Before Durya's eyes, the mirror swayed open like a portal between realms. It revealed a stone passageway that seemed to exist beyond the bounds of reality.

From this gateway, two figures emerged: a small Aelorian woman with a mane of fiery red hair and a constellation of freckles scattered across her cheeks. Her ears peeked through the tangle of locks, giving an air of otherworldly charm. Beside her stood a hulking form, an embodiment of both the orcish heritage that Durya recalled and the softer lines of humanity. He looked at her with a familiar warmth, yet she could not place him.

Her heart was a drumbeat, erratic and pounding against the walls of her chest. The familiarity was both comforting and terrifying. She was standing at the precipice of a fall or a tremendous leap into the unknown.

"What magic is this?" The question slipped from her lips. Less an inquiry and more utter wonder, a childlike grasp at the tendrils of a forgotten fairytale. Her voice betrayed the tremors of her inner turmoil, the dichotomy of fear and a trust trying to blossom through the cracks.

The Aelorian moved closer. "Magic?" she chuckled, her voice a lighthearted chime that seemed to fill the corners of the somber chamber. "No, my lady, unless you count carpentry as an arcane art. This," she gestured towards the swinging mirror, "is courtesy of your own clever designs."

Beside her, the large man lumbered into the room, his size imposing yet tempered by the gentleness in his eyes. He glanced down at the Aelorian woman, his expression concerned, then turned his gaze back to Durya. "It's not the woodwork she's confused about, Kaci," he said, his voice a rumble. "Something's not right."

The smaller woman's smile faltered as she stepped closer to Durya, her head tilting in a birdlike motion, sharp eyes scanning the noblewoman's face. "Lady Durya, it's me, Kaci. And this big lump of worry is Sharn," she said, her tone playful yet edged with a seriousness that seemed uncharacteristic of her. "Do you really not remember us?"

Sharn moved to Durya's side with a protector's vigilance. "We're here for you, my lady," he murmured, placing a hand on her shoulder with a tenderness that belied his warrior's physique. "What has befallen you?"

They exchanged a glance, an unspoken conversation passing between them. Kaci's brow creased with concern, her jesting demeanor slipping as the situation set in. "Great Mother, what have they done to you?"

Together, they stood by Durya, pillars of strength and levity, offering her the balance of their contrasting natures. Amid her confusion, Durya felt a flicker of warmth at the duo's odd camaraderie. It was a distant echo of affection and safety amidst the fog that clouded her thoughts.

She searched their faces, desperate for recognition, but found none. She was adrift in a sea of anonymity, clinging to the flotsam and jetsam of her fragmented identity. "I do not know you," she confessed, her words a lifeline cast into the waters of her uncertainty. "Yet you seem to know me. Tell me, please, who am I to you?"

Her plea was raw, stripped of the regal bearings she could not remember possessing. Durya stood at the mirror's threshold, flanked by guardians of a lost life.

Kaci stepped forward. "I am Kaci," she announced with a warm, reassuring smile. "We are the best of friends." Her eyes sparkled with a fondness that suggested shared memories, now lost to Durya.

"And this stoic guardian here is Sharn," Kaci continued,

gesturing toward the large man whose presence seemed to anchor the very air around them. Sharn bowed his head, his expression duty and something more.

"I've stood watch over you for more years than I can count," Sharn added, his voice carrying a tender note that seemed to wrap around Durya like a warm cloak. "We've faced much together, you and I."

Kaci caught Sharn's eye and offered him a wink. "And worry not about Marcus," she chimed in, her words cutting through the haze of Durya's uncertainty. "Your brother is safe. We've spirited him away from the clutches of his captors."

Durya's brows furrowed, the name setting off no sparks within her empty halls of memory.

"Marcus?" Her voice was a whisper, escaping the tightness in her throat.

Sharn, with his broad shoulders and the protective tilt of his head, seemed to sense her unspoken plea for stability. "Your brother," he said, his voice a steady anchor. "He waits for us."

Her brother. The word ricocheted through the hollow cavern of her amnesia, finding no purchase. Durya looked from Sharn to Kaci, seeking in their faces the pieces of herself she could not assemble alone. They were now her guides, protectors, and the sole connection to her forgotten past.

Marcus, her title of Lady, and the visible urgency in Kaci and Sharn's movements painted a picture of a tapestry torn, a rule challenged, a kingdom in the throes of upheaval. In this room, Durya stood at the edge of an unexpected journey. The path of a woman shrouded in mystery, standing at the crossroads.

In the refuge of her chamber, now stripped of its familiarity, Durya watched with a sense of detached curiosity as Kaci and Sharn gathered supplies. They moved with efficiency, cloaked in the urgency of their mission. They draped cloaks around their shoulders with hoods deep enough to shadow their faces from any prying eyes.

Sharn approached Durya with a cloak, its fabric heavy. As he draped it over her, his fingers brushed against the exposed skin of her neck. This sent an inexplicable shiver down her spine—a tingle of familiarity, of shared histories and battles side by side. She turned, her eyes clouded with questions. She felt a connection in that touch, finding comfort in this man's presence.

As they prepared to step through the mirror, the portal that had revealed itself as a secret passage, Durya's heart drummed and her body tensed. She sensed the peril that awaited them beyond the stone walls of her once-secure haven.

They traversed the hidden tunnels beneath the manor, the damp earthiness of the passage mingling with mold and ancient secrets. The walls, once familiar, now remained silent to Durya, just like her lost memories. Her feet seemed to know the way.

Emerging into the rough underbelly of the city, the trio navigated the labyrinthine streets. The city was a maze, its dark alleys and dimly lit corners mirrored Durya's fractured mind— both concealing and revealing in their shadowy embrace.

Her instincts flared as they passed close to danger, the distant clang of guard patrols or the shifty gaze of a thief. Muscle memory guided her reactions, a subconscious dance with the pulse of the city. She ducked when Sharn's hand signaled, stopped when Kaci's eyes hardened, all without understanding why she heeded these silent commands.

Finally, they reached the outskirts of the city, the gates behind them and the freedom of the wilds ahead.

Upon reaching their destination, the cave was nothing like

the grand caverns of lore but resembled a large mound on the side of a hill—a cozy hovel carved into the earth, humble and hidden.

Its entrance gave way to a cozy interior, its walls hugging them close as they stepped into its sanctuary. In the shadows, a man with skin the color of a twilight storm stood. His frame was slender, muscles taut and defined in the way of one who relied on speed and cunning rather than brute strength.

"Lord Marcus," Sharn announced with a respectful nod, the title carrying their shared heritage and struggle.

Marcus turned, his eyes bright in the low light. "Any troubles on the way?" Kaci queried, her voice a soft note in the hushed space.

"All quiet," Marcus responded. "I don't think they've realized I'm gone yet." The ease of his demeanor suggested a confidence forged in the fires of many escapes.

The cave itself was a natural haven, its confines whispering of ancient earth and steadfast stone. In the dimness, a large opening yawned in the floor, a black abyss that promised depths untold. "Careful of that, lady," Sharn cautioned with a grin, his voice a gentle rumble in the quietude.

Durya stepped closer, peering into the chasm with a mixture of trepidation and awe. Like the one within her, the void held unseen memories, waiting to be discovered.

They settled near the cave's heart, where a respite from the chaos of the world above waited. Though the comfort of the cave was unfamiliar to Durya, her body recognized the safety it offered, responding with a profound sense of relief that coursed through her tired limbs.

In this secluded refuge, Durya felt the comforting embrace of the cave's heartbeat, a whisper of home. Here, perhaps, she could piece together the fragments of her past.

The flicker of the small fire they had kindled cast a warm, dancing glow upon the cave walls, the shadows playing like phantoms from a half-remembered dream. Kaci and Sharn settled close, their voices weaving through the air, stitching together tales from Durya's past. Marcus sat apart, staring out into the night, looking like a bird ready to burst into flight.

Kaci recounted a vast library they swore they would return to someday, but had not yet. Sharn spoke of quieter times, moments stolen from the ever-encroaching duties of leadership. "We'd sneak away, just you and I, to train," he reminisced. "You always bested me, but claimed it was luck each time."

As they spoke, Durya's senses heightened, the cave itself seeming to respond to the tales. The cool dampness of the stone beneath her, the musty scent of earth—it all tugged at her awareness. A scurrying sound in the darkness pricked at her ears, the memory of rats that once had been her silent, ever-present audience, their beady eyes watching her every move.

Red hair in the firelight drew her gaze, a flash of Kaci's face—those same freckles, that same unbridled spirit—evoking familiarity. It was Kaci who found her. This cave was where an unexpected friendship had blossomed.

Flashes of a stranger's face—Micah, they called him—rippled through her thoughts. A figure who had left a mark upon her soul, now just a whisper of a vision, his laughter a ghostly sound that brought a fleeting smile to her lips.

With each story, Durya's heart stirred, a deep yearning to remember, to reclaim the bonds that had been her foundation. "This is where we first met," Kaci said, her hand reaching out to touch Durya's. "You, lost in two storms, the one outside and of your own mind, and I, a wandering girl, just wanting to fit in."

Tears brimmed in Durya's eyes. There was a sense of loss, of missing pieces, but also a burgeoning sense of hope. Hope that the sparks Kaci and Sharn were tending would burst into flame and the shadows that veiled her memories would be cast aside, revealing the path back to herself. Yet it remained just out of reach, a melody whose tune she could not quite recall.

Durya sat somewhat apart from the huddled trio of Marcus, Kaci, and Sharn. Their voices were an indistinct murmur that filled the cave. She felt like a specter at her own council, a presence disconnected from the plotting and planning of her once-familiar allies.

Marcus's tone was grave as he spoke of the precariousness of succession. His words were a litany of what might have been. "With no heirs from Durya and Edward, and with my abdication, Redmont sees a path to power," he said, his eyes darting to Durya, as if seeking her approval or a sign of recognition.

Kaci, ever the firebrand, was pacing, her hands animated as she laid out her bold proposal. "We take her to Isdralan," she insisted. "A guardian will know how to restore her memories."

Sharn shook his head. "She wouldn't want that," he countered, his gaze lingering on Durya. "It's not her way to run from a fight, even one within her own mind."

"But she wouldn't be running," Kaci argued.

Their words painted a portrait of a woman Durya no longer knew—a leader, a warrior, a friend. They spoke of her as if she were a legend, their tones imbued with admiration and fear. It was surreal. Her life was being dissected and discussed as though she were not there.

A helplessness settled over Durya, a sinking realization that she was at the mercy of her friends' decisions. The very concept of self was elusive to her. Who was she if not the sum of her experiences? And yet, the way Marcus's brow furrowed with worry, the way Kaci's lips curled into a smile when she mentioned Durya's past fierceness, the way Sharn's hand clenched into a fist as if ready to fight for her—it all hinted at an essence that remained, something intrinsic and indestructible.

The conversation shifted towards action, towards what steps they must take next. Despite the uncertainty, there was a determination in their voices, a shared resolve they would not allow Redmont to usurp the future of Westerfield or Marshfield—not without a fight.

Frustration furrowed her brow as she listened to the plans unfurl. The confidence and urgency in the voices of Kaci, Sharn, and Marcus only sharpened the edges of her own helplessness. Anger simmered within her, an emotion unattached to any memory, yet protective of the identity she could not grasp. She was tired of being discussed as a riddle to be solved. Her gaze shifted upwards, meeting the eyes of everyone in the room, a silent rage burning within her. She was more than the sum of memories she could not retrieve; she was present, breathing, and would not be sidelined.

With a defiant lift of her chin, Durya communicated her intent. Instead of waiting to be awakened, she would accompany them through the uncertain mists, actively working to reclaim what belonged to her. She would not yield to the darkness, but stand against it. From the very turmoil that sought to devour her, she would rise again.

5

Quest for the Forgotten

As the first blush of dawn crept across the horizon, it cast a pale light that seeped into the cave, signaling an end to the night. The group, huddled around the dying embers of the fire, had talked through the dark hours, each exchange weaving a tighter bond of shared purpose in the face of uncertainty.

Now Lady Durya sat apart, her silhouette etched against the burgeoning day. The morning brought clarity, and with it, the stark realization of the weight they all bore. Today was a crossroads for their fates, a moment that demanded action and resolve.

She listened as Marcus, Kaci, and Sharn mapped out their strategy, their voices a symphony of determination. When Durya spoke, her voice carried the timbre of command, an echo of the leader she once was. "We can deliberate no longer," she declared, her violet eyes reflecting the morning's resolve. "I may not recall the full measure of who I am or what I have done, but I will not be defined by the memories I have lost."

Durya rose to her feet. "I am the Baroness of these lands, by right and by blood," she continued, her gaze sweeping across the faces of her companions. "I will journey to Isdralan. I will face whatever trials await, and I will return with the power to restore what has been sundered."

Her proclamation stirred the air, a call to arms that resonated within the cave's confines. Marcus nodded in solemn agreement, his own resolve mirrored in his sister's words. Kaci's smile was supportive and warm.

Sharn's expression was harder to read. The muscles in his jaw tensed, a subtle dance of sinew that spoke volumes of his inner turmoil. He was a warrior, bred for the tangible reality of steel and blood, not the whimsical and unpredictable paths of Isdralan.

Lady Durya, observing him, could see the battle that raged within him—a war not of swords, but of loyalty against instinct. His hands, accustomed to holding a weapon, now opened and closed at his sides, as if grappling with invisible foes.

Kaci, ever attuned to the undercurrents of those around her, stepped closer to Sharn. "You don't need to go to Isdralan," she breathed, her hand reaching out to rest on his arm—a touch meant to steady. "Durya will be safe there."

But Sharn's eyes, when they met Kaci's, were stormy seas, his reluctance a force that seemed to fill the cave. He did not like this.

The cave seemed to lean in, listening as Marcus's voice broke the silence. "Isdralan might hold the answers, but time there is a fickle stream. We risk much if we return to find years have passed in our absence." His concern hung in the air like the mist that rose from the damp cave floor.

Durya felt a strange pull at his words, and fear at the thought of lost time—an enemy as formidable as any on the battlefield. She watched Kaci nod, her red hair reflecting the fire's glow, a subtle reminder of the morning's first light. "Well then, it seems we ought to whip up a plan, something to keep the lands from running amok while we jaunt off into uncharted territories."

Sharn's stance was one of a man bracing against a storm, his arms crossed, his brows knitted together. "Isdralan is no simple journey," he said, his voice a low rumble of concern. "Durya, you've always said the caves were a maze of madness. And Aeloria—" His eyes found hers, steady and protective, "—is a land we can touch and challenge together."

There was caution in his tone, a resonance of the same unease that gnawed at her own spirit. She remembered nothing of the caves, yet his words painted a picture of a place she had once known and spoken of with a warrior's wary respect.

Marcus, immersed in deep thought, absentmindedly twirled a small orb of glowing energy between his fingers. "The assassin's trail leads to Aeloria," he mused aloud. "My rights there may be dormant, but they are not dead. They will lend us their ears."

Kaci's solution was swift, like the strike of an arrow. "Sharn, you and Marcus have the right blend of knowledge and magic to search for a cure in Aeloria. Your skills in healing and Marcus' deep understanding of ancient lore could unlock what we need. While you're there, perhaps a brief investigation into the rebel faction. A bit of snooping could give us an edge. Meanwhile, Durya and I—" She paused, her gaze flicking to Durya, seeking affirmation, "—we'll consult the guardians of Isdralan."

"That's fine," Sharn interjected, his voice a deep note of dissent. "But Durya told me of the path you took to Isdralan, and she swore she'd never tread that way again." Durya watched the exchange, feeling like a bystander in her own story, as though her past exploits were legends told by the fireside. She could see the resistance etched into Sharn's stance. His broad shoulders tensed as if bracing against an unseen gale. He was rooted in the tangible, the known, and the idea of returning to Isdralan's embrace sat ill with him.

Kaci stood with an infectious energy. Her face, sprinkled with freckles, shone with a bright, irrepressible enthusiasm, drawing the attention of everyone around her. She chided Sharn. "Ease up on that scowl, Sharn, you great, brooding oak tree," she teased.

In her hand, she held a pennywhistle, its metallic surface gleaming in the cave's dim light. She raised it to her lips and blew. Though no sound echoed in the cave, a palpable sense of magic filled the air, hinting at secrets yet to be revealed. With a knowing smile, she implied, "I've found us a safer route to Isdralan." Her eyes sparkled, hinting at the enchanting journey ahead.

She winked at Sharn, a silent acknowledgment of his concern. "The sea calls us," she declared with a flair that seemed as much a part of her as her bright hair. "The Golden Gull was once Edward's own vessel, and the one that defied the shadows. Its new captain is an ally, and under her guidance, the waters will carry us to Isdralan's shores."

Sharn's frown deepened. His gaze flickered to Durya, then back to Kaci, as if her confidence could sway the very fates. With a rumble like distant thunder, he conceded, the word "Fine" falling from his lips. His grumble was a reluctant surrender to Kaci's plan, a warrior yielding to the strategist in their midst.

As Durya absorbed their words, the texture of each voice, the threads of each argument, she felt the grip of helplessness tighten. Despite the decisions and planning being centered on her, she felt directionless and vulnerable. The Durya they spoke of was a stranger to her now, a shadow she chased in vain.

But she was still Durya. The frustration, the yearning, the silent roar of a leader within—these were hers, memories or not. "We will move forward," she stated, her voice cutting through the doubt. "On both fronts."

Lady Durya watched as Sharn grappled with his sense of duty, his innate need to protect. "While you seek your past, we will secure your future here," he said, though the words seemed to claw their way out of his throat.

In the silent communication between them, there was an understanding—Sharn would stand guard over what remained while Durya reclaimed what was lost. The plan left no one at ease, but it was the path they walked. They all fought for the future of Westerfield, and maybe all of Elanthia.

* * *

In the secluded cove, far from the cacophony of the bustling port, the Golden Gull awaited like a silent promise of adventure. The trek had been quiet, each companion lost in their own thoughts. Durya walked with trepidation, the briny air filling her senses, whispering of the journey ahead.

The ship loomed out of the mist, a silhouette of liberation on the calm waters. A chaotic ballet unfolded on deck. The sailors—a motley crew of human, goblin and orc—navigated the ropes and wood with an effortless grace that belied the danger of their dance.

Before they could cross the threshold to the ship, Durya paused, casting a backward glance at Sharn and Marcus. Kaci, ever eager, had already sprung onto the gangplank with the lightness of a leaf on the wind.

Sharn's towering form loomed, a steadfast presence now marked by an uncharacteristic unease. The lines of his face, set in an unyielding mask of a warrior's resolve, now betrayed his inner conflict. His hands hovered midair, betraying his wish to offer comfort through embrace. Yet, within the space of a breath, his sense of duty reasserted itself, and his arms dropped to his sides. He settled for a bow, deep and respectful.

Marcus stood apart, his goodbye brief, a mere whisper of sentiment against the roar of the sea. "Safe travels, Sister," he murmured, his voice low but clear over the sound of the waves. His eyes locked onto Durya's for a moment, then he tuned to go.

As Durya stepped onto the gangplank, the image of Sharn bowing and Marcus's nod of farewell etched itself into her heart. She carried their silent goodbyes with her, stepping from the solid ground onto the swaying promise of the Golden Gull, ready to chase the horizon and the fragments of her lost self that lay beyond.

Once onboard, a goblin with a hat adorned by a vibrant red feather approached. His grin revealed a mismatched set of teeth, but his eyes sparkled with recognition. "Lady Durya, as I live and breathe! How fare Jeth and Meshach?" he asked, his voice carrying the rasp of the sea.

Durya's heart faltered, the names sparking no light in the dark recesses of her mind. Her lips parted, but it was Kaci who filled the silence, her voice a buoyant note amidst the sea of confusion. "Smeadun, the lady's memories are adrift," Kaci said, her hand giving Durya's arm a reassuring squeeze. "The details are lost to the tides."

It was then the Captain made herself known, her voice booming with a natural authority that demanded attention. Her red hair was like a fiery halo framing her face, each strand ablaze with the reflected light of the rising sun. Her piercing blue eyes, clear and commanding as they swept over her new passengers, were as keen as the edge of the horizon where the sky met the sea. "Ahoy there, noble travelers! Welcome to the Golden Gull, my pride and joy!" Her arms swept wide, as if to embrace the sea and sky alike.

Smeadun's chatter ceased as the Captain stepped forward, the very picture of command despite her diminutive stature. "Let's keep it lively, Smeadun," she called out, her voice ringing clear above the sound of lapping waves, a playful twinkle in her eye belying the firmness in her tone. "We've got guests to attend to, and the tide waits for no one."

The captain's stance was one of confidence, a hand resting on her cocked hip as she surveyed her domain. Durya noted the striking similarity between Kaci and the woman—had it not been for the pointed tips of Kaci's ears, one might wonder at a shared lineage. "I'm Captain Aanee, and I run a tight ship. But worry not," she winked at Durya, "you're in capable hands."

Durya, grappling with the unknown, couldn't help but feel a sliver of admiration for the captain's brash assurance. Captain Aanee's demeanor promised adventure and the potential for rediscovery, offering a silent vow she would not let them falter, not under her watch.

Sharns body looked relaxed as he watched from the shore, but as the gap between the ship and the land widened, his posture stiffened. He raised a hand in farewell, a salute to the bravery of their undertaking.

With a jolt, the ship lurched forward. Durya gripped the rail, the wood solid beneath her fingers. In that moment, as the Golden Gull cut through the water, Durya felt the chains of her uncertainty loosen.

* * *

As Durya and Kaci emerged into Isdralan, the sprawling cityscape of Illebridge unfurled before them, at once both alien and reminiscent of the familiar boulevards of Westerfield. Yet here, the orderliness she knew was replaced by a delightful disorder, a whirlwind of life that spun around them with vibrant intensity.

Illebridge was alive with a diversity that Westerfield's cobbled streets could scarcely dream of. Earthborn—their sturdy frames hewn as if from the mountains themselves — wore their beards like badges of honor. Slender elves moved among them, their silvery laughter weaving through the air, delicate and ethereal like spider silk. Humans of every shade and garb jostled shoulder to shoulder. The city was a melting pot of cultures and classes. Durya also noted her kin, orcs whose proud gait and gleaming tusks stood as emblems of their heritage.

Among these familiar peoples roamed beings that Durya could not name—creatures with scales that shimmered with iridescence, beings of pure energy that crackled as they passed, and small, mischievous entities that seemed to flicker in and out of existence with each blink of her eyes. The city was a breathing organism, pulsating with the lifeblood of a thousand races, each contributing to the wonder—and the overwhelming strangeness—of the place.

Her gaze followed the fluid architecture of the buildings, which morphed with each glance, walls curving and towers spiraling into fantastical shapes. "Does the city always change like this?"

Kaci glanced back at her with a knowing smile, her eyes reflecting the mutable landscape. "That's Isdralan for you," she explained. "It's like stepping into a dream where the dreamer is awake. The city shifts with the whims and wills of those who tread its paths."

As they ventured deeper into the heart of Illebridge, Durya braced herself for the imposing grandeur of a castle or a tower befitting the center of such a place. Instead, the urban maze gave way to an expanse of wild forest that seemed to have sprouted from the very cobblestones. The clamor of the city hushed, as if respecting the sanctity of this verdant haven.

With each step into the forest, the sounds of Illebridge receded, replaced by the symphony of nature—a chorus of rustling leaves, the soft murmur of brooks, and the distant call of creatures unseen. Durya felt the odd sensation of having stepped through another veil, leaving the dream of the city for the dream of the wilds. The contrast was jarring, yet mesmerizing.

Kaci led the way with unwavering certainty, the soft pine needles yielding beneath their steps, guiding Durya not towards a throne but towards an encounter with one of the guardians, in a realm where even the concept of a castle was too mundane to contain the magic that awaited them.

The sudden tranquility was almost tangible, like stepping into a sacred chamber where the world's whispers could not penetrate. Durya stood at the edge, her senses alert, her mind still grappling with a life she could not remember.

A being, indistinguishable from the land, trees, and sky, stood at the center of the clearing. Fia was divine, their form a tapestry of shifting elements that defied the binaries of existence. One moment, their silhouette bore the softness of the maiden; the next, it swelled with the strength of the warrior. Their skin was the rich hue of the fertile earth, and their hair, cropped close, was a dark canopy crowning their ever-changing features.

Fia's presence was both awe-inspiring and unnerving, an embodiment of nature's fluidity. Durya felt her preconceptions peeling away, layer by layer, as she observed Fia's form fluctuate with an effortless grace, a seamless transition that spoke of a being beyond the mortal coil.

Kaci stood beside Durya, her voice hushed as if in reverence. "Orcs of Elyndris revere them as Valkyriara," she murmured, her eyes never leaving the guardian. "And some human sects know them by a name that escapes me. They are the essence of Isdralan's heart."

Durya's gaze remained locked on Fia, a question burning behind her eyes. "Did I... worship Valkyriara?" she asked, her voice barely a whisper, as if afraid to disturb the sanctity of the space.

"Yes," Kaci replied, her affirmation gentle. "You held them in high esteem, a guardian for all seasons and reasons."

Fia's eyes met Durya's, steady and deep, a silent acknowledgment from a being whose existence spanned realms and realities. "Welcome, child of Elyndris," Fia spoke, their voice clear and rich, not imposing but enveloping, as if the air itself carried their words straight to Durya's core. "I am Fia, guardian of thresholds and keeper of the balance. By many names, I am called, and by many paths, I am reached."

Their gaze never wavered from Durya, and though their expression remained serene, there was an intensity there that spoke of immense power. "You come in search of your past," Fia continued, each word deliberate. "The journey to reclaim them will not be without its trials. But that which you seek also seeks you. Together, let us tread the path to restoration."

Fia's presence seemed to root itself in the earth as they unfurled the tapestry of existence before Durya's questioning gaze. "We are but echoes of possibility," they mused, their voice a meditative hum that seemed to weave through the leaves and wind. "Threads in a vast tapestry, stretching across the many looms of time and space. You, I, all of us are infinite— our stories etched into the cosmos in countless iterations, each shaped by the looms, turn."

Their eyes, dark and fathomless, held the wisdom of ages as they continued, "Memories are not merely recollections; they are the essence of our being, energy that cannot be extinguished. They persist, eternal, waiting to be reclaimed." Fia's hand moved with a grace that stirred the air, as if drawing the outline of worlds unseen. "The Caves of Chaos, a realm where lost things are found and time and reality intertwine. It is there you must venture to reclaim the shards of your essence."

Kaci's reaction was a silent tightening of her jaw, a subtle shift in stance. Her frown was brief but telling. A window into a past discomfort with the Caves of Chaos that even Durya, in her current state, could perceive. There was a history there, a shadow that danced behind Kaci's bright demeanor.

Fia's gaze shifted to Kaci, acknowledging but unyielding. "Child of fire, your path is your own to forge, but this journey is for the Lady to decide. She must be the one to walk the corridors of her own soul."

Durya felt Fia's words settle upon her shoulders, a mantle of both fear and purpose. The Caves of Chaos—a name that resonated with an instinctual fear, a primal warning of the trials that lay ahead. Yet within her, amidst the turbulence of forgotten self, stirred a resolve that felt older than her lost memories.

"I will go," she affirmed, despite the quiver of apprehension that threaded through her words. "I must find my past."

Fia nodded, a gesture that held the solemnity of a sacred pact. "So it shall be. The journey will test you, Lady of Elyndris, but remember—within you is the strength of many lifetimes. Trust in it to guide you back to what has been lost."

Durya's gaze lingered on Fia, a myriad of questions swirling in her mind. "But what exactly am I to search for in these caves?" she asked.

Fia regarded her with a serene confidence, the kind that was born from an intimate acquaintance with the ebb and flow of fate. "You seek the essence of your own history," they answered, their tone imbued with the patience of the eternal. "The fragments of your soul that hold the memories you've lost. They are beacons, pulsing with the life force you've left behind."

Durya frowned, the concept as elusive as the memories she yearned to retrieve. "But how will I find these fragments if I don't remember what I'm searching for?"

Fia's response was a smile, cryptic yet assuring. "Trust in

the journey, Lady Durya. What you seek also seeks you. Your memories will guide you—they've been waiting for you to listen."

She leaned closer, her words like a gentle yet compelling force. "You must endeavor to collect every memory, no matter how fleeting or distant it may seem. Some hide in the laughter of a forgotten day, others in the tears of lost nights. Do not overlook even the smallest, for in their entirety, they hold the power to unlock the truths you seek."

Fia's expression turned solemn, her eyes reflecting her words. "After this event unfolds, the landscape of your reality will shift. It's like the turning of a great wheel—inevitable and transformative. When that moment arrives, these memories, these echoes of your soul, will be your guiding stars. They will light your path, reveal secrets long buried, and grant you the clarity to understand the purpose of your journey."

She paused, letting her words sink in. "So, gather them close, Lady Durya. Let them be your strength, your wisdom. For when the world changes, it will be these memories that stand as pillars of your resilience, guiding you to your true destiny."

Beside her, Kaci exhaled a sigh that seemed to carry a thousand reluctant steps. "The Caves of Chaos are not my friend," she confessed, "but I'll stay by you, just as I've always done."

Fia turned their gaze upon Kaci, and their next words were laden with caution. "Beware, Child of Fire, for the caves reflect not only the seeker but also the darkness within. Keep your own shadows at bay, lest they rise to meet you."

Kaci squared her shoulders as Fia's words of caution settled over her, the usual spark that danced in her eyes flickering with a shadow of doubt. "I'll be careful," she responded, her voice a whisper against the guardian's warning.

Durya, observing her friend's change, felt the undercurrents of something deeper, something Kaci had carried with her all this time. "What is this darkness Fia speaks of?"

Kaci met her gaze, and in that moment, Durya saw the firebrand's hidden depths—a turmoil beneath the surface that Kaci had always masked with laughter and bravado. "We all have our battles," Kaci replied, her smile a wane echo of its usual brightness. "Some shadows are cast by our own light. I've learned to dance with mine."

The assurance in Kaci's words did little to veil the truth of her struggle, and Durya felt her friend's unspoken fears. It was a stark reminder that they each bore their own burdens, invisible and heavy.

Taking a breath, Durya reached out, her hand finding Kaci's in a grip that spoke of solidarity. "Whatever darkness we must face, we'll confront it as we always have, I think—together."

With Kaci by her side and Fia's presence guiding them, Durya felt confident. "It's decided, then," she announced, her words carving certainty into the moment. "We venture into the heart of chaos, and we reclaim what has been taken."

"Side by side, we walk this path, and from the shadows," Kaci added, "We will emerge into the light."

6

Departure into the Unknown

Sunlight pierced the forest canopy, throwing sharp shadows that flickered clearing. The usual chatter of the forest hushed, as if it too sensed the importance of their quest. Fia, standing tall and unwavering, was a striking contrast against the wild backdrop, both a part of it and yet somehow beyond it. Their eyes, deep pools of knowing, held an ageless wisdom, cutting through the present. "Your journey now takes you beyond these woods," Fia declared, their voice emotionless but commanding. "Ahead lie the Caves of Chaos, a crucible to test your mettle. Stand strong."

Durya met Fia's gaze, her feelings a tumultuous sea battling against the tides of uncertainty. She sensed the challenge in Fia's words, a call to confront not just the physical dangers that awaited but the deeper, more personal trials of identity and memory.

"Thank you, Fia," Durya replied, her voice carrying resolve despite the unease that lingered beneath. "I shall face what comes."

Kaci nodded in agreement, though her expression betrayed

apprehension. Together, they turned to leave, stepping away from the guardian's imposing presence and back into the realm of Illebridge.

As they made their way toward the Golden Gull, the city seemed to have shifted subtly. The streets, which had earlier bustled with an eclectic mix of inhabitants, now appeared more serene, almost reflective of their own internal journey. The buildings and pathways seemed to acknowledge their departure, the magical essence of the city sending them off with a silent blessing.

Durya couldn't help but feel a connection to the city, its ever-changing nature mirroring her own quest for identity. With each step, she felt the pull of her forgotten past.

The journey back to the Golden Gull was less a physical traversal and more a transition from Fia's guidance to the uncertainty of the unexplored. Durya's heart, though heavy, beat with the rhythm of a warrior setting forth into battle.

Aboard the ship, they sailed towards a remote island that harbored the entrance to the caves. The journey across the channel was akin to a passage from an old mariner's lore. The vessel, robust in build, glided through the water with unexpected elegance, its sails puffing out like the wings of a colossal seabird. On this brief sea trip, the horizon melded into a seamless line where sky and sea embraced, the world around them expanding into an immense expanse.

Captain Aanee navigated the vessel with a deft hand, her presence on deck as commanding as it was reassuring. She moved about with a sailor's ease, her eyes keenly watching the sails and the sea ahead. Now and then, she'd throw a quip or a story over her shoulder, her voice carrying over the wind, a mix of salt and sagacity.

With a red-feathered hat perched jauntily atop his head, the goblin Smeadun scurried about, attending to his duties with an earnest diligence. He often approached Durya, offering snippets of seafaring wisdom or inquiring about her well-being.

Durya was caught in a whirlpool of thoughts. The rhythmic creak of the timbers and the soothing rush of the sea provided a backdrop to her introspection. She pondered over the fragmented pieces of her past, the gaps in her memory like dark voids that seemed to grow deeper the more she tried to peer into them. Her identity felt adrift, untethered from the anchor of her experiences.

She stood at the rail, her gaze fixed on the churning waters below, wondering about the person she used to be. The warrior, the leader, the friend—these were titles given to her by others, but without her memories, they felt like borrowed garments, ill-fitting and unfamiliar.

As Isdralan's coastline became a distant memory, Durya found herself drawn to the bow. There, near the proud figurehead, she felt an inexplicable connection. It was a beautifully crafted golden gull that seemed to possess an aura of familiarity. Its wings were outstretched as if in mid-flight over the endless sea. Being near it felt like being near an old friend.

Durya stood close, her hand hovering but not quite touching the polished metal. It was almost as though the gull whispered to her, a murmuring in the back of her mind. Words, or perhaps memories, seemed to dance just beyond her reach, tantalizing and elusive.

Lost in this strange communion, she barely noticed Captain Aanee's approach until the captain stood beside her, her lively demeanor subdued. The captain's eyes were fixed on the figurehead as she reached out to touch the carving.

"You must be someone special if he speaks to you," Aanee murmured, her voice a low blend of reverence and wonder.

Durya, surprised, turned to face her. "He?" she asked, confusion in her voice. "Aren't ships referred to as 'she'?"

Aanee gave a small smile, her eyes still on the figurehead. "Most are," she conceded. "But not this one. He's different, always has been. There's more to the Golden Gull than just wood and sails."

The captain's words hung in the air, a riddle wrapped in the ship's mystery. Captain Aanee seemed to hesitate, as if on the brink of divulging a secret.

"I'll leave you to your thoughts," she said, patting the figurehead before turning to walk away. "Keep in mind, the sea holds countless tales, and some are whispered only to those destined to hear them."

Left alone with the golden gull, Durya gazed out across the water, pondering Aanee's words. The sense of connection to the ship, to the figurehead, was a puzzle that added another layer to her forgotten past. She wondered what secrets the gull held, what stories it might share if only she could understand its silent language.

Before long, the Gull anchored off a rugged, untamed shoreline, where the relentless waves crashed against jagged rocks. There was no dock in this land seldom visited, a secret kept by the sea and the wild. Lady Durya and Kaci prepared to disembark, their journey to the shore requiring a smaller vessel. They lowered a dinghy into the churning waters, the small boat bobbing like a cork in the ocean's vastness.

As they rowed toward the shore, Durya's gaze swept over the wild landscape, its untamed beauty different that the structured elegance of Isdralan's cities. The shoreline was a jumble of rocks and sand, overgrown with hardy vegetation that clung to life amidst the spray of saltwater.

Upon reaching the shore, they were greeted by a young girl, barely ten, with an air of wisdom that seemed too profound for her years. Her eyes, bright and curious, sparkled with a hidden knowledge as she watched them approach.

"Hello," the girl called out, her voice carried the lilt of youth. "I know you! You are Lady Durya and Kaci. I'm Muirenn, Mir's daughter."

Kaci's face lit up with recognition. "Muirenn! We met you the last time we were here. You helped us navigate the caves," she said, her tone warm.

Durya looked at the young girl, feeling a pang of frustration at her own blank slate of memories. "I'm sorry, I don't remember," she admitted, the words heavy with the loss of not knowing this bright-eyed child who seemed to know her.

Muirenn's smile didn't waver. "That's alright," she said. "The caves take as much as they give. But I remember you."

Durya nodded. It was disconcerting, meeting someone who knew a part of her she could not access, a piece of her history that remained shrouded in the fog of amnesia.

"Are you heading to the caves again?" Muirenn asked, tilting her head, her gaze shifting between the two women.

Kaci nodded. "We are. Lady Durya is hoping to find some answers about her past."

Muirenn's expression turned thoughtful, a seriousness settling over her young features. "The caves can be tricky," she said. "But I can show you the way. I've learned a lot since we last met."

As they made their way to the Caves of Chaos, Muirenn led

the trio with a skip in her step. The path wound through dense underbrush and over rocky outcrops, each turn and twist revealing more of the wild, untamed landscape.

Muirenn chattered away, her voice a steady stream of anecdotes and observations that filled the air with a sense of adventure. "Last time you were here, I saw a family of shadow foxes near the entrance," she recounted. "They're shy, but if you're quiet, you can glimpse them. Their fur changes color with the light!"

Kaci laughed, her spirits lifted by Muirenn's cheerfulness. "I've never seen one," she said. "But I heard if to follow one, it vanishes like smoke."

Durya listened with a sense of detachment. She observed Muirenn's animated gestures and bright eyes, her mind grappling with the inability to recall any past encounters with this remarkable child. Muirenn's presence was like a living bridge to a part of Durya's life that remained out of reach.

As they approached the mouth of the caves, Muirenn's demeanor shifted, solemnity tempering her youthful exuberance. "The caves can be tricky," she warned, her tone more serious. "They change all the time, like they're alive. You need to be careful."

Durya eyed the looming entrance, its dark maw an ominous invitation to the unknown. She could feel the history within its shadows, a history she was a part of yet estranged from.

"And watch for the whispering stones," Muirenn added, her voice dropping. "They say the caves talk to those who listen. But not all whispers are friendly."

Kaci nodded, her expression turning pensive. "We'll be on our guard," she assured the young girl.

"Oh! and if you see Illyan, tell him I say hi!" Muirenn

brightened. "But I do not think he will be there." She shrugged.

Muirenn's words, though spoken with the innocence of youth, carried a depth of understanding. The child was a fount of knowledge and lore about a place that seemed as mysterious and complex as Durya's own lost memories.

With a deep breath, Durya steeled herself for the journey ahead. The Caves of Chaos awaited. A labyrinth that promised answers but threatened with its unpredictable nature.

As they entered, Durya, Kaci, and their young guide, Muirenn, shared a moment of quiet understanding. The mouth of the cave yawned before them, dark and foreboding.

"Thank you, Muirenn," Kaci said, offering a grateful smile to the girl. "We owe our progress to you."

Muirenn's eyes sparkled. "I wish I could go with you, but mother says I am not ready yet," she replied, her tone tinged with disappointment yet firm with resolve. "Don't forget, the caves are different for everyone. You'll find what you're meant to find."

Durya looked down at Muirenn, feeling a swell of gratitude. "Your help has been invaluable," she said, the words sincere even though they came from a stranger to Muirenn's past kindness.

With a last wave, Muirenn turned and disappeared back onto the beach, leaving Durya and Kaci at the threshold of their journey into the unknown.

As they stepped into the cave, the cool, musty air enveloped them, a tangible shift from the world outside. The initial cavern was vast, the walls rough and dotted with stalactites and stalagmites. Their footsteps echoed, a reminder of the surrounding emptiness. But as they ventured deeper, the cavern changed. The rough walls gave way to smooth, almost polished stone, and the cavern narrowed into a long, winding hallway.

"This... doesn't seem like a natural formation," Durya observed, her voice echoing off the walls. "Is this normal?"

Kaci glanced back with a wry smile. "In the Caves of Chaos, 'normal' isn't a word you should count on. These caves have a mind of their own."

The flickering torchlight cast dancing shadows on the walls, creating shapes that seemed to move just at the edge of her vision.

"What happened last time you were here?" Durya asked.

Kaci's expression turned somber for a moment. "Last time, we began from Aeloria. Things were different. We were different," she said, her voice trailing off as if lost in memories that Durya couldn't access. "We lost someone important. This place... it tests you, in ways you can't imagine."

Durya nodded, understanding that the caves held more than just physical challenges. They were a place where one confronted more than just the darkness of the earth.

As they continued down the hallway, the sense of entering another world grew stronger. The air felt charged, the silence pregnant with unspoken secrets. The passage twisted and turned, branching off into multiple corridors that seemed to defy logic. With no doors or clear markings, each choice of path felt like a leap into a dark abyss.

"This place is like a maze," Durya murmured. She ran her hand along the smooth stone wall, feeling a slight vibration under her fingertips. "Which way we should go?"

Kaci, holding the torch ahead, paused at a fork in the path. "Last time, we just followed our instincts," she replied, peering down each corridor. "But the caves change. The path that was once correct may now be a dead end."

Durya looked down each pathway, a sense of unease creeping over her. Despite having no memory of this place, there was a familiarity in the air. It had an oppressive silence, and the shadows seemed to move just beyond the torchlight.

"Let's go left," Durya decided, her voice more confident than she felt. As they took the left path, the corridor narrowed, the ceiling lowering until they had to stoop to proceed.

The deeper they went, the more Durya felt a growing sense of dread. It was as if the cave itself was aware of their presence, watching and waiting with bated breath. Her heart beat faster, not just from the physical exertion but from a primal fear that seemed to seep from the very walls.

"Do you feel you are being watched?" Durya asked, her voice barely above a whisper.

Kaci nodded, her face illuminated by the flickering torch. "Yes. It's part of the cave's charm, or curse, depending on how you see it. It tests not just your body, but your mind and spirit."

They encountered their first obstacle, a narrow crevice that split the path in two. The gap was just wide enough for them to squeeze through, but it was a tight fit, the rocks cold and unyielding against their skin.

"This place," Durya grunted as she pushed her way through the crevice, "it's like it's alive."

Kaci emerged on the other side, helping Durya out. "That's because it is. The Caves of Chaos are more than just rock. They're a part of Isdralan's magic, its heart and soul."

Once past the crevice, the path opened up into a larger chamber, the walls here glowing with an ethereal light. Durya looked around, her eyes wide. The chamber exuded an aura of power and mystery, almost like a sanctuary.

As they moved through the chamber, Durya couldn't shake the feeling that she was walking through her own forgotten past. In the chamber, the cave's strange nature continued to unfold. The whispering walls, with their subtle, almost inaudible murmurs, seemed to speak to Durya's soul. It was as if the cave itself beckoned her to uncover its secrets, much like the forgotten corners of her mind urged her to remember.

Suddenly, a soft glow caught Durya's eye. Floating in the air before her was an orb, its surface shimmering with a soft light. It pulsated, casting a mesmerizing luminescence that filled the chamber with a dreamlike quality. Durya found herself drawn to it, her steps slow but deliberate, as if an invisible thread pulled her towards the mysterious sphere.

Kaci, noticing the orb and Durya's trance-like approach, reached out a hand. "Durya, wait! Don't touch—"

But Kaci's words were lost in the echo of the chamber. Durya, entranced by the orb's presence, couldn't resist the urge to reach out. Her fingers brushed against the surface and a surge of energy coursed through her. She felt the world whirl and twist around her, as if spiraling into an abyss that yawned open beneath her feet, pulling her into its depths.

The sensation was disorienting, a whirlwind of colors and sounds enveloping her. Durya's heart raced, her mind a storm of confusion and panic. She was no longer in the cave, no longer standing beside Kaci. Instead, she was being pulled in, a fragment of time captured within the orb.

Durya's senses reeled as she acclimatized to the sudden shift in her surroundings. The ground beneath her was soft and damp, the air smelling like marsh and earth. She stood at the edge of a marshland, surrounded by a group of orcs. Their rugged features and imposing statures were familiar.

As her gaze swept across the faces in the clan, recognition dawned on her. These were her people, her orc clan. A sense of belonging, long lost and buried, stirred within her.

Before the group stood two human nobles, flanked by a contingent of guards. The nobles' attire was elegant, a vivid reminder of a life vastly different from the one the orcs led. Durya's heart skipped a beat as she recognized them—they were her foster parents, the ones who had raised her after she was separated from her clan.

This realization hit her with the force of a thunderclap. She remembered! This was her memory, a piece of her past unfolding before her eyes.

Durya observed, as a bystander, the younger version of herself, cradled in the arms of an orc elder. She was tiny, two years old at most, her bluish-gray skin and budding tusks marking her as orcish. Beside her, an older orc child stood, his features similar to hers. Durya understood this was her brother, a fellow piece of her fragmented past.

During this solemn gathering, a human child, only three or four years old, stood by the side of Durya's future foster parents. The scene unfolding before her was one of diplomatic exchange, a mutual agreement steeped in hope and apprehension. The children, though too young to comprehend, were central figures in a cultural exchange designed to foster understanding and peace between the orc and human worlds.

Durya watched as her foster parents interacted with the orc leaders. Her foster father spoke with a voice that wove threads of hope into every word, his eyes shining with sincerity and his posture humble, embodying respect and earnestness in every gesture. The conversation, though silent to Durya's ears, resonated, signifying the moment—a gesture of trust and a bid for lasting peace.

Her foster mother, pregnant, stood with a hand resting on her swollen belly, her eyes full of compassion as she looked upon the orc children. The exchange was not just a diplomatic arrangement but a heartfelt commitment to raising these children as their own, to bridge the gap between their disparate cultures.

As Durya stood within the memory, deep, visceral emotions engulfed her. She looked upon her younger self, a small orc child, and felt a surge of protectiveness and sorrow. She knew the challenges that lay ahead for these children, raised in a world that viewed them with distrust and fear. A world that was not their own.

She turned her gaze to the human child being welcomed by the orcs, a sense of foreboding washing over her. She possessed a deep intuition that this child wouldn't make it in the orc realm. The realization hit her like a physical blow, and she felt an overwhelming urge to scream, to warn them, to stop this exchange from happening.

But her shouts went unheard, her pleas lost in the memory's fabric. It was then she noticed Fia, the guardian, standing at the periphery of the scene. Fia's presence was both comforting and unsettling.

Fia's voice echoed around Durya, imparting a crucial truth. *Altering this moment won't erase what has been,* they explained. *It will fracture the memory, creating a divergence. Infinite possibilities exist, and while you can forge a new path, the one you've known won't vanish. It simply becomes one of many truths, a fragment among countless others in the tapestry of your existence.*

Durya's heart raced with conflict. The urge to intervene, to save the children from their fates, was powerful. She stepped forward, her resolve hardening. But as she neared the scene, a profound sadness overwhelmed her. Tears streamed down her face as her decision bore down on her.

Fia's words lingered in the air. *The journey ahead will not be easy. It will only grow more challenging. But remember, the choice is always yours.*

Durya collapsed to her knees, her sobs echoing in the memory's stillness. The pain of the moment, realizing what these children, her younger self included, would endure, was unbearable. Yet, she understood the gravity of changing the past. The lives they led, the paths they forged, were all part of a greater story.

With a heavy heart, Durya stood. She couldn't change the past, not without losing herself and the journey that had made her who she was. With one last, lingering look at the scene, she turned away, her spirit fortified by the knowledge that her past had shaped her, but it did not define her.

Durya was pulled back into the present by Kaci's voice. "Durya! Durya, are you alright?" Kaci's hands were on her shoulders, shaking her.

Blinking, Durya looked around, disoriented. The walls of the cave closed in around her, the light of the orb gone. She was back in the Caves of Chaos, staring into Kaci's worried eyes.

"I... yes, I think so," Durya stammered, her mind still reeling from the vividness of the memory. "What happened?"

Kaci's relief was palpable, but her expression remained tense. "When you touched that orb, it just... it grew, enveloped you in this blinding light. It was as if it was consuming you. You started shaking, and I thought..." Kaci trailed off, swallowing hard. "But then, the light calmed down, became gentle, and faded away. It was like watching a storm turn into a calm sea."

Durya tried to steady herself. The memory orb's power had been overwhelming, transporting her into her past with a force that had left her shaken.

"I saw... I saw a memory," Durya murmured, still processing the experience. "From when I was very young. It was about how I came to be with my foster parents, about the pact between the orcs and humans."

Kaci listened, her expression turning from worry to fascination. "That's incredible. It sounds like these orbs don't just hold memories; they let you live them."

Durya nodded, understanding dawning on her. The caves were a repository of time, and each orb a gateway to the past. Fia's words echoed in her mind. *The choice is always yours.* It was a reminder that her path, though fraught with pain and uncertainty, was hers to walk. The journey to rediscover herself was just beginning.

"We should keep moving," Durya said, her voice firmer now. "There may be more to find, more pieces of my past that can help me understand who I am."

Kaci agreed, and they continued deeper into the caves, their path illuminated by the torches' flickering flame. The experience with the orb had changed something within Durya. Though the amnesia still clouded much of her history, the connection to her past had been reignited, filling her with a determination to uncover the full truth of her identity.

7

Echos of Shadows

Silence shrouded Lady Durya and Kaci as they traversed the caverns' paths. Durya's mind was a tumultuous sea. As she grappled with Fia's presence, uncertainty gnawed at her. Had Fia been there in flesh and blood, or a ghostly figment born Durya's memories?

In the throes of the memory, Durya had remembered herself and everything that would come. This clarity now slipped through her fingers like grains of sand. All that remained were the images of what she had just witnessed, as ephemeral as a dream at dawn. Her lips pressed into a thin line.

Kaci sensed the shift in Durya's mood. "You okay?" she asked, her voice gentle.

"No," Durya huffed. "I am not okay! It's all right there, within my grasp, but I can't reach it. When I was in the memory, everything was lucid, connected. Now, it's like trying to catch mist."

Kaci's brow furrowed. "Do you remember what happened in that memory?" she probed, hoping to untangle the threads of Durya's thoughts.

Lady Durya paused. "I do," she responded, her voice distant, reflective.

"It's fascinating," Durya mused, more to herself than to Kaci. "In that memory, I saw not just the past but what was to be, glimpses of the future. It's as if the memory orbs hold not just recollections, but keys to understanding the paths not taken."

Kaci's face lit up with determination. "Then we'll find more orbs."

Durya nodded, her resolve hardening. "Yes, more orbs. They are the keys to unlocking my life."

The caverns unfolded before them, revealing chambers filled with crystal formations that glittered like stars. Here, in the bowels of the earth, time seemed to stand still, and the line between past, present, and future blurred.

A sudden, eerie skittering noise shattered the silence behind them, echoing off the cavern walls like a whispered warning. Kaci spun around with a swift, practiced grace, her eyes darting through the dimness. The caverns lay still and silent around them, an oppressive quietude descending as if the very shadows themselves were holding their breath. Durya stood motionless, her own gaze piercing the shadows, trying to discern what secrets the ancient caverns might hide within their stony embrace.

They moved onward, their steps cautious, when the distinct sound of footsteps reverberated through the cavern.

"Hello?" Kaci called out. "Who's there?"

The caverns responded with silence.

"It can't be anything good," Lady Durya murmured, her senses on high alert.

Kaci nodded, raising a hand to signal Durya. "It's probably nothing," she said, a little too loudly. Her pace slowed, a subtle cue. It took a moment, but Durya understood Kaci's intent. See rambled about the memory orb, a distraction to cover Kaci's stealthy movements into the shadows.

As Durya continued her monologue, she couldn't help but marvel at Kaci's skill in vanishing unseen. She glanced over her shoulder, searching the darkness for a sign of Kaci, only to collide with a warm, solid figure.

"OUCH!" a male voice exclaimed.

"Durya!" Kaci's voice rang out from the shadows, appearing at Durya's side in an instant.

"Who are you?" Kaci demanded, her stance defensive. "What are you doing here? Are you following us?" Her questions came rapid-fire, her eyes narrowing. "Micah?"

The man, taken aback by the barrage of questions, opened and closed his mouth, struggling to find words. He had dark hair, long and adorned with a feather, and when he finally smiled, the lines around his eyes deepened. "Hawke," he introduced himself. "I'm looking for my son. I do not know who Micah is, and no, I'm not following you. You bumped into me, remember?"

His gaze shifted to Durya, widening, as he took a step back. "I'm not in Kansas anymore."

"Kansas?" Kaci echoed, her brow furrowing. "I've read about that place, back when I was on Earth..."

Hawke chuckled, inching closer to Kaci. "Yeah, I'm not from around here. Wherever here is."

As the conversation unfolded, Durya noticed Hawke's continued attempts to maintain distance from her. He was intimidated, which satisfied her. Standing tall, she drew upon her full titles she did not remember, but had been assured by her friends were hers. She introduced herself with a regal poise. "I am Lady Durya Barclay-Conwyn, Baroness of Westerfield, and Duchess intended of Marshfield, second only to the King. You shall address me with the respect my position commands."

Kaci struggled to suppress a giggle, while Hawke took another cautious step back.

"Just Hawke," he replied, giving an awkward bow.

"What are you doing here?" Kaci's eyes narrowed as she questioned him. "This place is not safe!"

Hawke's expression twisted into a visage of confusion and worry. "My son," he began, his voice tinged with desperation. "He..." He paused, struggling to articulate the bizarre nature of his predicament. "He disappeared. Just vanished. I tracked him all the way to the shore, and then..." He sighed, his gaze flickering between Durya and Kaci. "A rat led me here. I swear, I'm not on any sort of mind-altering substances," he added, his hands raised in a defensive gesture.

Durya exchanged a glance with Kaci, who shrugged in response. The tale was odd, yet not unbelievable.

"You haven't seen a young man in his twenties, have you?" Hawke asked.

Both women shook their heads in unison. The caverns were vast, a place where many mysteries remained unsolved.

"Then I must keep looking." Hawke declared.

Durya opened her mouth to offer help, but Kaci interjected, "Good luck in your search!" There was a subtle nudge to move him along.

The man turned and continued down the passage. They watched until he was out of hearing range.

Lady Durya frowned, her mind wrestling with the decision. "If this place is so dangerous, shouldn't we help this man?" she queried, her tone laced with concern.

Kaci let out a small giggle. "Baroness, how uncharacteristic of you to suggest such a thing!" She then continued, more seriously, "If the caves are anything like the rest of Isdralan, he'll likely wake in his own bed, pondering over the strange dream he just had."

Yet Durya's frown deepened, her intuition stirring within her. "I'm not sure I agree. Something about him felt significant, as if he might be a part of a memory, a piece of this intricate puzzle we're trying to solve."

Kaci cast a lingering look in the direction Hawke had retreated, her expression turning somber, a shadow passing over her usually bright features. She shook her head. "I don't think he's involved in our quest, not in the way you think."

Lady Durya noticed the subtle change in Kaci's demeanor. Despite the gaps in her memory, Durya's sharpness and keen observation had not dulled. She could sense there was more behind Kaci's words, a depth of thought or doubt perhaps, that Kaci herself might not have acknowledged.

As they continued their journey through the caverns, the encounter with Hawke lingered in Durya's mind, mingling with the shift she had seen in Kaci. The caverns were more than mere stone, and in their echoing halls, Durya sensed that every meeting, every shadowed corner, might hold the key to unraveling the mysteries of her past and perhaps the future.

After wandering the paths of the cavern for the better part of the day, Kaci slumped onto the ground with a heavy sigh, her shoulders drooping in frustration. "Nothing!" she exclaimed, throwing her hands up in exasperation. "Not even another memory found. It's like chasing shadows in here."

Durya, leaning against a nearby stalagmite, raised an eyebrow in her friend's direction, a slight smile playing on her lips.

"Did you expect this quest to be a walk in the park?" she asked.

Kaci let out a light giggle, the sound echoing on the stone walls. "Well... no. But you know, usually, you're the one who's impatient. I guess it's a... cavernous difference this time," she said, a twinkle in her eye.

Durya couldn't help but chuckle, her usual stoic demeanor forgotten. "Cavernous difference, really? That's so... deep," she retorted.

Kaci's grin widened. "Ah, I see what you did there! That's boulder than I expected from you, Durya."

The rare sound of Durya's laughter filled the air, warm and genuine. "Well, I guess I'm just full of surprises," she said, her guard lowered in this moment of camaraderie.

Kaci sat up, brushing off her clothes. "Alright, let's keep moving. Who knows, maybe we'll stumble upon a memory or a... stalactite joke along the way?"

Durya offered Kaci a hand up. "Lead the way."

As they paused, a distant clatter, like stone clacking against stone, reached their ears. They froze, holding their breath, listening, but the sound was swallowed by the encompassing silence of the caverns.

Kaci's voice broke the quiet, laced with unease. "Do you get the feeling that someone, or something, is following us?"

Lady Durya nodded. "I do. At first, I thought it was just that man Hawke, but the sensation persists."

Kaci didn't respond. She sat in contemplative silence, rummaging through her pack before pulling out some rations. "Hungry?" she offered some food.

Durya's stomach growled in response, a sound that seemed to echo in the cavern. She hadn't realized her hunger until the food was in her hands. She bit into the square, the taste bland but satisfying. The ration, known as field bread, was a dense mix of nuts and grains, designed not to spoil during long journeys. The recipe was Aelorian, though humans had adapted it, replacing the exotic nuts from the Arba Vitae tree with more common varieties.

Suddenly, Durya's eyes widened. "Kaci!" she exclaimed. "I remember field bread."

The smile that spread across Kaci's face was radiant, lighting up the gloom. "That's incredible, Durya! Perhaps you recovered more from the memory orb than you realized!"

"And the Arba Vitae," Durya continued, memories beginning to piece together. "The tree of your people."

At the mention of the Arba Vitae, Kaci's expression shifted, the joy fading into a somber reflection. "Yes, the Arba Vitae," she mumbled.

"What's wrong?" Durya asked.

"The Arba vitae is dead." Kaci answered. "Part of her demise... it's my fault. If I had been stronger, figured things out sooner, my people might not be in such turmoil."

Durya, sensing the depth of Kaci's guilt, laid a comforting hand on her friend's shoulder. "From what I've seen and known of you, that's probably far from the truth," she reassured. She tried to find a memory of Kaci, to offer a more personal comfort, but the past remained shrouded in fog. "You are clearly brave, strong, and fearless. And I don't believe I would have chosen a weak person as a friend." She offered Kaci a supportive grin, trying to lighten the heavy atmosphere.

Kaci's attempt at a smile was tinged with sadness. "No... No, you wouldn't have," she agreed, her eyes glistening. "But you don't remember, Durya. After the shadows were defeated, you stayed to help your people rebuild. Both your peoples. Even after everything that happened with Edward, after all that was taken from you, you remained brave."

"And you didn't?" Durya's voice held no judgment, only curiosity.

Kaci's voice dropped to a whisper, heavy with unspoken emotion. "I left as soon as I could. I always wished you could have come with me. But you refused."

The shadows in the cavern played across Kaci's face, casting one side in light, highlighting her freckles and the traces of joy that once were, and the other in darkness, mirroring the hidden depths of her soul.

Durya studied Kaci for a moment, her eyes thoughtful. "Why did you leave, Kaci?"

Kaci hesitated, struggling with her answer. "I... I had to," she finally said. "I lost more than I ever let on in that fight, and I needed... I needed to resolve that."

"And did you?" Durya pressed.

Kaci turned her face away, letting the shadows consume her features. "No," she admitted.

This revelation deepened the complexity of their journey. The caverns, with their ancient secrets and echoing silence, seemed to mirror the labyrinth of emotions and memories that Durya and Kaci were navigating. As Durya reflected on Kaci's confession, she realized their quest was not just about recovering the past, but also about confronting the unresolved sorrows and losses that had shaped them both.

Lady Durya and Kaci found themselves enveloped in an introspective silence. Durya reached out and took Kaci's hand, offering a silent gesture of solidarity and understanding. They sat together, lost in their thoughts, when, as if summoned by their stillness, another memory orb floated into the room.

Both women burst into laughter. "We walk all day, and when we finally stop looking, it comes to us," Kaci giggled.

Durya gazed at the orb, watching the motes of color swirling around it. She knew what she needed to do, yet a hesitation gripped her. The orb held not just memories, but potential truths about herself and the path she might choose.

Kaci's voice broke through her contemplation. "What's wrong? Was the last memory that bad?"

Durya struggled to articulate her feelings. "No... Yes..." she started, her voice trailing off. "The memory wasn't bad. It was filled with... hope, I think. But it's what I knew would come after that troubles me."

Kaci nodded in understanding. "I suppose that's a bit of a curse, huh? Not knowing if you can change things."

"That's the trouble," Durya replied. "I'm pretty sure I can change things if I choose to. But Fia warned me that if I do, it will not make a difference."

Kaci looked thoughtful, her gaze introspective. "Is that so bad?" she asked.

Durya sighed. "I don't know myself well enough to know the answer. And what else changes as a result? Fia was clear that changing things was complicated."

"So it seems you have choices," Kaci observed, her eyes meeting Durya's. "We can walk away, find our way home, and you can start life anew. Or you can reclaim the memories that are yours. You even have the power to direct your life as you wish."

Durya let out a heavy sigh, the enormity of her decision weighing on her. "But what does that mean for everyone else?"

After a moment of reflection, Durya squared her shoulders and strode towards the orb, determination in her every step.

She clasped it with both hands and braced herself for the flood of memories.

The orb glowed brighter as she touched the light in the darkness. As her fingers made contact, the orb pulsed, and she was tumbling through time and space again until she landed with a soft thump on the ground.

This time, Durya found herself concealed behind a large tree, observing two orcish children engaged in a playful sword fight. The girl, a younger version of herself, wielded her wooden sword with skill and intensity. The boy, slightly older, held back, allowing the young Durya to claim victory in their mock battles.

In the distance, a woman's voice called out, "Durya? Durya, where have you run off to? It's time for afternoon tea." The familiarity of the voice stirred a deep nostalgia in Durya. she was witnessing a fragment of her own childhood.

The boy grinned at the young Durya. "You probably ought to go. Your mama is quite formidable when she's angry."

"I don't want to," her younger self protested, stamping her foot. "I just want to fight."

The boy watched her, his expression a mix of affection and something deeper, something unspoken. He looked as if he wanted to say more, but remained quiet.

In a burst of youthful exuberance, the young Durya exclaimed, "We should run away! You and me, we can join a clan and always be friends."

A look of sadness crossed the boy's face, and a rush of memories flooded the older Durya's mind. This boy was her Sharn, her dearest childhood friend, the only one who had understood her inner fire, a fire that even her magic-entangled brother could not comprehend.

"Let me go have some tea and crackers, then I'll be back, and we will run away," her younger self promised.

Sharn gave a small bow. "Yes, lady," he answered. "When we do, I will be your knight, always watching over you. I swear it!"

The younger Durya giggled and bonked him on the head with her wooden sword. "More like I'll be watching over you!"

After watching this tender moment from her hidden vantage point, Durya felt an overwhelming desire to step out, to warn her younger self, to alter the course of events. But she made a resolute decision then and there. She would not change who she was; she would endure all the pain to come once again.

As the younger Durya ran off towards the manor, intercepted by one of her mother's ladies, the older Durya knew this was the last time her younger self would ever play at swords with Sharn. Her childhood would now shift towards the rigid training of a lady, in a world unwilling to accept a blue-skinned orc as one of their own.

Sharn gazed after her with a look of love and care, and Durya realized his words had always been true. He had always watched over her, always been her protector, her confidant. As the memory faded, Durya was left with a bittersweet sense of gratitude and sorrow, understanding the depth of their bond and the sacrifices they both had made.

Emerging from the memory felt gentler this time, its echoes fading into the cavern's silence, leaving Durya wrapped in contemplation. Each memory, she knew, carried a lesson about her true self. Yet, all she could discern now was the image of a naïve child, blind to the genuine love and care that was so clear in hindsight.

Kaci remained where she had been when the memory claimed

Durya, sitting cross-legged on the ground, her eyes closed in a meditative state.

"I'm back," Durya whispered.

"Ready to talk about it?" Kaci asked without opening her eyes.

"Not yet," Durya replied. The puzzle pieces of her past were still assembling, too fragmented to share. "Let's move on. Maybe we'll find another orb before we need rest."

Kaci nodded, rising to her feet. They soon found themselves in a chamber different from the rest.

"What's this place?" Durya inquired, her curiosity piqued.

"Not sure," Kaci responded, peering into the unknown. "It's new to me."

The air was dense with history, every relic pulsating with untold stories. Tapestries adorned the walls, their threads weaving the cosmic dance of stars and planets, while shelves bore vials filled with twilight essences and devices twinkling with celestial light.

Kaci looked around, her eyes scanning the room. "We should be careful in here," she advised in a subdued voice.

Drawn to the relics, Durya approached a shelf. Her gaze fixed on a crystal orb, similar to those she sought, but imbued with a deeper, more significant energy. It seemed to embody the universe's pulse, a rhythm that resonated with the very core of her being.

A faint noise from deeper within the chamber caught Kaci's attention. She raised a hand, signaling Durya to silence. As they advanced, they spotted a woman standing before an obsidian mirror, its surface undulating like a dark, liquid portal. The mirror, a gateway or perhaps a soul's reflection, contained only shadows.

The woman's pale hair cascaded down her back, shimmering as she murmured unheard words to the mirror. Kaci touched Durya's arm, guiding her behind a massive pillar for cover.

The woman stepped away from the obsidian mirror, her movements frantic as she searched through the chamber's relics. Her voice was urgent and echoed through the cavern, "It must be here. It has to be. Mir wouldn't have entrusted it to her daughter this early."

Durya's heart skipped a beat at the mention of Mir, a name she recognized as one of the Guardians of Isdralan. She exchanged a meaningful glance with Kaci, and they agreed on their next move. Emerging from their concealment, they revealed themselves. The woman whirled around, her eyes as black as the abyss, a sharp contrast to her sweet demeanor.

For a fleeting moment, Kaci's eyes seemed to darken, a change so subtle Durya questioned if it was a trick of the light. Yet, the air around them felt charged, laden with hidden truths.

"Oh, what a surprise to find others here," the woman said, her voice dripping with insincerity. "And who might you be?"

Kaci's gaze, now returning to its usual green hue, hardened. "You don't recognize us, Keres?"

The woman tilted her head, feigning ignorance. "Should I?"

A sly smile crept onto Kaci's face, her eyes flickering with an uncharacteristic darkness. "Of course you should, child."

Durya felt adrift, her mind racing to make sense of the exchange.

The tension escalated, each moment stretching like an age, thick with unspoken words and lingering gazes. Kaci and Keres, standing at opposite ends of the room, shared a history that Durya was yet to decipher. Their eyes met, revealing a connection that went beyond mere acquaintance. Durya, observing from the sidelines, felt like an outsider trying to read a book with half the pages missing, aware of the underlying currents but unable to grasp their significance.

Kaci's behavior fluctuated between affection and hostility, a duality that was unsettling. Keres, though maintaining a calm exterior, couldn't hide the calculating glint in her pitch-black eyes. "Well, it's always lovely to meet new people, especially in a place as intriguing as this."

Suddenly, Kaci shifted her weight. "We must take our leave," she stated, her tone urgent. Then she grabbed Durya's arm and pulled her from the room.

Kaci maintained a brisk pace, remarkable considering the difference in their leg lengths, and slowed after what felt like an endless march.

Durya, gasping for air, inquired, "Are you going to explain what just happened?"

Kaci, her expression a canvas of inner turmoil, let out a deep sigh. "There's something I've kept from you."

"You mean since I lost my memories?" Durya inquired, her brow furrowing.

"No, not just that," Kaci replied, a seriousness overtaking her tone. "When we vanquished the shadows, a fragment of the darkness latched onto me. I left to learn to control it, to prevent it from overwhelming me."

Durya's face grew pensive. "It's troubling that you hid this from me," she said.

Kaci met her gaze. "I have everything under control now. I wouldn't have come back if I didn't."

An unyielding silence fell between them. It dawned on Durya that Kaci's eyes turning black was not a mere trick of the shadows. There she stood, Durya, engulfed in a war she couldn't recall, facing an adversary, or perhaps a comrade, whose loyalties were as fluid as her own forgotten past.

"It's fine," Kaci said, piercing the silence. "Something in that chamber, something about Keres, set it off."

Before Durya could respond, a voice emerged. "I knew I shouldn't have left you alone."

Both Durya and Kaci spun around. "Sharn?" they exclaimed in unison.

"What are you doing here? You're supposed to be with Marcus!" Kaci said.

"My lady is always my priority," Sharn replied, his gaze fixed on Durya.

Durya studied him, the boy's face from her memory still vivid in her mind. Then, acting on impulse, she ran to him and wrapped her arms around him, her actions surprising both Sharn and Kaci.

Kaci slumped to the ground. "I'm sorry. I thought I had mastered this," she confessed. "It's like she woke something within me, something I thought I had tamed."

Durya felt a surge of empathy for her friend. The turmoil Kaci faced was not just an external battle but an internal one, grappling with shadows that ran deeper than she had imagined.

It was Sharn who broke the contemplative silence. "To answer your question, I came because I knew you were both walking into danger," he began, his tone serious. "Marcus released me from my duties when he sensed the shift in energies. I couldn't let you face this alone."

Durya turned towards him. "But how did you follow us here? Isdralan isn't a place you go to."

Sharn gave a wry smile. "It wasn't easy. I swam to the Golden Gull while you guys were doing introductions, then stowed away on the ship. The captain found me, but after hearing my story, she let me stay. She said something about the foolish things men and women do for love." Sharn blushed.

Kaci, despite her troubled state, couldn't help but chuckle.

Sharn shrugged, his gaze steady. "I do what I must for those I care about."

Durya's heart warmed at his dedication. "We're lucky to have you with us, Sharn," she said, her voice filled with sincerity.

Kaci sighed, her expression softening. "I just wish I could be as sure of myself as you are, Sharn. Keres seemed like she has a hold on the darkness within me."

Durya squeezed Kaci's hand. "We all have our battles."

The trio sat without speaking, each lost in their thoughts. Durya broke the silence. "We've all been pushing hard," she said, her voice gentle yet firm. "We don't know when day turns to night in these caves, but our bodies know when it's time to rest."

Sharn nodded, the fatigue in his eyes. "Rest will do us good. We'll need our strength for what's coming."

Kaci, looking drained, managed a weary smile. "Rest sounds like a blessing right now."

They found a comfortable spot within the cave, sheltered and secure. As they settled down, each wrapped in their own cloaks, the flickering light of a small campfire cast dancing shadows on the walls. Tomorrow, they would rise again, united and ready to face whatever the caverns held. For now, sleep beckoned, offering a brief escape.

8

The Labyrinth of Self

Durya awoke in the dimly lit cavern, the remnants of their last night's fire reduced to cold embers. She observed Sharn and Kaci, who were already up, moving quietly around their makeshift camp. Her query about their rest was met with silence, an unspoken confirmation that sleep had eluded them both. Kaci handed her a square of field bread, which Durya nibbled on thoughtfully as she studied her companions.

"So, obviously, we have encountered this woman before. What can you tell me?" Durya asked.

Kaci exhaled deeply. "I'm not sure," she admitted. "This Keres, or at least this version of her, didn't seem to recognize me. The Caves of Chaos are a conundrum. They exist outside of normal time. We could meet her again, and it might be a completely different version of her." Kaci's face scrunched in contemplation. "We need to be cautious. Maybe we can use this to our advantage?"

Sharn frowned, his expression betraying a deep-rooted distrust. "If she's an enemy, she's always an enemy."

Kaci countered, "It's not so simple."

Sharn's frustration was palpable. "Then make it simple, for a 'stupid orc' like me."

Kaci's smile was gentle, yet tinged with sadness. "You're not stupid, Sharn. I don't fully understand it myself, so I'm just trying to navigate this cautiously."

Durya, feeling the tension between her friends, placed a reassuring hand on each of them. "Let's take a moment. Kaci, gather your thoughts and explain when you're ready. For now, our focus should be on finding my memories."

Kaci nodded in agreement, "I can agree to that."

"Me too," Sharn added, his tone softening.

Durya felt a swell of pride. She was their leader, guiding them through uncertainty and darkness. She pondered for a moment. Had she always relished this role of leadership so much? Durya felt more than ever the burden and the honor of her role, ready to face whatever the caverns and fate had in store for them.

They hadn't walked far through the winding passages of the Caves of Chaos before a new orb, glowing with an ethereal light, floated towards them. Durya watched, a hint of amusement in her eyes, as Sharn's expression transformed from curiosity to awe. He had not yet witnessed the peculiar phenomenon of Durya interacting with her memory orbs.

"I'm getting better at this, but don't be alarmed if my actions seem odd. It's like I'm reliving these memories from outside my own body," Durya explained to Sharn, her tone a mix of reassurance and caution.

"It's as terrifying as a banshee in a thunderstorm," Kaci added with a wry half-smile, attempting to lighten the mood.

Sharn gave a solemn nod, his warrior's demeanor unshaken. "Thank you for the warning," he said, bracing himself for the unknown.

As Durya brushed her fingers against the orb, she surrendered to the familiar sensation of falling. The experience, once disconcerting, was now something she navigated with a sense of mastery.

She found herself in a delicately furnished sitting room, the very picture of refined elegance. Her present self stood in the corner alongside two human girls, yet her demeanor perfectly mirroring that of her human counterparts. What did the others see when they looked at her?

Her foster mother, Lady Evelyn, the only mother figure she had ever known, was engrossed in an embroidery piece. The room was filled with other noblewomen, the air thick with the subtle fragrance of perfumed teas and the soft clatter of fine china.

Durya observed her younger self sipping tea with practiced grace, a skill hard-earned to avoid the clink of the cup against her tusks.

Lady Evelyn rose to leave the room for a moment, prompting a respectful stand from everyone present. Once the duchess exited, the room relaxed into its previous state.

The memory carried a bittersweet undertone. A pang of sadness echoed in Durya's heart as she remembered her mother's fate — a casualty of the shadows. Lady Evelyn, though not a perfect mother, had tried her best to mold Durya into her own image, often forgetting that Durya was not a human, but an orc, with her own heritage. Despite the societal pressures and the subtle disregard of others when not in the lady's presence, Lady Evelyn's love for Durya had been unconditional.

In this memory, Durya saw the complexities of her upbringing—a dance between acceptance and the struggle to fit into a world that wasn't entirely her own. It was a poignant reminder of the duality of her existence, both orc and human, and the journey she had embarked upon to embrace every facet of her identity.

As Lady Evelyn's footsteps receded, the room's delicate air of nobility unraveled. The noble girls, once restrained by the Duchess's presence, turned their attention towards young Durya, their faces morphing from feigned sweetness to barely concealed scorn.

One girl, a blonde named Sara, who had always maintained a neutral stance, spoke up first. "Lady Durya," she said, her voice dripping with mock politeness, "it must be so hard for you, adapting to our ways. Do you ever miss the... wildness of your people?"

The other girls tittered, their eyes gleaming with cruel amusement. Young Durya stood tall.

"I have learned to appreciate the finer aspects of all cultures," young Durya replied, her voice steady, betraying none of the hurt that Sara's words had intended to inflict.

Sara's words cut through the silence with a sharpness that belied her feigned concern. "But surely, it must be difficult. I mean, learning to eat with utensils, speaking our language without that... rough accent."

The room responded with a chorus of soft, calculated laughter, the sound echoing off the walls like a delicate yet sinister melody. Young Durya stood amidst them, her hands clenched into fists at her sides. Despite the tension coursing through her, her face was an impassive mask, giving nothing away.

Her voice, when she spoke, was cool and measured, each word carefully chosen. "I find the challenge invigorating," young Durya responded. She locked eyes with Sara, her gaze unwavering. "It's always enlightening to rise above one's limitations. Wouldn't you agree, Sara?"

The subtle barb in Durya's words was clear to those who knew the undercurrents of their interactions. Sara, known for her own struggles with mastering the etiquette of courtly speech and often the subject of whispered criticisms, visibly stiffened. The implication that she, too, had limitations to overcome was a subtle yet pointed dig.

Before the tension could escalate, Marianne, seizing the opportunity to divert attention, chimed in with a question veiled in mock curiosity. "And what of your... tusks? Does it not make things like drinking tea rather cumbersome?"

As if to answer, young Durya gracefully lifted her teacup to her lips, taking a sip with such finesse that there was no hint of a clink against her tusks. It was a skill hard-won, a sign of her adaptability and determination.

"It requires a certain finesse," young Durya stated, setting the cup back down with a quiet assurance. Her calm demeanor in the face of their veiled insults was her armor, her way of maintaining dignity in an environment that sought to undermine her at every turn.

Watching this memory unfold, older Durya felt a complex mix of emotions. Pride swelled in her for the young orc's resilience and cleverness in navigating the treacherous waters of court politics. Yet, there was also a profound sadness for the isolation and constant scrutiny she had endured. These experiences, she realized, had helped to shape her into the leader she was now—one who understood the power of words and the importance of maintaining one's composure in the face of adversity.

As the memory receded, pulling Durya back to the dim, echoing space of the Caves of Chaos, she was enveloped in a profound sense of melancholy mixed with a fleeting joy. The experience of reliving those moments in the sitting room, the sight of her younger self enduring veiled barbs with stoic grace, stirred a deep sadness within her. Yet, alongside this sadness, there was a spark of joy at seeing her foster mother, Lady Evelyn, again—a reminder of the love and security she had provided in a world that often felt cold and unwelcoming.

Durya felt a desperate longing as the memory faded. "No! I want to see my mother one more time," she thought, her heart aching with the need to relive when Lady Evelyn would re-enter the room and set things right with her commanding presence. That was the part of the memory she yearned to experience again — the feeling of being defended and cherished.

But the memory slipped away like sand through her fingers, leaving her on her knees in the cavern, tears streaming down her face in a rare moment of vulnerability. The raw emotions from the memory had breached the walls she had carefully built around her heart.

As she faced Sharn and Kaci, Durya's training and experiences kicked in. Just like her younger self, she swiftly composed herself, her face settling into a stoic mask. Yet, the tears that had already fallen were proof of the emotions that had momentarily broken through her defenses.

Durya's breaths were slow and measured as she regained her composure, a silent war raging within her between the need to express her emotions and the instinct to maintain a strong front. She stood up, wiping the remnants of tears from her cheeks, her eyes reflecting a complex tapestry of strength, sadness, and resilience.

Sharn's voice was gentle, breaking the heavy silence that had fallen over the group. "You don't have to be heartless in front of us, lady," he said.

Durya gave a small, appreciative nod, feeling a sense of solace in Sharn's words. It was a rare comfort to let down her guard, even if just for a moment.

Kaci, who had been quietly observing, took a deep breath, as if bracing herself to open up about her own struggles. "It's this darkness within me," she began. "A part of Javina lingers, like a shadow. When we defeated the shadows, a piece of that darkness fused with me. And a part of me... it stayed with her."

Durya, her brow furrowed in confusion, admitted, "I'm sorry. I do not know this Javina of whom you speak." There was a hint of embarrassment in her voice, a rare admission of vulnerability from someone who was always so assured.

Kaci's expression turned solemn as she delved into the explanation. "Javina... she was the one who instigated the shadows we fought against. When she tried to escape her dark prison, she sent an army of shadows ahead of her. They opened portals, and these shadows possessed people, causing chaos and fear."

Durya listened intently, absorbing every word. The story was like a piece of a puzzle she was desperately trying to complete.

Kaci continued, "We overcame them—you, me, and Micah." She paused briefly, a fleeting shadow crossing her face. The silence that followed spoke volumes, hinting at a mystery yet to be unraveled.

Durya's heart ached for her friend, understanding the immense burden she carried. "And this Javina," she asked, "where is she now?"

Kaci shook her head. "Defeated, but not destroyed. She's a lingering threat, like an ember that could reignite at any moment. She possessed me." Kaci said, her voice barely above a whisper. "But I fought her off with my light... mostly."

"That must be awful," Durya said, her voice soft with empathy.

"You would think," Kaci replied with a wry twist of her lips. "But it's become a part of me now. It's hard to explain. It's a constant battle, especially when she stirs and tries to control me. But when she's quiet, it feels like a piece of me is missing." She sighed, a sound filled with weariness and complexity.

Sharn, who had been listening quietly, added, "It's why we must remain vigilant. The battle might have ended, but the war is far from over."

Durya reached out, placing a comforting hand on Kaci's shoulder. "I can't pretend to fully understand what you're going through, Kaci."

Kaci looked up, her eyes glistening with unshed tears. "Thank you, Durya. It means more than you know."

As they sat together in the cavern, a bond of shared struggles and mutual support grew stronger between them. It was a moment of vulnerability and strength.

After a while, Durya stood up, a determined look in her eyes. "Let's continue. There are more memories to find, more pieces of this puzzle to put together."

Kaci paused, her hesitation lingering a moment too long before she turned to face Durya. "I know this quest is about finding your memories, but I think we need to go back. There's something about that mirror in the room I can't shake off," she admitted.

Durya contemplated her options. The memory orbs seemed to drift in and out of existence on their own accord; perhaps their location in the caves didn't dictate their appearance. Besides, that room with the mirror had indeed been filled with intriguing artifacts. She glanced at Sharn, feeling a flutter in her chest as their eyes met.

"I go where you go," Sharn said, his lopsided smile reassuring. "Besides, I'd rather face an enemy head-on than run from one."

"Back to the room, it is then," Durya announced, her voice laced with a resolve that seemed to resonate against the cavern walls.

Their journey back, however, quickly took an unexpected turn. The familiar, glowing walls of the caves they had traversed just hours before had transformed, as if by some unseen hand. Now, they found themselves in a corridor more akin to the halls of a grand castle, yet there was an oddness to it that Durya couldn't quite place.

"These walls... they weren't like this before," Kaci muttered, her eyes scanning the rich wood paneling and the intricate plasterwork. The elegance of the decor was at odds with the natural beauty of the cave they remembered.

Durya touched the paneling, feeling its unfamiliar texture. "The caves are playing tricks on us," she said, a hint of annoyance creeping into her tone. "Shifting and changing with every step we take."

Sharn, who had been quiet, joined in. "It's like walking through a dream," he observed, his deep voice echoing slightly in the grand hallway. "A dream that keeps changing its mind."

Kaci leaned back against the wall, a frown creasing her forehead. "How are we to find that room again when the very path keeps changing?"

Durya exhaled slowly, steadying her nerves. "We push forward," she declared. "The caves may change, but our goal remains the same. We can't let this place deter us."

Their path seemed to weave through a series of increasingly

elaborate and foreign corridors. The transformation was subtle yet relentless, an ever-changing landscape that seemed to defy logic and challenge their resolve.

Ornate tapestries, unlike any they had seen in their travels, hung from the walls, depicting scenes that were both exquisite and unfamiliar, featuring landscapes and creatures that defied their understanding of the world. The floor beneath their feet was covered with plush carpets, woven with intricate patterns and vibrant colors, a luxury that should be foreign to the rugged terrain of the caves.

Elegant sconces lined the walls, casting a warm glow that was comforting, yet surreal in this subterranean setting. The transformation was so complete, so thorough, that it felt as though they had stepped into another world—a place that mimicked the grandeur of a noble estate but twisted with an otherworldly essence.

The air was still, filled with a silence that was almost oppressive, as if the very atmosphere was waiting, watching.

As they continued down the corridor, Durya, Kaci, and Sharn exchanged looks of caution. This place, whatever it was, felt dangerous. It was a reminder that the Caves of Chaos were a realm of endless possibilities and unpredictable transformations, where the boundaries between the real and the surreal were blurred.

"This isn't right," Kaci said, panic coloring her tone.

Durya inspected the hallway, her brow furrowed in concentration. "We turn back," she suggested. But upon turning, they were met with the same endless corridor stretching behind them.

"Look!" Sharn pointed ahead. A door stood in the hallway, its knob ornate and unusual.

Kaci rushed towards it, eager to escape the unnerving corridor. But Durya raised her hand, signaling caution. Approaching the door, she knocked three times, respecting the decorum of their former world.

No response came. Kaci shot Durya a grin, her earlier apprehension momentarily forgotten. "Locked," she announced after a brief attempt to turn the knob.

"Let's keep moving," Lady Durya suggested, though a sense of dread was taking root in her gut. The caves, already a labyrinth of mysteries, were proving to be more unpredictable than she had expected.

As they continued, doors appeared more frequently, spaced at regular intervals. The dissonance between the cave's natural formations and this bizarre, constructed pathway deepened Durya's unease.

She couldn't shake the feeling that they were being led somewhere, that the caves themselves were shifting and changing around them, guiding them towards an unknown destination. The Caves of Chaos, living up to their name, were a place where reality seemed to bend and twist, challenging their perceptions and understanding.

Time seemed to stretch and bend within the surreal corridors. Kaci, driven by frustration, had taken to wiggling the handles of every door they passed, hoping against hope that one would yield to her efforts. Finally, a knob turned under her insistent fingers, and the door creaked open, revealing a room bathed in an inexplicably bright light. It was neither the warm glow of the sun nor the flicker of a sconce, but something altogether different and more intense.

Inside the room, illuminated by the strange, intense light, a woman sat at a wooden desk, her attention wholly absorbed by an object that bore a resemblance to a mirror. This was no ordinary mirror, however. Words appeared within it, shifting as if endowed with a life of their own. They danced across the surface in a mesmerizing display, forming and reforming before the woman's watchful eyes. This had to be some form of enchantment or sorcery, a magic they had never encountered.

The woman herself was an oddity to Durya. She had dark hair that cascaded over her shoulders in gentle waves, and she was dressed in attire unlike anything Durya had seen before. The garments that seemed both practical and peculiar—a form-fitting material that covered her legs, much like trousers, but these were made of a strange, soft fabric. Her upper body was clothed in a loose, long-sleeved garment, akin to a tunic but with no laces or embroidery, an attire so simple yet so foreign.

Durya stepped closer, her curiosity piqued by this magical spectacle. The woman at the desk seemed oblivious to their presence, her fingers moving rapidly over a flat, rectangular object that lay in front of the mirror. This too seemed to be a part of the enchantment, an instrument of the strange magic at work.

The scene was a confluence of the familiar and the bizarre. A desk and a woman, both recognizable elements, were inter-twined with the inexplicable magic of the dancing words and the woman's unusual attire.

As Durya stepped forward, poised to enter the room, a voice resonated from behind them. "You might not want to go in there."

As they turned, they were met by the sight of an elderly man, his long, flowing beard giving him an air of ancient wisdom. His eyes, deep and piercing, seemed to capture the very essence of the night sky, with stars and nebulae swirling in their depths, hinting at a knowledge far beyond their understanding.

Durya, surprised by his sudden appearance, couldn't help but respond, "Who are you to tell me what to do? I am the Baroness." The authority in her voice surprised her. She had known of her title, yes, but it had always felt like a garment too large for her to fill. Why now did it fit so naturally?

Sharn, standing beside her, wore an expression of confusion, as taken aback as she was. Kaci, however, seemed to study the old man intently, her head tilted slightly, eyes narrowed in concentration, as if trying to decipher a puzzle.

The man's chuckle broke the tension, a rich sound that seemed to resonate with the very walls of the caves. He crossed his arms over his chest, his gaze lingering on each of them with a knowing look.

"Do I know you? Have we met?" Durya asked, her tone now tinged with genuine curiosity despite her initial irritation.

"No. But I know you. We have crossed paths many times before and will do so again. What brings you to my caves?" he replied, his voice echoing with a timbre that suggested both age and timelessness.

"Your caves?" Durya couldn't hide her skepticism. The notion that this man could claim ownership of such a place was almost laughable to her.

Kaci's silence persisted, adding to the mystery of the encounter. Her gaze never left the man, as if she was attempting to read an unspoken language in his eyes.

The man seemed unperturbed by Durya's challenging tone. "You will not find what you are looking for here," he stated, his voice imbued with a cryptic certainty.

Durya's frustration was palpable. "Well, I KNOW that," she snapped, her patience thinning. "What I want is to leave this place."

The man nodded, a hint of solemnity in his expression. "I can guide you out this once. But remember, the journey through these caves is a journey through fate itself, and not every thread is meant to be pulled."

Durya, puzzled and irked, shot back, "Why must you speak in riddles?"

It was then that Kaci broke her silence. "What is your name?" she asked.

The old man's eyes twinkled as he smiled at her. "You may call me Aeon."

With a gentle gesture, he pointed towards a grand archway that seemed to materialize out of the cave's ever-shifting walls. "There lies your path to the relic room," he said.

Durya turned to behold the archway, its promise of a return to the familiar filling her with a surge of hope. "See, helping us wasn't so hard!" she exclaimed, relief washing over her.

Yet, when she turned to thank the man, Aeon was gone, as if he had been nothing more than a wisp of cave mist, leaving them with more questions than answers.

9

Reflections in the Dark

As Durya entered the strange relic room through the archway, evidence of recent occupancy was apparent. Her eyes were drawn to the obsidian mirror, standing tall and imposing, but it was the subtle signs around the room that caught her attention. The stillness of the space was laced with fresh disturbances, but the woman, Keres, was nowhere to be seen. Despite its calm, the room was tense, as if the very air vibrated with the remnants of recent conversations and hasty movements.

Durya observed Kaci advancing towards the mirror. Its allure was palpable, and the aura was tangible. This stirred a twinge of apprehension in Durya. Accustomed to taking charge and deciding, she now wrestled with uncertainty in this unfamiliar situation.

Sharn maintained a careful distance, giving Kaci and Durya space to inspect the artifact. Durya respected his silent fortitude, valuing his consistent stability amidst their chaotic surroundings.

Entranced by the mirror, Kaci's eyes fixated on its surface. Durya inquired, "What is it, Kaci?" Kaci's silence only intensified Durya's anxiety. Assisted by Sharn, Durya shook Kaci, disrupting the mirror's mesmerizing hold on her.

"It whispers," Kaci murmured, her focus still locked on the mirror. "But I can't understand the words." She leaned in closer, as if being drawn back into the mirror's cryptic embrace.

Durya knew the dangers of such enchantments, the peril of being swept away by forces beyond their understanding. She found her lack of memory was frustrating, leaving her feeling unanchored like these when she needed to rely on her experiences.

"It's like this mirror connects to Kashara, where Javina is," Kaci said, drawing Durya's attention back to the task at hand. "I can hear her plotting, but only fragments. She could have connections to others."

"Kashara?" Durya questioned, her mind trying to connect the dots. The name felt important, but her memories offered no answers.

"Kashara and Isdralan were once a singular realm. Isdralan is the fabric of magic, the place where dreams spark into creation, where artists and seers find their muse. It's a realm of light and inspiration."

"And Kashara?" Durya pressed, seeking to understand the full picture.

"It was once part of Isdralan. But greed led some to misuse its magic. I read about it in 'The Birth of Magic.' Javina was connected to the rift, creating Kashara as darkness, opposite Isdralan's light."

Durya's face shadowed with thought. "Did I know of this book?"

"You skimmed it," Kaci replied. "The split created two realms—Kashara, the shadowed echo of Isdralan. Now, Javina is consumed by vengeance and hate, seeking escape from her dark prison."

"And Etharion's role in this?" Durya asked, piecing together the elusive threads of their conversation. "What do we have to do with this?"

"That's the puzzle I'm trying to solve," Kaci admitted, her gaze returning to the mirror. "Our world is somehow key to her plan."

Kaci's explanation of Kashara and Isdralan had only deepened Durya's frustration. She should know these things, should remember. 'The Birth of Magic' sparked a faint recognition, but nothing concrete.

Durya stood beside Kaci as she grappled with her emotions. Her friends painted her as a natural leader, strong and decisive. However, at that moment, she didn't feel like the confident leader they perceived.

The responsibilities that came with leadership weighed on her. She was expected to lead, make decisions, and be a guiding light. But how could she lead when her own past was a puzzle with missing pieces?

Leadership wasn't just about having all the answers; it was about forging ahead even when the path was clouded in mystery. The mirror before them, shrouded in mystery and linked to realms and plots far beyond their comprehension, was a problem to be faced after she got her memory back.

Durya steeled herself. She might not feel like the leader her friends believed her to be, but she would not shy away from the role. She was determined to resolve the mysteries of her own past, recognizing that understanding her own story was crucial to guiding them through the deciphering the riddles of Javina and this mirror.

As Durya's thoughts wandered through the fragmented landscapes of her life, a memory materialized before her. This one, however, was different from the others she had encountered. It shimmered into existence, an orb surrounded by motes of light that danced with a dark, almost foreboding haze.

"What do you think it means?" Durya asked.

Kaci pursed her lips. "I'm not sure," she admitted. "But perhaps it's best to leave this one untouched."

Durya's gaze remained fixed on the swirling memory. "I don't think I can," she responded, her voice reflecting her inner turmoil. "Fia told me I needed to face all of them, to confront every fragment of my past."

Sharn, who had been observing, chimed in with a note of caution. "I'm with Kaci on this one," he said, his eyes never leaving the memory. "It looks dangerous. What if it's not a memory, but some trick conjured by that mirror?" He gestured towards the dark mirror, its surface still and inscrutable.

Despite their concerns, Durya felt an undeniable pull towards the memory. It whispered to her, a siren call that resonated with something deep within her soul. She sensed that this memory, dark and unsettling as it appeared, held something vital, a key to understanding not only her past but also the path she must take.

Durya stepped forward. "This mirror may be influential, but I can't disregard it. There's something within it, something I must confront." Her voice remained steady, betraying none of the shakiness she felt inside.

Kaci and Sharn shared a knowing look, communicating their understanding. Familiar with Durya's determination once her mind was made up, they acknowledged her decision and took their places by her side.

Durya extended her hand. The orb reacted to her touch, emanating a pulse of light. In that instant, Durya transitioned into the memory, bridging the gap between certainty and the unknown. The cave's surroundings faded, giving way to her past. She was in the grandiose hall of Marshfield Estate, alive with anticipation for an important gathering. As with her other recollections, she found herself whole, embodying her true self. There, she observed her foster father, the Duke of Marshfield, engaged in discussion with a familiar figure—Edward Barclay, the Baron of Westerfield.

Edward was a figure of ambition and calculated charm and stood before the Duke. His words were smooth, his demeanor polite, as he made his proposal—a request for the hand of the Duke's foster daughter in marriage. Durya watched, a sense of surrealism washing over her as she observed her younger self entering the room, eyes wide with a mixture of naivety and tentative excitement.

The young girl was thrilled at the prospect of marriage, of being desired, now appeared to her older self as innocent and unaware of the true nature of the man before her. Edward's ambition was clear. He would unite their houses, positioning his future children as heirs to Marshfield, securing a path to greater power.

The Duke considered Edward's proposal. He spoke of his foster children, acknowledging Marcus's reluctance to lead and expressing his hope for Durya's happiness.

As the memory shifted, the scene transformed to the night of the wedding. After the ceremony's grandeur faded, the cruel truth of Edward's nature revealed itself. His sweetness, displayed in public, dissolved away, leaving in its place a cold, calculating cruelty.

In the depths of the memory, young Durya stood in the wedding chamber shivering in her nightclothes, her heart fluttering with a mix of excitement and nerves. The conversations she had with Lady Evelyn about what to expect, the duties and intimacies of marriage, played over in her mind. Nothing could have prepared her for the reality that was about to unfold.

Edward entered the room, his expression devoid of the warmth he had shown in public. The door closed with a sense of finality.

"You understand, don't you, Durya?" Edward's voice was icy. "This marriage is merely a means to an end. A strategic move for power."

Durya, her excitement turning to confusion and then to dread, could only nod, trying to process his words.

"It's official now. You can't back out," he continued, his eyes hard and unyielding. "But know this—I could never touch a filthy orc like you."

The words struck Durya like a physical blow. The realization that she was just a pawn in his ambitions, a mere tool for his ascent to power, was devastating.

As Edward turned away from her, he disappeared into the adjoining sitting room. The sounds of hushed conversation followed by the soft, unmistakable noises of intimacy with one of the serving girls filtered through the door. Durya sat frozen, the reality of her situation sinking in.

Alone in the room, the young bride grappled with a whirlwind of emotions — betrayal, disgust, and a profound sense of isolation. What was supposed to be a new beginning turned into a harsh awakening to the world's cruelty.

The memory shifted, transitioning from the painful revelations of the wedding night to the life that followed in Westerfield. Durya and Edward shared chambers in their grand estate, but they lived separately within its walls. It was a cold, hollow arrangement, a far cry from the loving home Durya remembered from her foster family.

One night, driven by a mix of curiosity and a desperate need for understanding, Durya slipped into Edward's private room. There, she saw a mirror, its surface dark and foreboding. Now, from the perspective of her older self, she recognized it with a start—it was the same as the obsidian mirror they had found in the Caves of Chaos.

To the outside world, Durya was the iron-handed ruler of her household. She was efficient, strong, and carried herself with pride. But behind closed doors, the reality was different. Edward subjected her to constant abuse, both emotional and physical, treating her with disdain and cruelty. His true nature often revealed itself in his unguarded moments. Durya endured his cruel words that cut deeper than any blade.

One evening, as they sat in the privacy of their quarters, Edward's voice broke the silence. "Our child will inherit it all, Durya," he said, his eyes cold and calculating. "But don't delude yourself into thinking I'd ever sully myself by fathering a child with an orc."

Durya flinched at his words, the pain clear in her eyes, but she remained silent, a growing sense of despair enveloping her.

Edward leaned back in his chair, a smirk playing on his lips. "And your dear brother Marcus, running off to live with the Aelorians," he sneered. "Another Conwyn out of the way. It makes things so much simpler for us."

Durya's hands clenched into fists at her sides, but she held her tongue, knowing any response would only fuel his cruelty.

But nothing prepared her for the chilling casualness of his next revelation. One night, as they were getting ready for bed, Edward remarked, "You know, if your father were to meet an untimely end, it would certainly expedite our rise to power."

The words hung in the air, a dark cloud that threatened everything Durya held dear. From that moment on, she found excuses to avoid visiting her childhood home, the fear of what Edward might do if given the chance paralyzing her.

"I'm not feeling well. We cannot visit the Duke this season," Durya would say, her voice barely more than a whisper, but Edward's piercing gaze always seemed to see right through her.

It wasn't long before Edward grew tired of her excuses. "Enough of this charade, Durya," he snapped one evening. "You can't fool me anymore. We're going to visit your family, and that's final."

It shifted again, and they were boarding a ship called the Golden Gull. But this time, she carried with her a deadly resolve, armed with a vial of poison bought from the apothecary—a toxic solution for herself and for Edward, to end the torment he had inflicted upon her. This would ensure her father's safety.

The quarters were cramped, unlike the spacious luxury of Westerfield. Within these confined walls, young Durya grappled with the potential consequences of her decision. She had the silent and deadly resolve in a small vial, but doubts gnawed at her. Poison was a coward's weapon. Instead, she could confess everything to her father, and he would make it right. She would fight her way out of this horrid life!

Then came the night that changed everything. Edward, drunk and belligerent, laughing at her huge and ghastly body, and how he could not wait to get off the wretched boat and tend to his needs.

"No more, Edward," young Durya's voice rang out, filled with a courage that belied her fear. "I refuse to let you control me any longer. I will tell my father everything, and he will free me from this mockery of a marriage."

The cabin had a charged atmosphere, hinting at the upcoming storm. Edward, fueled by alcohol and anger, turned his wrath towards Durya. His words were laced with malice and contempt as he advanced towards her.

"You think you can defy me?" he sneered, his voice dripping with scorn. "You're nothing but a tool, a means to an end."

Durya, her heart pounding in her chest, backed away, but Edward was relentless. With a sudden, violent motion, he pushed her towards the bed. His hands were rough, his strength overpowering.

"No. Stop!" Durya cried.

"You don't get to say no to me. We are married," he growled, his face twisted in anger. He held her with one hand and punched her in the jaw with the other. Then he put a pillow over her face, almost suffocating her. "I don't need to look at your ugly face. You have all the right parts."

Durya struggled beneath his grip, her spirit refusing to break despite the physical assault. But Edward's cruelty knew no bounds.

"And if you conceive," he hissed, his voice cold and menacing, "I'll rip any child out myself."

After he had his way, he passed out, snoring.

As the older Durya relived this memory, the pain and fear she had felt that night flooded back. She watched her younger self curl into a ball- trying not to move, in fear she would wake Edward. She wanted to run and hide, but there was nowhere to go. Who would believe her? They were married!

The following morning, Young Durya's resolve was steeled. As she prepared Edward's tea, her hands were steady. She added the all the poison to his cup, each drop a testament to her will to break free from the chains he had placed around her.

Edward, oblivious to his fate, accepted the tea. As he drank, turned to gasps of confusion and pain, and fell to the ground. In his last moments, he raged against her, but young Durya stood unflinching.

"I am the Baroness of Westerfield," she declared, her voice a fierce whisper as Edward's life ebbed away. "Through blood and thorns, I will rise."

Durya stood tall, her fists clenched at her sides as the last tendrils of the memory dissipated. A righteous anger surged within her, a fierce response to the injustice she had endured and overcome. She remembered what Edward had taken from her, and more importantly, how she had reclaimed her power, her life.

Sharn and Kaci observed her with shock and surprise. It was clear they had never seen her in such a state. Kaci, breaking the silence, asked, "Are you okay?"

Lady Durya, her breathing steady and controlled, didn't respond. She needed a moment to gather her thoughts, to temper the storm of emotions that raged within her. Finally, she spoke, her voice soft yet resolute, "I am the baroness..."

"You said that out loud during your vision," Sharn interjected, looking hurt. Durya wondered if he had misunderstood her words, thinking them affection for Edward.

A wicked laugh escaped her, rich and liberating. "Yes, I said that. I claim that title and will wear it like armor. I earned it through blood and tears." She reached out, her touch gentle as she brushed Sharn's cheek and then rested her hand on Kaci's shoulder. "But it is not an armor forged from love. That," she said, her eyes softening, "I reserve for a select few."

The moment marked a turning point for Durya, not just in her understanding of her past, but in how she viewed herself. She refused to let her memories define her as a victim. The title of Baroness, once a symbol of her subjugation, was now a testament to her strength, her resilience.

The memory, though fraught with pain, had illuminated the path forward. Durya knew who she was now—a leader, a survivor, a Baroness in her own right. She had faced darkness in her past and had come out armed with the knowledge and strength that would guide her in the challenges ahead. She would prevail.

Gathering her composure, Lady Durya inhaled, steadying herself for the tasks that still lay ahead. Although her memory journey was incomplete, this pivotal recollection brought profound transformation.

"We have work to do, and I still have memories to gather," she stated. "My journey isn't over here, but this memory... it was a turning point for me." She gestured towards the dark mirror, its surface a portal to a past she was only now beginning to piece together. "Without revisiting my past, I wouldn't have recognized this," she mused, showing the mirror. "It seems the darkness of Kashara and Javina's influence may have been entwined in our lives long before I even met you. For I had no memory of you in that vision." Her gaze flickered to Kaci, an acknowledgment of their shared history.

"I think we met shortly after that," Kaci responded. "When we first crossed paths, you had just survived a shipwreck. It was the Golden Gull."

Lady Durya's eyebrow arched. "Interesting," she murmured, the pieces of her past knitting together, more intricate and expansive than she had imagined.

"And what of Edward?" she questioned, her voice steady. "I watched him die in that memory. Did I face repercussions for his death?"

"No," came the response from both Kaci and Sharn, almost in unison, accompanied by a shared glance that spoke volumes.

The revelation brought a mix of relief and introspection to Durya. Her actions, the decision she had made on that ship, had been a burden she had carried, even without her memories. To learn that she had not faced consequences for it was both liberating and sobering.

"We must continue. There are more memories to uncover, more truths to unearth. And I must understand how all these threads tie together—for my sake, and perhaps for the sake of our worlds."

Durya turned to Kaci, "this mirror... it was dark in my memory like it is now, but when Keres was here, there was something more to it. Why? What does he have to do with this?"

Kaci sighed. "The darkness within me, the part that's connected to Javina... it's complicated. I think Javina's reach extends far beyond Kashara. She's entangled in our worlds in ways we're only beginning to understand."

"But why can't I remember? It's like I'm trying to navigate a labyrinth in the dark." Her hands clenched into fists.

Kaci placed a reassuring hand on Durya's shoulder. "Its appears we met after much of this had begun. Your lack of memories... it's a puzzle we need to piece together. But I believe Edward's ambitions in Elanthia are a part of Javina's larger plan.

She seeks control, influence... and somehow our world might be key to that."

Durya pondered this. "So, it could be the linchpin in preventing a greater catastrophe."

Kaci nodded. "Exactly. If Edward and now Redmont overthrows Elyndris under Javina's influence, the consequences could be dire, not just for your world but for all realms connected to Isdralan and Kashara. It's like a doorway in."

The gravity of the situation settled over them. Durya realized that her personal quest was intertwined with a conflict much larger than she had imagined.

Sharn hesitated, his posture conflicting with his words. "Our clearest path is to keep collecting your memories, Durya. We'll only get the full picture and tackle this threat once you've got all your memories back." Durya noticed the inconsistency but chalked it up to Sharn's discomfort with the Isdralan magic involved in their quest.

Durya nodded, undeterred by Sharn's noticeable unease. Despite the discomfort and unknowns that lay ahead, she was eager to confront more of her memories. This quest for her past was not just a journey of self-discovery, but a step in understanding the challenges they faced together. Her anxiety mingled with a sense of anticipation for the truths yet to be revealed.

10

The Darkness Within

In the ever-twisting passages of the Caves of Chaos, Durya sifted through more fragments of her past, each memory a piece of the puzzle that was her life. Some were snapshots of her childhood, innocent and carefree moments that seemed a world away. She saw herself playing with Sharn, their laughter in the rounds surrounding of her family's estate. Even after she was forbidden to interact with the help, Sharn was always there, a silent, steadfast presence in the background of her memories, a source of strength she hadn't fully recognized until now.

Another memory flickered into view—Durya relived a memory fraught with tension and uncertainty. The scene unfolded in a rugged cave, a shelter against the violent storm raging outside. The cave's inhabitants, brought together by fate or some unseen magic, were an unlikely assembly.

Her younger self had a demeanor cold and dismissive, especially towards the goblins huddled in a corner of the cave. She recognized Smeadun, Jeth, and Meshach. Her recent experiences with Edward had left her wary and untrusting, her gaze often flickering to the cave entrance as if expecting more trouble.

There was a young man, Micah, with floppy dark hair and a rebellious streak, that sat opposite her. His attitude, a mix of bravado and nonchalance, seemed at odds with the severity of the storm outside. Kaci, ever the mediator, tried to ease the tension in the air.

The memory was a mosaic of emotions and interactions, painting a picture of how their paths had crossed under the most unlikely circumstances. It was a convergence shaped by the storm, a moment that would lay the foundation for relationships that would grow in depth and significance. When they left the Earthborn mausoleum, they were planning a journey to the Mountain Kingdom.

Kaci, after listening to Durya describe the memory, leaned in eagerly. "Who led us there?" she asked, full of hope. "To the Mountain Kingdom."

Durya frowned as she recalled. "Some Earthborn, named Thom, or something like that," she replied, trying to grasp the elusive details.

Kaci's face fell, disappointment clouding her features. As though she had hoped for a different answer.

The next memory she processed was with the same group of people, but in addition, she learned where she knew Keres from.

Lady Durya watched herself stand beside Kaci, gazing out over the sea where the sun danced on the waves. The sound of footsteps pierced the air. They turned to see a woman approaching – Keres.

As Keres introduced herself, Durya observed a subtle tension in Kaci's posture, her eyes narrowing with suspicion. Their conversation was cordial, yet Durya felt a knot of unease in her stomach. In this memory, she recalled the grim outcome of this encounter.

Keres, offering assistance, led them to a quaint cottage. Durya noticed Kaci blushing as she adorned a rich green dress, feeling a surge of pride for her friend's beauty and jealousy for her own lack of it. Yet, Kaci seemed distant, her gaze lost in the fire, hinting at her gift of scrying.

Durya watched as fear flickered across Kaci's face, a premonition unsettling her. The scene shifted. Kaci and Micah running, with Keres's enraged footsteps thundering behind them.

Watching this, Durya felt a pang of guilt for aiding Keres in separating Micah from his twin sister. She empathized with his anger, but felt justified, now understanding the peril of tampering with the past.

The memory led her to a cliff's edge where Keres appeared, engulfed in fiery wrath. Chaos ensued, ending with Durya and her friends reaching the deck of the Golden Gull, escaping Keres's fury. The scene faded, leaving Durya to ponder her actions.

Durya, now immersed in her quest for memories, led Sharn and Kaci with an unrelenting urgency. Her hunger for the past propelled them forward, regardless of their fatigue. They navigated the passages, their path illuminated by the faint, eerie glow of the cave walls until they stumbled upon another memory orb. This one, however, pulsed with an odd frequency, its light shimmering with an unsettling intensity.

"There's another one," Durya pointed out..

Sharn stepped forward, his eyes narrowing as he observed the orb. "Be careful," he warned. "This one seems different."

Kaci moved closer, her curiosity clear. As they approached, the orb morphed, its serene glow contorting into a shadowy form. It expanded, twisting into a monstrous entity that seemed to pulsate with a malevolent energy.

The transformation was abrupt and startling. Kaci's reaction was immediate; her eyes darkened to an inky blackness, a visual manifestation of her inner darkness being triggered. Without a word, she dashed towards the creature, an almost feral determination in her stride.

"Kaci, wait!" Durya called out, but Kaci was already gone, swallowed up by the shadows as she pursued the creature.

With a glance full of panic between Durya and Sharn, they sprang into action, racing after Kaci. Their footsteps thundered through the caverns, resounding off the walls as they dashed down the corridors, their hearts pounding in sync with their hurried pace.

The desperate pursuit culminated in a staggering, open expanse that struck them with its bizarre and ominous atmosphere. Before them unfolded a scene bordering on the surreal. Kaci teetered at the brink of a vast, abyss-like portal, a gateway to an unfathomable dimension. Alongside her, the shadow creature towered, its presence more menacing and tangible than ever, yet cloaked in an impenetrable veil of darkness.

Kaci's eyes, deep pools of blackness, were not fixed on the creature but on the portal. From within its depths, a figure reached out towards her—a woman whose form was both familiar and strange. As Durya and Sharn drew closer, they saw that the woman's face bore a striking resemblance to Kaci's, yet overlaid with another visage, creating an eerie, dual appearance.

With a lightning-fast motion, Kaci reached out towards the figure. The surrounding air seemed charged with a strange energy, the lines between reality and something otherworldly blurred.

"Kaci!" Durya called out again, her voice echoing.

Kaci, lost in the moment, didn't respond. The figure in the darkness continued to reach out, beckoning her.

Durya catapulted into motion. She bolted forward, seizing Kaci's arm with a fierce grip, trying to yank her back from the portal. "Kaci, ignore its whispers! This is an illusion!" she cried out.

By now, the trance-like state had lifted from Kaci, and her eyes had returned to their normal green as she was pulled away from the portal. The figure within the darkness reached out a last time before fading away, the portal closing in on itself, vanishing as if it had never been there.

As the immediate danger passed, Durya held Kaci close, concern etched on her face. "You're safe now," she whispered.

The creature beside Kaci let out a low, menacing growl, its form dissipating as they broke its hold over her. Before their eyes, its form reshaped and solidified into a figure they recognized. Keres stood there, a look of defeat and tears in her eyes.

"I have failed," she murmured, her voice breaking.

Durya's grip on Kaci tightened as she turned a piercing glare towards Keres. "Explain yourself," she commanded, ice in her voice.

Keres wiped away a tear, composing herself. "It's not what you think," she said, her voice stronger now. "I... I was trying to reach out, to protect you."

"Protect us? From what?" Kaci interjected, her eyes narrowing as she assessed Keres, trying to discern the truth in her words.

Keres, her expression a complex mix of resolve and despair,

inhaled before continuing her revelation. "The darkness... it binds us all," she said. "It's growing, becoming more than I can control. I thought I could use it to guide you, to help in my way, but it's slipping from my grasp."

Durya, Kaci, and Sharn listened as her words hung in the air.

"My mother, Mir, will not listen to me," Keres continued, her eyes reflecting a deep inner turmoil. "We need to close the doors between our worlds. Everyone speaks of balance, but they don't understand. If Javina wins, balance won't matter. Kashara and Isdralan can exist separately. It's what's best."

"Mir thought that if there was a child born of both worlds— me — then they could safely merge and balance would be restored," Keres explained, her voice bitter. "She thought it would be a good idea to free Javina. But she was so wrong."

Keres paused, her face contorting into a strange expression. "My existence was a mistake. She sent me back to Kashara. I was alone until Javina reached out. She was like a mother to me, more than Mir ever was. But it was all fake, fueled by jealousy. Now, I have no mother. I have no one." Her voice hardened. "My only goal now is to close the door. Close the caves."

"But people need to touch Isdralan, and even Kashara." Kaci interrupted. "It's where dreams and ideas come from."

Keres's reply was cold, her resolve unwavering. "Not if Javina has her way. She wants all to come from her. She seeks to dominate, to control everything and everyone."

Durya studied Keres, piecing together fragments of memories that now resurfaced. But the woman standing before them seemed different from the one she had known—not just in demeanor, but almost as if they existed in separate strands of time. The Keres she had met in Isdralan had been deceptive, even dangerous, attempting to kill them.

Yet, as this Keres spoke, her words carried some truth. There was a conviction in her voice that resonated with Durya, a sense that, despite their past encounters, she was being sincere.

"Sharn," Durya said, turning to her companion. "Bind her, for now. We need to decide our next move, and we can't risk any more surprises."

Sharn moved, securing the ropes around Keres with expert precision. As he finished, the cavern's air shifted, thick with an unspoken magic. Keres's form wavered, like a shadow caught in the light, and then transformed. Her human shape dissolved into a cloud of dark mist.

From the mist emerged a small creature, unlike any they had seen before. It was furry, with a compact body and a pair of bright, intelligent eyes that held an eerie depth. Its limbs were agile, tipped with claws that hinted at a potential for danger, and its mouth, though small, was filled with sharp teeth.

The creature that Keres had become looked up at them, a silent challenge in its gaze. Before they could react, it darted away with surprising speed, its nimble form slipping through the ropes that had bound the woman moments before. It scurried across the cavern floor and disappeared into a narrow crevice in the cave wall.

In the wake of Keres's escape, a heavy silence fell over the cavern. Kaci's face crumpled as she turned to Durya and Sharn. "This was a mistake," she murmured. "I should have never come back. I am a danger to everyone around me."

Durya's heart raced. Before her memory loss, connecting with others' emotions had been a challenge. Her own feelings were concealed that comprehending those of others often eluded her. However, now, witnessing Kaci's vulnerability, something within her awakened—an emerging capacity for understanding and a powerful urge to safeguard her friend.

She stepped closer, her expression softening. "Kaci, don't say that. You're not alone in this," she reassured, placing a hand on Kaci's shoulder. "We're in this together, remember? Whatever darkness you're facing, we'll face it as one."

Sharn looked to Durya, then nodded, his demeanor showing solidarity. "We've faced worse, Kaci. You've always seen the best in us, and that will not change now."

Kaci looked at them, her eyes glistening with unshed tears. "But what if I lose control again? What if I hurt one of you?" The fear in her voice was palpable, her usual confidence shaken.

Durya's resolve hardened. "Then we'll help you regain control. We've overcome every challenge thrown at us so far. This is just another hurdle in our path."

Kaci's gaze flickered between Durya and Sharn, searching for the conviction in their faces. The trust and determination she saw there seemed to offer her some comfort, a glimmer of hope in the face of her doubts.

As Sharn's gaze swept over the cavern, there was a moment of contemplation before he addressed his companions. His expression was one of careful consideration, his words measured. "Perhaps it's not just about gathering more memories right now," he proposed. "Our immediate focus might need to be on understanding the current mysteries—the caves, Keres, and your situation, Kaci." There was an almost imperceptible caution in his suggestion.

Kaci nodded, agreeing with Sharn. "You're right, Sharn. Maybe understanding our present situation should be our priority. Rushing into uncovering more memories without fully grasping our current predicament could be reckless," she said.

Durya, however, furrowed her brow in disagreement. "I respect your caution, but I feel differently. Each memory we uncover is a piece of the puzzle," she countered, her tone firm. "We can't afford to pause. The more we know about our past, the better we can navigate these challenges. We must continue to seek memories—it's the only way to truly understand and confront what we're facing."

Kaci paused before responding. "I understand the urgency, Durya, but I need time to rest and meditate. I'm overwhelmed, and a rational mind is a happy mind." she smiled.

Durya paused. After a moment, she nodded, her expression softening. "Alright, we'll take a quick break. Rest and clarity are important too," she conceded. "But let's not delay for too long."

As they wandered through the caves, it seemed as if the passages themselves responded to their needs. They stumbled upon a secluded alcove, a quiet refuge from the chaos of their journey. The serendipity of their discovery led Durya to wonder if they were indeed on the right path, guided by some unseen force or fate.

Kaci found a smooth rock to sit on and settled into a meditative pose, closing her eyes and taking deep, measured breaths. Sharn offered to take watch. "Get some rest," he said to Durya, moving to a vantage point that allowed him a view of the alcove's entrance.

Left alone, Durya sat near Kaci, her mind racing. The recent events had been tumultuous, and this moment of calm provided an opportunity for introspection.

Kaci opened her eyes, turning to Durya. "I've been carrying this darkness inside me," she began, her voice a whisper. "I fear it might one day harm those I care about. All I've ever wanted is to belong somewhere, to be part of something greater."

Durya nodded. "I can relate to that, Kaci," she said in a voice low enough Sharn could not hear. "For so long, I've shut myself off from feeling, from truly connecting. But now, finding these memories, understanding my past... it's opened a part of me I didn't realize was closed."

Kaci gave a small, bittersweet smile. "In a way, I'm grateful for this journey. I never would have wished the loss of memory on anyone, but it's shown me a side of you that feels more... real. We're sisters, not by blood, but in every way that counts."

The two women sat in silence, a bond of understanding and shared experience between them. As fatigue settled in, they leaned against the cave wall, allowing the exhaustion to lull them into a gentle sleep.

Later, Durya felt a gentle nudge from Sharn. Sensing his touch, she leaned back, creating a small but significant distance between them. While his presence brought reassurance, this subtle shift in space highlighted the complexities of their evolving relationship. Noticing her reaction, Sharn drew back a little more.

Confused and hurt, Sharn broke the silence. "Did I do something wrong?" He asked.

Sharn faced Durya. "I'm wary of the situation with your memories," he began. "You've endured so much, and before your memory loss, our relationship was just starting to... evolve," he hesitated, struggling to find the right words. "From acquaintances to something more."

Durya's laughter, light and sincere, resonated in the cavern, "I appreciate your concern. But from the fragments I've recalled, I can sense you've been a constant in my life."

Sharn shook his head. "But there were times I wasn't there for you," he admitted. "Times when I should have protected you, but didn't."

"Protected me from whom?" Durya asked, a sudden tightness gripping her heart. The name 'Edward' echoed in her mind, an unsettling presence from her past.

"Do you feel I'm... somehow less now?" Durya's voice was a mere whisper, exposing her deep-seated insecurities.

Sharn's response was fervent and immediate. "You are not less, absolutely not. I blame myself. I vowed to look out for you since we were kids. But when Edward entered our lives, I..." He faltered, overwhelmed with emotion. "I let you down."

Tears welled up in Durya's eyes. "Was I so oblivious?" She looked at Sharn. "You've always been there for me. It's me who didn't fully recognize your commitment, your affection."

As their gazes locked, a profound connection formed, bridging the gap between years and unsaid words. Durya added softly, "In these caverns, amidst these memories, I'm rediscovering not just my past but also what I truly desire."

Sharn's eyes conveyed a blend of relief and tenderness. "Durya, I—"

Their heartfelt conversation was interrupted by a rustling nearby. Alerted, Durya and Sharn turned to see a small creature stepping out from the shadows, its dense fur, razor-sharp claws, and keen eyes belying an intelligence uncommon for an animal.

Sharn's protective instincts kicked in. His posture shifted from relaxed to alert, his hand reaching for his weapon. He positioned himself between Durya and the creature, a silent guardian ready to defend against any threat.

The creature paused, its eyes locked onto theirs, conveying a sense of recognition and intelligence. There was no mistaking it. Keres was back.

As they watched, the creature changed. Its form shimmered and shifted, the fur receding and the body reshaping into a familiar figure. In moments, where the animal-like creature had stood, now stood Keres.

Durya shook Kaci awake, her movements cautious in the dim light of the cavern. As Kaci's eyes fluttered open, a sharp alertness replaced her initial grogginess. She sat up, her gaze darting between Durya and the figure of Keres.

Keres, with a noticeable weariness, held her hands up in a non-threatening gesture. "Please, don't hurt me," she implored, her voice strained with a sincerity that Durya couldn't dismiss. "I've just escaped from the life that was my prison. I'm only seeking a way home."

Kaci, however, was far from convinced. Her eyes narrowed into a skeptical squint. "I don't trust you," she stated flatly. "You were talking to her in the mirror. Collaborating with our enemy."

Keres retorted with a biting sharpness, "And I should trust you? The shadow of her lingers in you. She could overpower you at any moment."

"No, she can't," Kaci shot back, but her voice wavered, betraying doubt. Durya could sense the internal battle raging within her friend.

Keres, however, seemed to relent a fraction. "I saw a part of you in her as well," she admitted, her tone less confrontational. "Perhaps that's why she hasn't taken me over completely. Javina is desperate to escape, and she'll stop at nothing to achieve that. I want to prevent it as much as you do. Doesn't that make us allies? If I can sever her tie to Isdralan, perhaps I can sever her tie with you, Kaci."

Durya pondered Keres's words, feeling their truth. She remembered Kaci's warnings about their encounters with Keres in Isdralan. Yet, standing before her was a woman who seemed as much a victim of her circumstances as they were of theirs.

"Perhaps we should trust her," Durya ventured, wondering how much this choice would disturb the balance of their fates.

Kaci whirled around, her eyes flashing with a fire that rivaled the energy crackling through her hair. "Trust her? Again?" The words were sharp. "Have you forgotten what happened last time? You'll regret this, Durya. Mark my words."

Durya's resolve wavered. She knew the dangers of trusting someone like Keres were as real as the scars they bore from past betrayals. Yet, the promise of the insights Keres could offer loomed large. This was a gamble, but one worth taking.

The weight of the decision pressed down on her. In the world of shadows and secrets, trust was a rare commodity, once shattered, seldom restored. Durya's mind raced, weighing every outcome. Could they afford to walk this razor's edge?

As the silence stretched between them, thick with unspoken fears and unyielding resolve, Durya's next words hovered on the brink, a choice that could alter their path forever.

11

Betrayal and Bargains

The air was thick around them and the previous words were still hanging between them like a suspended verdict. "Do you really think you can influence Isdralan?" Durya asked. She stood tall, her presence commanding even in the dim light. Her eyes, unwavering, bore into Keres. The skepticism in her voice was clear, but so was the newfound authority she wielded.

Keres met her gaze and stepped out of the enveloping shadows. Her movements were smooth and deliberate, like a cat stalking unseen prey. "Isdralan is my goal," she murmured.

"And what of these caves?" Lady Durya stood with an unyielding straightness that seemed to command the very air around her. "What do you know of them?"

Hesitation flickered across Keres's face, a subtle crack in her otherwise composed demeanor. "My knowledge is sparse, fragments from my mother's tales before I was sent away. They exist outside of time. Outside of everything," she said, her eyes darting away, betraying a wariness she masked.

Her gaze then shifted to Kaci, who was rigid, fists clenched at her sides. "Why this hostility? Have our paths crossed before?"

Keres asked, her tone laced with a sly curiosity.

Kaci's eyes flashed, a tumult of emotions swirling in their depths. "You ask why I don't trust you?" she spat. "Once another life, you tried to kill me. Worse than that, you fooled me. I actually believed what you said made sense."

Keres's expression shifted, a mask of innocence belying the cunning beneath. "You know these deeds are my other selves and not mine. Yet, here we stand, our paths intertwined."

Kaci's gaze hardened. "The caves may twist time, Keres, but it's curious how each of your 'selves' plays the same game. You withhold truths, grasp at control without seeing the full picture, always leaving a trail of half-told stories and broken trust. Different times, same deceptions. You say these selves aren't you, but the pattern, it seems, is hard to break. It's not about betrayal; it's about never knowing if you're standing on solid ground or quicksand with you."

"Fair point," Keres conceded. "At this moment, our goals seem to align. Don't forget I hold information that might help us rid us of Javina."

Durya, maintaining her composed exterior, felt a ripple of concern. Her eyes, adept at reading the subtleties of power and tension, settled on Kaci. The harshness and anger radiating from her warm and composed friend struck her as out of character. Durya pondered if the darkness of the caves was warping Kaci's emotions, or if this was a raw, honest reaction to the intricate weave of half-truths and manipulations spun by Keres.

Disturbed by this thought yet hiding her worry, Durya offered a dry chuckle, aiming to ease the mounting tension. "Regarding a path to Isdralan, we don't have a clear map. We are on our own quest, trusting that the right path will unveil itself when necessary."

Keres leaned forward, her eyes alight with an intensity that had been absent moments before. "And in your journey, have you found any clues to reaching Isdralan? I must reach that place. Any guidance would be helpful."

Durya, sensing there was more at play, pressed. "You mentioned you had something to offer us. What might that be?"

The corners of Keres's mouth turned up in a knowing smile. "Kashara," she revealed, her eyes glinting with unspoken knowledge.

Kaci bristled at the name, her fiery temperament flashing through her jovial facade, though she held her tongue.

Durya let out a measured sigh. "Then enlighten us about Kashara."

With the intent of using her skills in court diplomacy, Durya watched, attempting to unravel the mystery of Keres and Kashara. As she observed Keres discussing the interconnected nature of Kashara and Isdralan, she learned that Kashara, misunderstood as a mere shadow realm, represented a version of the same reality as Isdralan. It was a realm where darker desires and the lure of power were more clear, in contrast to Isdralan, which symbolized light, creativity, and inspiration.

As Keres's words painted a picture of these twin realms, Durya pondered the equilibrium that existed between them. The portals and rifts that linked Elyndris (and all worlds, for that matter) to Kashara were not physical pathways, but also metaphors for the balance between darkness and light, chaos and order. There was a depth to Keres's understanding, a certain familiarity with Kashara's darker aspects that made Durya pause. Could the more sinister traits have influenced

Keres?

"It's not all what you think, you know. The power you can gain there is essential to defeat Javina," Keres stated, casting a wary glance at Kaci.

"Go on," Durya prompted. "How would one get to Kashara?"

Keres leaned forward, her voice lowering. "It's actually quite simple. That's how I returned. A life for a life. There are countless rituals to achieve this. I seized my chance during a ritual gone awry, a group sacrificing one of their own. In that moment, I traded places with the victim, stepping into the light as darkness consumed him." Her smile was unsettling, hinting at a deeper, darker understanding of these forces. "Unfortunately, I ended up here, and not Isdralan."

Kaci, her expression a mixture of horror and disbelief, interjected, "So, to confront Javina, we need to trade a soul?"

Keres nodded, a grim satisfaction in her tone. "Easy as that."

Kaci, her temper flaring, declared, "Then let's trade me. I'll face her and end this."

Keres shook her head, a condescending smirk playing on her lips. "You foolish child, meddling in forces beyond your comprehension. There's a better way to *end this*. We seal the doors to both Isdralan and Kashara."

Kaci hesitated. "We can't do that. What about the dreamers? The ones with ties to both worlds?"

Keres's answer was cold and dismissive. "They'll have to learn to dream without the realms."

As the Baroness, her decisions now were pivotal, with consequences that would ripple far and wide. Her mind wandered to her own journey of self-recovery, the need to reclaim her full sense of self. Durya knew she couldn't make any far-reaching decisions until she herself was whole again. With this resolve, she declared, "Our immediate task is to complete our own mission. Keres, you may accompany us to Isdralan."

Kaci, bristling with an objection, spoke, but Durya raised a hand, asserting her authority

"We will proceed with our plan," she stated, her voice leaving no room for debate.

"Of course," Keres replied, but her eyes gleamed with an unspoken malice that did not escape Durya's notice.

Kaci protested again, "No!"

But Durya reiterated, "This is my quest. I am the Baroness. We will do this my way."

As the group reached a tenuous agreement, Durya couldn't shake the feeling that they were treading on dangerous ground. Keres's desire to seal the realms was a drastic step, one that could have unforeseen consequences. Durya knew she needed to tread carefully, balancing the immediate needs of their quest with the long-term implications of their actions.

She shared a brief, meaningful glance with Sharn, who had remained silent throughout the exchange. Her eyes communicated a message clear only to him. With a subtle nod, Sharn understood, shifting his position to stand closer to Keres. His quiet demeanor belied the vigilance of a seasoned warrior, ready to act should Keres show any sign of deceit.

As they navigated the twisting pathways of the Caves of Chaos, Durya signaled for Kaci to stay behind, seeking a moment of private conversation. The dim, flickering cave lights cast an eerie glow on their faces.

"We're nearing the end, I think," Durya whispered, her voice low and intense. "Every memory I regain makes me feel more like myself. Once we're done here, our next goal is to liberate you from Javina's hold."

Kaci's expression was fraught with worry. "But Keres, she's not trustworthy. We're making a mistake."

"Sometimes, we must keep our adversaries close" She swept her hand around them, encompassing the daunting expanse of the caves. "I learned that lesson too late. If only I had known, I might have avoided this trap," she said, her gesture encompassing both the physical labyrinth and the maze of her fragmented memories.

To trust Keres was risky, yet it was a well-considered decision. She was familiar with the intricacies of power plays and deceit. The Baroness aspect of her personality was strategic, prepared to employ any required methods to attain their objectives.

Sharn's silent vigilance by Keres's side was a comforting presence. His loyalty and strength were pillars she could rely on. The path ahead was shrouded in uncertainty, but Durya knew they were not without their own resources and cunning.

As Durya and her companions continued, the experience became more than a mere journey. The voyage into the depths of her own soul. Each memory orb they encountered brought forth fragments of Durya's past, stitching together the tapestry of her identity in a way she had never imagined possible. The curse that Lord Redmont had inflicted upon her, which once felt like a relentless storm, now revealed itself as an unexpected blessing, a gateway to self-discovery.

Each time she touched an orb, a torrent of emotions washed over her. They pulsated with scenes from her life, each one a key unlocking the hidden chambers of her heart. She saw herself, a young orc, in a world that often felt alien. The confusion, ache for acceptance, and struggle to belong remained vivid. Yet amidst these turbulent waters, there were islands of warmth and love. The fond memories of her foster parents, their flawed but genuine affection, filled her with a sense of gratitude. Her father's proud, unwavering support in the face of judgment was a beacon of unconditional love.

But not all memories were tender. The sharp sting of rejection from her orc kin left a mark on her soul, a reminder of the pain of not belonging. And then, the memory of Marcus's departure to the Aelorians–a chapter of her life that brought both joy and sorrow, his absence a void that lingered long after he was gone.

Each memory, whether joyous or painful, wove into the fabric of her being, shaping the warrior, the leader, the woman she had become. With each step, with each revelation, Durya felt a growing sense of empowerment. She was a complex being, not just an orc or a human.

Then, in the cavern's heart, where the echoes of their initial gathering still seemed to resonate, she found it. An orb unlike any she had seen before. It throbbed with an almost sacred energy. Its glow was not just light but a physical manifestation of her journey's culmination.

Durya approached, her heart pounding in her chest, a mixture of excitement and reverence coursing through her veins. "This is it," she whispered, her voice barely audible. "The last piece of my story." She reached out, her hand trembling. This orb felt like the key to unlocking the deepest parts of her soul, the part she had yearned to understand.

As her fingers brushed against its surface, a surge of understanding, acceptance, and peace flooded through her. It was as if the orb was not just showing her memories, but also affirming her identity, her worth, her place in the world. At that moment, Durya wasn't just recalling her past; she was embracing her entire essence, the sum of all her experiences. This was more than memory—it was realization, it was coming home.

Sharn, loyal to a fault, moved to stand next to her, taking her hand in a comforting grasp. "We'll leave you to have some time alone, my lady," he suggested. Kaci nodded, her eyes meeting Durya, a silent gesture of agreement.

"Wait," Durya said, her voice steadier than she felt. "I want a moment with Sharn."

As Kaci and Keres retreated into the cavern's shadows, Sharn remained, his gaze tender and attentive. "I will always be here," he promised, his voice a comforting balm to her soul.

Durya raised her eyes to meet his, feeling a rush of emotions. "I'm different now, because of everything we've been through," she admitted. "I realize the love that's been around me all this time. Power doesn't matter to me anymore." Her smile was sincere, revealing a seldom-seen side of her she usually concealed. "At least not as much. It's you I want."

Sharn moved, hesitated. "But being a leader... it's part of who you are," he reminded her.

Durya was more certain than ever. "We will return to Elyndris. We'll persuade Marcus to take up the mantle in Marshfield." Her words were not just plans but affirmations of a future she yearned for.

"I don't care who leads Westerfield, as long as they truly care for the people and remain free from Javina and Redmont's influence," she added.

"Then we'll find a quaint cottage in Marshfield," she continued, her eyes sparkling with dreams of a simple yet fulfilling life. "We'll build a home, a family... our own little world."

Sharn, his eyes reflecting a deep sense of joy and contentment, leaned forward and kissed her.

"I'm ready," Lady Durya declared with newfound resolve as Sharn moved away to join Kaci and Keres.

Alone now, Durya approached the orb, her heart full of love and her mind clear of doubt. This was her last memory, the last key to unlocking her complete self. She stepped into the orb, ready to embrace whatever truths lay within, fortified by the love and choices that had led her to this defining moment.

In the deepest recess of her last memory orb, Durya found herself in her quarters at Westerfield estate. The memory unfolded with a serving girl handing her a steaming cup of tea. Shortly thereafter, Lord Redmont's voice, harsh and scolding, permeated the room. She observed as her former self accused him of poisoning the tea, his face a picture of genuine bewilderment.

Then, her past self collapsed onto the bed, and Durya braced herself for the memory to dissipate. This was her last recollection before her memory had been erased. Yet, it lingered. Her earlier self's eyes flew open with panic, her body immobile and paralyzed. The hidden door behind the mirror swung open, and to her astonishment, in walked Sharn, her trusted confidant, her beloved.

Relief and love filled Durya's heart as she watched him approach her bedridden former self. "It's okay, I will always care for you," Sharn murmured, planting a tender kiss on her forehead. Durya's mind raced, anticipating this as the moment of her salvation, the story she had always believed. However, Sharn turned and walked away, crossing the room and opening the door to the serving girl's chamber. Ellie, her favorite lady-in-waiting, stood, trembling.

"She is awake. Did she drink the whole thing?" Sharn asked.

"Yes, sir," Ellie stammered, "I swear it!"

"Then why is she awake?" Sharn paced the room, each step a sharp echo against the stone floor. His hands clenched and unclenched at his sides, and every so often, he ran them through his hair, pulling at the strands in a visible sign of agitation.

Ellie, on the verge of tears, could only shrug. "I don't know!"

Sharn's expression shifted to one of concern as he returned to Durya's side, scooping her up in his arms. "Don't you worry," he assured her, "I will take you away from all of this, to a life of love you deserve."

Turning to Ellie, he instructed, "I must go. I need to find Kaci and rescue Marcus. Stay with her, please? I'll knock on the mirror as a signal before we enter, to give you time to disappear."

"Yes, sir," Ellie responded, bobbing her head.

As Sharn vanished through the mirror, Durya remained, a solitary figure amidst the shadows of her memory. The truth, stark and merciless, bore down on her. Sharn, her unwavering pillar of trust, was the architect of her downfall. It just sting, it razed her world, leaving a smoldering crater where trust and affection had just been flourishing. Why show her all this, and build her up to love, just to tear it down again? It wasn't fair!

In the bedroom's silence, the ghosts of her past whispered of the loneliness that was Durya Barcley-Conwyn. A lone tear made its pilgrimage down her cheek. Inside her, emotions churned, threatening to overflow. Her fists clenched, nails biting into flesh, anchoring her in a reality that threatened to spiral into chaos, forcing the rest of her body to calm.

I will not kill him, she repeated to herself, again and again in a silent mantra. Confrontation loomed like a darkened horizon.

The future they had just painted now lay in ruins, a mosaic of broken dreams.

12

Love and Sacrifice

Durya inhaled and stood tall. "I am the baroness," she declared, her voice clear and firm.

"Have you learned nothing? You are more than that," emerged a voice from the shadows. As it spoke, the air shimmered, and Fia materialized, her form coalescing like mist turning into a solid shape. "You are a warrior," Fia continued, her voice a mirror of Durya's countless struggles. "But you are also the mother, the maiden, and the crone."

Upon seeing Fia, Durya experienced a blend of relief and anticipation—a sign of her journey's conclusion, yet the start of something new. But her feelings swiftly turned to anger upon absorbing Fia's words. The term 'mother' mocked her, a painful reminder of a dream she had relinquished. Her hopes of nurturing a child, sharing her love, had been shattered by Edward's cruelty.

"I am not a mother. I will never be one."

"Is that your focus?" Fia asked. "You do not have to birth children to embody the spirit of a mother."

"I don't understand," Durya whispered.

Fia explained, "We are all composed of various facets, but no one embodies them in quite the same way. You have sought to be an orc, a noble, a wife, a mother, a warrior. However, you are all."

Durya took a moment to reflect. Her past, a tapestry of roles and identities, came into focus. She realized she had been trying to fit into a single mold, yet she was a complex amalgamation. After breathing deeply to calm her turmoil, she spoke again, "I am the baroness." This time, the words resonated differently. They affirmed her multifaceted truth, not merely a title she hid behind.

Fia's eyes locked onto Durya. "You are blood and thorns, the tempest's fury and the serenity of a clear sky. You encompass all these attributes, acting as the bridge that brings them together. I have watched you," Fia continued, her gaze piercing yet kind. "While other guardians choose their kin to pass down their legacy, I choose you."

"What do you mean?" Durya's heart skipped a beat. "You want me to replace you?"

Fia inclined their head. "All worlds are linked to Isdralan, but there appears to be a unique connection with Elyndris. You will suit us well."

"You want me to be a guardian?" Durya asked, blinking. "But aren't you immortal?"

Fia laughed, and the sound was like a soft lullaby filling the room. "No more than you. Just like me, you can be eternal, too. It is just a matter of understanding the nature of things."

"I am not ready," Durya confessed.

"no one ever is. But you have the potential to grow, to learn. Come with me to Isdralan, and you shall be guided on this path."

Durya felt a gentle tug at her being, and in moments, she stood in the grove where her journey had started. The air was fragrant with the scent of ancient trees and blooming flowers.

Fia's eyes, as deep and fathomless as the night sky, seemed to pierce through Durya. "The grove is where we confront the many facets of our being. It mirrors the complexities of your journey."

As Durya absorbed the tranquility, she shared her turmoil. "I thought I had learned so much. I rediscovered myself and felt... Happy. But it ended with betrayal."

What you have gained should not be overshadowed by the last moment. "Life's journey is a battlefield of experiences. Each memory you reclaimed was a victory in understanding your true self."

Durya pondered Fia's words. "How do I reconcile the warrior with the noble, the lover with the betrayed?"

Fia's form softened, embodying the nurturing aspect of a mother. "You are a tapestry woven from these experiences. Like the trees of this grove, you are rooted yet ever-growing, your strength lying in your diverse nature."

Durya's eyes flickered. "And what of my role, Fia? You see something in me I'm yet to grasp."

Fia transformed again, this time embodying the wisdom of the crone. "Readiness is a path, not a destination. In seeking balance, embrace change and accept the immutable."

Realization dawned in Durya. "A balance between action and acceptance..."

Fia smiled, now exuding the warmth of the maiden, her energy gentle and inviting. "Contemplate my offer. Here, time flows with the needs of the heart."

"I need time to reflect, to choose my way forward." Durya

whispered.

"Time here is your ally," Fia assured, their presence now a harmonious blend of many aspects. "In the grove, it is a guide, not a constraint."

Durya remained firm and undaunted. "I don't mean here, in the grove. I need to finish what I started and go back to Elyndris to make things right.

Fia's presence suddenly intensified, becoming larger and more formidable. A great sword materialized beside them, its blade gleaming with an ancient power. They were a fearsome warrior, embodying strength and authority.

"You are not bound by any duty," Fia declared, their voice echoing around the grove like a storm. "You let your perceived identities dictate your actions. True power lies in shaping your destiny, not being led by it." With a swift motion, they swung the great sword towards Durya, who cringed, only for the blade to halt mere inches from her neck.

Durya's heart pounded, but she looked into Fia's eyes, finding a depth of meaning in the act. Fia's transformation was not just a display of power, but a lesson in the dynamics of identity and choice.

"You have much to learn," Fia spoke again, their form shifting to that of a small, quiet old woman. "Go, complete what you have begun. When the time is right, I will be here, waiting for you."

Durya was moved by Fia's words. It was a moment that went beyond mere identity revelation.

"I'll return when I shape my story's conclusion."

Fia smiled with understanding. "When you're ready, come back. Your journey of discovery is far from over."

"How will I find my way back to Isdralan when the time

comes?" Durya asked.

Fia regarded her. "In the relic room, there's a door," she began, her voice soft yet clear. "You've seen it before, Durya. You always knew the way."

"The relic room? The one with the mirror." Durya's brow furrowed.

"Yes, this is one path of many." Fia's voice carried a hint of mystery. "The relic room holds a door for your return. Once guarded, now the tides are shifting, unbinding old roles."

Durya absorbed this, her mind racing. "And Keres? She came from a dark mirror. What are your thoughts about her?"

Fia's eyes seemed to look through time itself as they answered. "What will happen with Keres has already happened."

Durya felt a wave of confusion but remained silent, pondering Fia's cryptic words. The mysteries of time and fate were still beyond her grasp, yet she sensed their importance.

The Grove, once tranquil and beautiful, melted away from Durya's surroundings, vanishing like mist in the morning light. Towering ancient trees, vibrant flowers, and even Fia's wise figure receded into nothingness. Durya found herself alone in the Caves of Chaos in the place where she had declared her love for Sharn.

Everything from before felt like a fading dream, but Durya was changed. She was reshaped in the place that was once a confusing maze of forgotten memories. Sharn's betrayal, her heartache, and Fia's teachings had changed her. Durya Barclay–Conwyn was ready.

Ready to face the consequences of her past decisions, ready to confront the challenges that lay ahead in Elyndris, and ready to write the next chapter of her life. She was no longer just reacting to the surrounding events. She was now an active participant, the author of her destiny.

With each step Durya took towards the others, a bittersweet certainty grew within her. She was changed, forever different from the person who had once confessed her love to Sharn in this very cave. The revelations and self-reflection had left an indelible mark on her soul.

As she neared, Sharn's eyes caught hers. He offered no words, only a silent, understanding nod. His presence was steadfast as always, but Durya sensed a subtle shift in him. Perhaps he, too, felt the change in her. There was a distance in her eyes, a guardedness that hadn't been there before. Durya wasn't sure if she would confront him about the betrayal revealed in her memory. That decision would require more reflection.

Kaci appeared next, her light-hearted demeanor replaced with a thoughtful, contemplative look. She studied Durya for a moment, as if trying to read the changes etched in her face. There was uncertainty in Kaci's eyes. Yet, she offered Durya a small, supportive smile, a silent acknowledgment of the trials they had both endured.

Keres stood apart from the others, and kept her distance, watching. Her role in their journey was complicated, filled with motives and intentions Durya had yet to grasp. Her reaction to Durya's transformation was understated—a faint narrowing of her eyes, a contemplative tilt of her head, signaling she was weighing the impact of Durya's change on her own plans.

As Durya stood among them, she felt a sense of detachment. She was part of this group, yet apart from it. She had come to a crossroads in her life, and the path she would choose was hers alone.

The journey ahead was clear. She would first return to Elyndris and confront her past, her identity, and her future.

Only then would she feel free enough to learn more from Fia. The decisions in Elyndris she would make were no longer influenced by her emotions or duty. They were guided by a deeper understanding of herself and the world.

The surrounding silence wasn't the comforting kind, filled with companionship and mutual understanding. It was a silence fraught with tension, an uneasy lull in a storm of unspoken thoughts and feelings. They all watched, waiting.

Durya addressed Keres first, stepping toward the woman with an air of nobility that was second nature to her. As Keres slid beside her, Durya's voice was a hushed murmur, meant only for the ears of the dark lady.

"You seek passage to Isdralan?" Durya inquired.

Keres's nod was cautious.

"There is a hidden passage in the room of relics, behind the tapestry near the mirror that brings you to Kashara," she divulged. There was no turning from this path.

Keres's reaction was a mix of surprise and concealed eagerness. "It's been there all this time?"

Durya's subtle touch on Keres's arm halted her sudden movement. "Do not make your intentions too obvious," she suggested.

Keres resettled by the fire, her sly smile betraying her satisfaction. Durya's statement was unequivocal. "Our paths as allies end here."

Keres seemed on the verge of probing further but held back — two souls shaped by worlds of light and shadow, forever marked by their journeys.

Then Durya rejoined the silent circle by the fire, motioning Keres to join them. As she contemplated the web of events she had just set in motion.

In the cavern's dim light, the sense of departure was palpable. Durya, distant, especially from Sharn, had lost her once warm gaze towards him, now replaced by a coldness.

Durya broke the silence and confirmed their suspicions. "I've retrieved the final fragment of my memory. I am now complete," she declared.

The group exhaled in unison, gathering their belongings. Kaci asked, "How do we find our way back to the entrance?"

Durya, with newfound assurance, responded, "Our exit won't be the same as our entry. The chamber holding the relics leads to both Kashara and Isdralan."

As the group started on their way, Sharn seized the opportunity to draw Durya aside. The others averted their gaze, granting them privacy.

"Durya, you seem far away," Sharn began, his voice shaky. "Is everything okay?"

Durya met his gaze, her eyes like windows to a stormy sea, revealing nothing of the chaos within. "I'm fine, Sharn. Just thinking about the future."

Sharn hesitated, picking his words. "You remember everything now, don't you? About... before."

Her face remained impassive, a mask hiding her inner thoughts. "I remember a lot of things, Sharn. Why do you ask?" She refused to make this easy for him.

He fidgeted, his unspoken confession hanging between them. "It's just that... if there's anything you want to talk about, I'm here."

Durya studied him, her gaze piercing. She waited, hoping he would speak, unveil the truth they both knew. But Sharn faltered, his confession teetering on the edge of his lips but never materializing.

"I appreciate that, Sharn," she said, stepping back from him. "Right now, I need to focus on what lies ahead." Now was not the time to deal with her hurt.

Sharn's expression flickered was unreadable. "Of course, Durya. Whatever you need."

She strode forward, pushing past to distance herself from the group. Her heavy steps betrayed a restrained anger. Sharn, like a lost puppy, trailed behind her, weaving through Kaci and Keres, driven by a need to reconnect.

"Durya, I just want to take care of you, to make sure you're safe," Sharn said, a note of panic in his voice.

Durya stopped, turning to face him. "I don't need someone to take care of me, Sharn," she snapped. her voice was sharp. "I never have. I need a partner, someone who stands with me, not for me."

Sharn recoiled. "I... I've always been there for you. Ever since we were kids."

"Yes, you have," Durya acknowledged, her voice softening just a fraction. "But some things can't be undone. This changed me in ways that can't be reversed."

Sharn searched her face, looking for a hint of the woman he knew, the woman he loved. "I can change too, Durya. I can be whatever you need."

"It's about more than just reacting to what I've seen. I don't care if you change or not. In this new chapter, you don't fit," Durya said, her voice steady, concealing the turmoil of hurt and anger within. Just hours before, she was prepared to escape from the world to be with her love. Her words struck him with devastating force. Sharn's face crumpled, pain clouding his features. His body seemed to falter, and his shoulders slumped.

"What about our future? Our home, our life together, away

from all this chaos? Don't you think we deserve that?"

Durya paused, meeting his eyes. "A life away from it all... that was a dream. But it's not my reality. Not anymore."

"But we could make it our reality, you said..." Sharn insisted, his voice now desperate. "We could find peace, build something together. You deserve happiness. Don't I deserve a chance to be a part of that?"

Durya's gaze turned steely, her emotions long bottled up, now surging forth. "Happiness built on what?" she demanded. She shook her head, a bitter laugh breaking free. "You should have thought about that before you played a part in erasing my memories."

Sharn flinched as if struck, the raw truth of her words slicing through him. "I..."

"You poisoned me," Durya's voice rose, laden with anguish and anger. "How can I forget that? How can I ever trust you again?"

Behind them, Kaci and Keres exchanged shocked glances, the intensity of Durya's revelation reaching them.

Sharn's face crumpled, his composure shattered. "I was trying to protect you," he stammered, his voice breaking under the strain. "I thought it was right, but..." His words faded, overwhelmed by the impact of her anger and the stunned reactions of their companions.

"Protect me?" Durya's voice rose, tinged with anger and disbelief. "By allowing me to be manipulated and controlled? By standing by while my agency was stripped away?"

"I was wrong," Sharn admitted, his eyes pleading for understanding. "Terribly wrong. But I love you, Durya. That has never changed. I will spend every moment of my life trying to make this right, if you'll just give me a chance."

Durya looked at him. "Love isn't just about intentions, Sharn. It's about actions, about respect. I can't see past what you did."

Sharn reached out, attempting to bridge the gap between them, but Durya stepped back, her body language firm and final. "I need to be on my own, Sharn. To understand who I will be, after all this. I can't do that with you."

Sharn's hand fell to his side, his expression one of resignation and sorrow. "I understand," he mumbled, though his eyes betrayed the pain of his words.

Durya, despite her pain, resolved to move forward. Then she turned away, walking with the firm, commanding stride.

"I'll do anything, Durya. I'll spend my life making it up to you," Sharn called out to her back.

Hearing Sharn's plea, Durya felt a twinge of sorrow, yet she knew forgiveness wasn't simple. His words, sincere as they were, couldn't undo the past. She walked on, acknowledging the pain but choosing her future over what had been. In her heart, there was a bittersweet acceptance that some things, once broken, couldn't be mended.

As they navigated the ever-changing caves, the group felt the tedium of their journey. Kaci broke the silence. "How are we going find that room again?"

Durya, confident as ever, replied, "It will find us," her smile tinged with sadness. She led more by instinct than certainty. Their progress halted at a dead-end, revealing an ancient mirror that caught the dim cave light.

Keres voiced her frustration. "This is a waste of time." But they were startled to find their return path had disappeared, the cave shifting around them.

"Another mirror?" Kaci joked. "Seems these caves fancy a bit of reflection." No one was in the mood to laugh.

Above the mirror, an inscription read:

Behold in this glass, your essence deep,
Where truest selves their vigil keep.
In this reflection, falsehoods fall,
As heart's unmasked truth stands tall.

The words seemed to hold ancient power, pulsating with energy. The mirror was a test, a mystical snare designed to confront them with something far more daunting than physical barriers: the truths of their own souls.

Sharn's composure, already fragile, shifted to panic, reflecting the anxiety rippling through them all. In this chamber, a nexus of ancient mystery, the mirror loomed like a sentinel, daring them to confront the secrets within its depths.

"I hate this place," Keres muttered, her voice echoing. With a resigned breath, she stepped forward, positioning herself in front of the mirror. As her gaze met the reflective surface, an intense light flared from within its depths, engulfing the chamber. The brilliance was so overpowering that Durya had to shield her eyes. When the light subsided, Keres was nowhere to be seen, as if the mirror had absorbed her very essence.

"What did she see?" Sharn's voice cut through the heavy silence that followed.

Durya, trying to dispel the disquiet left by the mirror's revelation, felt a sudden spike of annoyance towards Sharn. She replied, her tone clipped, "I believe this mirror is meant for individual reflection, not public display."

"Do you think she... died?" Sharn's voice trembled.

It was Kaci who spoke up, her voice edged with fear. "I'm not sure 'died' has any meaning here. What happens to any of us when we face our true selves? Does a part of us... disappear?"

Resolved to maintain control of the situation, Durya declared, "I will go last. Sharn, you're next, then Kaci." She paused, her gaze piercing as she laid out the plan. "Wherever you end up, wait one hour. If no one shows up, consider yourself or the others lost, and continue as you would."

"As you would?" There was a noticeable edge of anger in Sharn's voice, his words heavy with emotion. "I live for you, my Lady."

Durya's response was bitter, her voice sharp as a blade. "Then perhaps it is time you live for yourself." It was a challenge to Sharn, a push to reconsider his own existence beyond his devotion to her.

Sharn hesitated as he faced the mirror. The cavern's light cast shadows across his face, accentuating the lines of anxiety. This was an adversary he couldn't combat with his sword or shield. It was a battle that demanded he confront something far more daunting—the depths of his own soul.

Durya watched as Sharn's large hands clenched and un-clenched at his sides. He took a step forward, then paused, a silent battle raging within him. His gaze shifted toward Durya, seeking an assurance she couldn't give. In his eyes, she saw a vulnerability that he rarely exposed, a glimpse into the man who had always been her steadfast protector.

The mirror's surface rippled, and a light emanated from it, surrounding Sharn in a luminous embrace. His reflection blurred, the light growing in intensity until it was all Durya could see. For a fleeting moment, she thought she saw a myriad of emotions crossing his face–fear, acceptance, and perhaps a glimpse of understanding.

Then, the light flared brightly, and when it dimmed, Sharn

was gone. The place where he had stood mere moments ago was now empty, the mirror calm once again, as if nothing had happened.

"It's my turn, then," Kaci said. She stepped forward, her stride betraying her uncertainty as she approached the mirror.

Before she faced the mirror's power, Kaci turned to Durya, their eyes locking. They had faced countless challenges together, their bond forged in the fires of adversity and deepened through shared victories and losses. Now, as Kaci stood on the brink of her own confrontation with the unknown, the depth of their connection was stronger than ever.

Durya reached out, her hand finding Kaci's. Their fingers intertwined, a silent symbol of their friendship. In that brief clasp, a surge of emotions passed between them - fear, courage, and solidarity. It was a reassurance, a promise that no matter what the mirror revealed or where it took them, their sisterhood would remain unbroken.

Then, Durya pulled Kaci into a tight hug, a rare display of open affection that contrasted with her composed exterior. In this embrace, there was a sense of fierce protectiveness, a deep love that Durya felt for Kaci as a sister, a friend, a confidant. Then, turning to face the mirror, Kaci squared her shoulders.

Durya, observing from a distance, noticed the mirror's surface ripple, its soft glow enveloping Kaci. However, as the glow grew, an unforeseen event occurred. The light flickered wildly, alternating between brightness and darkness, suggesting the mirror's struggle to resolve two opposing aspects within Kaci. It appeared as if two forces were in a tug of war, each striving to emerge as the dominant reflection in the glass.

The cavern's ambient light dimmed in response to the mirror's turmoil, casting the chamber into a realm of half-light, half-shadow. Durya watched, her heart in her throat, as the struggle in the mirror reached a crescendo. The light didn't flare as it had with the others; instead, it was an abyssal void that seemed to consume everything, including Kaci.

This sudden engulfment of darkness was terrifying. The very air felt heavy, charged with an unseen energy, and a chill run down her spine.

Slowly, painfully, the light crept back into the cavern, a gradual return to normalcy that seemed to take an eternity. The mirror calmed, its surface once again still and clear. But Kaci was gone, the space where she had stood now empty.

Durya, left alone in the cavern, felt a profound sense of loss and isolation. Kaci's disappearance, engulfed in that terrifying darkness, weighed on her. What had been different?

She stepped forward, her heart a tumult of emotions as she faced the mirror. The cavern around her felt silent, as if the very stones were holding their breath, anticipating the revelation that was about to unfold. As she gazed into the mirror, her own reflection stared back – the image of Lady Durya, Baroness of Westerfield, a figure of power and resilience. But this was the surface.

The mirror rippled, its surface shimmering like the surface of a tranquil lake disturbed by a gentle breeze. The first layer to fall away was her title, the mantle of Baroness dissolving into the ether. Regal attire, the symbol of her authority and status, faded from her reflection, leaving her in simpler garb, a visual stripping away of her societal role.

Next to vanish were the more personal identifiers. The mirror shed her identity as an orc, erasing the physical traits that marked her as different, both in the eyes of her people and those of the orcs who had never fully accepted her. The tusks, the bluish-gray skin, all melted away, leaving a figure unmarked by race or species.

Then, the mirror peeled away her roles as a sister, a friend, a wife. The loving memories of Kaci, the complex bond with Sharn, the turbulent history with Edward - each relationship unraveled and dissipated, leaving her devoid of these connections that had shaped her.

With each layer that fell away, the voices that had haunted her—the sneering, the doubts, the constant murmurs of "You will never be one of us" from both humans and orcs alike—grew louder, then were silenced. The cacophony of external judgments and self-imposed constraints that had always clawed at her mind was stripped away, leaving a stark, unadorned silence.

Next was her gender. The defining characteristics that the world used to categorize her as female faded from her reflection. In their place was a being unbound by gender norms or expectations, a pure embodiment of self beyond the binary constructs of male or female.

Then, the mirror stripped away even the most primal aspects. The sensations of hunger and desire, the basic urges that drive so much behavior, evaporated. What remained was a being not driven by bodily needs or earthly wants, but by something more ethereal.

The process continued, peeling away layer after layer until all that was left in the mirror was a form of pure, radiant energy. It was Durya, but not as anyone, including herself, had ever known her. She was vitality, knowledge, and love — the fundamental elements of existence that underpin the universe itself.

It was the core of her being, stripped of titles, of race, of societal roles. Her true self was resilient, compassionate, independent, and defined by her experiences, choices, and innate character, not by the external factors that had always sought to define her, just ways in which the universe expressed and experienced itself through her.

She closed her eyes, and when she opened them, she found herself in the relic room. Right where she needed to be.

13

The Heart of Darkness

For a fleeting moment, calm enveloped Durya. The encounter with the mirror had been liberating. A sense of freedom, like shedding a heavy cloak, coursed through her. She wondered if the others had experienced a similar revelation. Her gaze drifted, unfocused, as her mind wandered to Kaci, imagining her as a radiant, warm energy - like the comforting embrace of sunshine after a cold, relentless rain. However, her thoughts of Sharn were still tinged with unresolved anger. And Keres... Keres was a puzzle that evaded easy understanding.

Durya scanned the relic room, her attention drawn to Sharn and Keres. They were having a conversation with an Earthborn man, stout and sporting a braided beard—a clear symbol of royalty. His presence in this place piqued her curiosity, stirring a sense of familiarity she couldn't quite pinpoint. She racked her brain, sifting through memories. There was that night she, Kaci, and Micah had spent in the king's stronghold. Each time she felt close to recognizing him, the memory eluded her, slipping away like a wisp of smoke carried off by the wind.

Kaci was absent from the scene.

Durya cleared her throat and addressed the group. "Where's Kaci?"

The Earthborn man turned, a warm smile spreading across his face. "Baroness Durya Barclay-Conwyn, it is an honor to make your acquaintance."

Durya's response was curt, her mind racing with concern. "Do I know you?" she asked, dispensing with the niceties afforded to royalty. "I need to find Kaci."

"In a sense," the man replied, his eyes holding a hidden depth of understanding.

Keres interrupted, "She went through the mirror."

"I know," Durya sighed, her patience thinning. "We all did."

"Not that one," Keres continued. "She went to Kashara."

The mention of Kashara sent a chill through Durya's veins. Her blood ran cold at the thought of what awaited Kaci in that realm.

"Why didn't you stop her?" Her voice cracked with a blend of fear and anger.

"I am not her keeper," Keres shot back. "If she chooses to surrender her light, that's on her. And you."

"And you, Sharn," Durya spat out his name, her tone venomous.

"I needed to wait for you," Sharn replied, his voice steady.

Durya felt a storm of emotions brewing within her. Frustration at Keres' indifference, betrayal at Sharn's inaction, and an overwhelming sense of responsibility for Kaci's safety. She had always been the one to look out for her, to shield her from the harsh realities of their world. And now, Kaci was alone in Kashara. Kashara where the Javina and the shadows came from. Kashara, the place of Kaci's nightmares.

The Earthborn man, now absorbed in the surrounding relics,

moved with a sense of wonder and respect. His fingers traced the intricate carvings on an ancient sword, his eyes wide with awe at the shimmering robes that hung from the walls. Each thread spun from the moonlight. He paused before a set of scrolls, their pages yellowed with age, containing lore and spells long forgotten by the modern world. His curiosity was palpable, a contrast to the tension-filled interaction between Durya and her companions.

Determined to focus on the task at hand, Durya turned back to Keres. "You. Help me find her. You know Kashara, guide me there."

Keres' lips curled into a sneer, a silent but unmistakable display of her disdain. "I have been very clear that I am not going back there."

Sharn, clearing his throat, interjected. "It was *her* that told Kaci the words."

"What words?" Durya demanded, her patience wearing thin.

"The magic words that let her pass through to the world," Sharn explained.

In a swift motion driven by urgency and anger, Durya grabbed Keres by the throat. "Tell. Me. How to get there." Her voice was a low growl, her grip tightening. All other plans were now forgotten.

Keres, struggling for breath, gestured with her hands, indicating her inability to speak. Durya released her grip, allowing Keres to cough and regain her breath.

Durya repeated her demand and watched as Keres uttered the spell, the words heavy with ancient power and mystery.

As Durya recited the incantation, the Earthborn man interrupted, "Perhaps..." But Durya paid him no heed and focused on the incantation. With each word spoken, the mirror before her responded. The surface, once solid and reflective, rippled like the surface of a disturbed pond. Durya reached out. It yielded to her touch, feeling almost liquid under her fingertips.

Keres couldn't hold back her commentary. "You don't know what you're doing," she sneered. "You don't know who is waiting on the other side to leave Kashara. It could be as bad as Javina herself."

Durya, however, was undeterred. Her thoughts were on Kaci, on rescuing her friend from whatever fate had befallen her in that place. With one last look at the others, Durya pushed her hand further into the mirror's surface. Cowards, the lot of them.

As she stepped forward, the mirror's surface stretched and enveloped her, pulling her through. The sensation was disorienting, being stretched and compressed all at once, until she emerged on the other side.

In the realm of Kashara, she found herself enveloped in a strange atmosphere. The surrounding environment was thick, a realm of shadows and twilight where the landscape lay in a dusky state. Jagged mountains rose like silent sentinels against the dim sky, their peaks seeming to pierce the veil of twilight. Deep valleys yawned below, and mysterious forests, dense and absorbing, sprawled across the terrain, appearing to swallow light rather than reflect it.

Durya felt utterly alone. The landscape stretched out before her, barren and devoid of any visible signs of life. She pondered where Kaci might have wandered in such a desolate place. A fleeting thought crossed her mind—maybe she should have strategized before plunging in. With a sigh, Durya steeled herself. She was determined to find her friend.

The air felt heavy, laden with ancient magic and untold

secrets. It was neither harmful nor benign, but it carried a weight that pressed upon Durya's chest, affecting her mood and perceptions. She could feel the gravity in every breath she took, an ever-present reminder of the strange nature of this place.

With a sigh, Durya chose a direction at random and walked. She harbored a hope that, just as in Isdralan, what she sought in Kashara would find its way to her. Every so often, she called out for Kaci, her voice piercing the stillness, only to be met with the eerie echo of her own words and the unyielding silence of the land.

As she journeyed, the initial sense of desolation yielded to the subtler, hidden aspects of the realm. At first, these nuances eluded her, blending into the backdrop of the environment. It took a moment for her senses to adjust, to attune to the peculiarities of this land. The more she walked, the more she noticed the life that thrived in the shadows and the twilight.

Faint glimmers of bioluminescent flora revealed themselves, their gentle glow painting the landscape with soft hues of blue and green. The air, though still heavy with ancient magic, carried whispers of movement—the rustling of leaves, the soft scuttling of creatures adapted to the dim light, and the distant, almost imperceptible, murmur of a stream.

Durya's eyes eventually adjusted to the strange twilight, allowing her to discern shapes and forms that she had missed. She noticed that the jagged mountains were not merely geological formations, but were adorned with intricate carvings. The deep valleys hid small oases, pockets of life where water pooled and nourished the surrounding flora, creating an oasis in the barren landscape she had first encountered.

Before long, her eyes catching the vague outlines of a settlement etched against the dusky horizon. The distance was deceptive in this twilight realm, making it hard to gauge how far she had to travel, but she adjusted her path, aiming toward it. In her heart, she harbored hope that Kaci, too, might have spotted this haven and made her way there.

As she ventured closer, a subtle but distinct sound punctuated the silence — the sound of footsteps trailing behind her. Durya paused, her senses heightened, trying to listen for movement or presence, but the sound ceased, leaving her in an unsettling quiet. When she resumed her trek, the footsteps echoed once again, their rhythm a haunting mimicry of her own.

This time, Durya chose not to stop. Instead, she focused on the sound, allowing it to fill her ears as she continued her steady pace. Then, in a swift motion, she spun around, hoping to confront whatever followed her. Her eyes met only a shadowy form, shifting and elusive. A chill ran down her spine, her heart pounding against her chest. Memories of past confrontations with shadow beings flooded her mind, each one a reminder of the realm's insidious nature.

Fear enveloped her, her breaths sharp and rapid. Hands balled into fists, she faced not only the entity before her but also what it symbolized—the darker, concealed facets of Kashara and of herself.

With a voice that she fought to keep steady, Durya addressed the shadowy form. "Hello," she said, her tone measured, betraying none of the fear that surged within her.

The shadow regarded her for what seemed forever until it answered back in her own voice. "Hello"

A shiver went down her spine, and she struggled to know what to do next. The shadow, an amorphous silhouette that seemed to absorb the faint light around it, paused. It didn't have a clear shape, but its presence was unmistakable—a dark, unsettling echo of Durya herself.

"Who are you? What do you want?" Durya demanded.

For a moment, the shadow remained silent, its form rippling as if it were a part of the darkness itself. Then, in a voice that mirrored Durya's own but carried a chilling resonance, it replied, "I am what you refuse to see, the part of you that lurks in the shadows of your soul."

Durya's fists clenched. "Are you a threat?" she asked, defiance in her tone.

The shadow's form shifted, growing taller, then shrinking back, as if it were breathing. "Threat? No. I am truth. The anger you hide, the power you covet, the fears you bury."

Durya shuddered. It was as if the shadow peeled back layers she had built over the years. "I have controlled those parts of me for the good of my people," she countered, her voice steady but her heart racing.

"Control? Or denial?" the shadow pressed, its voice a whisper that seemed to come from all around her. "Here, you cannot hide from yourself, Durya."

"I don't have time for this," Durya snapped, frustration seeping into her voice. "I must find Kaci. That's all that matters now."

"But isn't this search also a distraction? From facing what lies within?" the shadow asked, its tone almost taunting.

Durya paused, the words striking closer to home than she cared to admit. "My duty is to my people, to Kaci. I cannot be swayed by... by shadows and doubts."

The shadow seemed to nod, its form becoming more defined, more like a mirror image of Durya. "Yet here I am, a part of you that even Kaci doesn't know. The part that questions, that rages, that desires more. Would she love you if she knew this, Durya?"

Durya's emotions churned, and she reacted to the shadow's insinuation. "Would she love you if she knew this, Durya?" The words cut deep, igniting the anger within her. She swiped at the shadow, to silence it by force. But her hands met only air.

The shadow, unfazed by her aggression, continued, its voice a sibilant whisper. "You possess more power than you realize, Durya. Power that can help you find Kaci. All you need to do is embrace it, grasp it."

Durya's eyes flickered around, noticing small creatures skittering in the shadows of Kashara. They moved with an eerie grace, part of the realm's mysterious wildlife.

"Use them," the shadow urged. "Bend them to your will. They can lead you to Kaci."

Torn between her urgency to find Kaci and the unsettling proposition of the shadow, Durya hesitated for only a moment before reaching out towards the creatures, attempting to exert her will upon them.

At first, the creatures paused, as if sensing her intentions. Then, as she tried to command them, something unexpected happened. The creatures recoiled, their bioluminescent lights flickering. They let out a series of distressing sounds, a reminder that no being, no matter how small or strange, desired to be controlled.

Durya froze, her hand still outstretched. The realization hit her like a wave—control, power. These were the desires of her shadow self, not her true nature. She withdrew her hand, guilt washing over her.

The shadow observed, its form now still, almost contemplative. It spoke again, its voice a haunting echo of her own. "You see, the power you hold, the control you could exert. But there's more, isn't there? Deep down, you've always known."

Durya, her emotions still raw from the encounter with the creatures, turned to face the shadow. "What more do you want from me?" she asked.

"Embrace the part of you that craves recognition," the shadow suggested, its form shifting. "You've always sought validation for your deeds, haven't you? The hero, the savior—isn't that what you desire to be seen as?"

Her life had been a series of battles and decisions, often thankless, often in the shadows. The desire for acknowledgment, for her sacrifices to be recognized, was a thought she seldom allowed herself to entertain.

"You could make them see, make them all understand the sacrifices you've made," the shadow continued. "You could force the recognition you deserve."

Durya's heart raced. The temptation was there, a whispering thought she had always silenced. But as she stood there, considering the shadow's words, Durya remembered the faces of those she had sworn to protect, the trust they had placed in her. This wasn't just about her; it was about them, their lives, their futures.

"No," Durya said. "Recognition earned through manipulation is hollow. My duty is to serve, not to seek glory."

The shadow's form flickered, as if reacting to her determination. "And what of your own happiness? Have you not sacrificed enough of yourself? Don't you deserve happiness?" It asked, its voice a haunting reflection of her innermost thoughts.

The notion of personal happiness struck a deep chord within

Durya. For so long, she had submerged these desires beneath a sea of duty and responsibility. The longing for a connection, for someone to share not just her responsibility but the joys and sorrows of her life, was a silent whisper in her heart.

But then, the shadow's form twisted, its voice taking on a sharper edge. "Oh, not that," It laughed a bitter laugh. "Think of Sharn," it said, and Durya's heart clenched. "His betrayal cut deep, did it not? How can you trust? How can you open your heart when those closest to you can turn their backs?"

Durya's fists tightened at her sides. The mention of Sharn brought a surge of pain and anger. She had trusted him, relied on him, and his betrayal was a wound that had not yet healed.

"You see," the shadow continued, "even those you hold dear can leave scars. How can you seek companionship when trust is such a fragile thing?"

The words stung. The shadow was probing at her vulnerabilities, at the fear and doubt that lurked beneath her surface of strength. The fear of being hurt again, of opening up only to be betrayed, was a reality she couldn't ignore.

"I..." Durya began, her voice faltering. The certainty she had felt moments ago was wavering under the shadow's relentless assault.

Durya stood silent, wrestling with the conflict within. Her deepest fears and desires were lay bare, challenging the walls she had built around her heart. Trust, companionship, love— these were not just abstract concepts but tangible possibilities that she had denied herself.

"Why indeed?" Durya countered. "Why seek companionship when it only leads to disappointment and pain?"

The shadow, now a dark reflection of Durya's own anguish, moved closer. "You see the pattern, don't you? Trust leads to betrayal, companionship to abandonment. Sharn was just the beginning. What if Kaci, too, betrays you? What if all you sacrifice for others is in vain?"

Its words dropped her to her knees. The shadow was unbuilding her brick by brick. The thought of Kaci, her closest ally, turning on her, was almost too much to bear.

"And yet," Durya said, rising to her feet, "I cannot let fear rule me. Yes, Sharn betrayed me, and yes, it hurt more than I care to admit. But that pain cannot define all my relationships. It cannot dictate my actions."

The shadow tilted its head, almost mockingly. "Noble words, but can you live by them? When every instinct tells you to guard your heart, can you open it again?"

Collapsed on the ground, Durya buried her face in her hands, her shoulders shaking. The shadow's words continued to echo around her, a relentless whisper.

"Let Kaci go. She chose her battle. It is not your fight," the shadow urged. "Come, let's find a way home."

Durya's heart ached at the thought. Kaci, her steadfast companion, would have dropped everything to aid her without a second thought. The idea of abandoning her now, when she might be in need, conflicted with everything Durya stood for.

"No," Durya murmured, her voice muffled by her hands. "Kaci's fight is my fight. We stand together."

The shadow seemed to pulse with a dark energy. "Think of the power, Durya. We can even take Sharn back. He would follow us in an instant—and YOU would be in control forever more."

Durya lifted her head, a fierce determination in her eyes. "Control is not what I seek. I will not use others for my gain. That's not who I am."

As the shadow advanced, its form twisting into something more menacing. "But it's who you could be. Imagine it, Durya. No more betrayal, no more pain. Just power, control, respect," it hissed, the words echoing around her like a dark temptation.

After rising to her feet, Durya felt her body tense, a rush of memories flooding her senses. The shadow's words conjured echoes of her past, of Edward, whose reign had been a paradigm of fear and control. She remembered the chill of those nights under Edward's cold eyes, the way his presence instilled a deep-seated terror, the kind that seeped into your bones, leaving you feeling small and powerless.

"That's not respect. That's fear. And I will not be a person who rules by fear," Durya declared. Memories of Edward's tyranny, now intertwined with her own actions, haunted her. She saw in her mind's eye Edward's dying moments, poisoned by her hand, a necessary act born of desperation and pain. She remembered the trail of destruction she had left behind, a path fraught with heartache and loss, where trust and loyalty lay torn, leaving behind a scarred landscape marked by blood and thorns.

As she confronted the shadow, it transformed before her eyes, its edges becoming nebulous. Durya saw a version of herself within the shadow, one that bore the darkest potentialities of her being. The shadow was marred with the scars of her internal battles and external conflicts—ragged edges dripping with blood, interlaced with briers representing the pain of betrayal and the harshness of a fear-driven rule.

This reflection was the embodiment of what Durya might become if she yielded to the darker urges that lingered in her subconscious — a ruler who led through intimidation and cruelty rather than with the noble strength of her convictions.

SHe would become Edward.

Confronted with this twisted mirror image, Durya under-stood what this shadow represented and the choice it presented. She dropped her arms to her sides and faced the shadow with a somber acceptance. "I am sorry for the pain you have felt," she said, her voice a whisper of regret. "I forgive you."

"You have the power to make it all go away!" the shadow growled, lunging towards her with desperation.

"I know," Durya whispered, tears streaking her cheeks.

She bridged the chasm between them. She realized that her true battle lay within—choosing compassion, fairness, and integrity over the seductive call of tyranny and control.

Durya took a steadying breath and stepped toward the shadow. Herself. "I see you for what you are," she stated. "A part of me, but not all of me. I acknowledge you and accept you as a part of my whole being." She remembered the anger that had kept her alive, when she had only wished for death, and whispered thanks for that protection. But now she needed to move forward, past the hurt.

As Durya confronted the shadow with the full strength of her true self, it began to waver and dissolve. Its form, once a looming presence, lost its substance, fading and merging into both her and into the darkness of Kashara.

The shadow's retreat wasn't a defeat. It affirmed Durya's inner strength and dedication to her principles. In facing the depths of her own darkness, she didn't claim victory, but gained insight. Now, with a deeper self-awareness, she was better prepared to resume her quest for Kaci.

14

The Turning Tides

As Durya approached the settlement, its true magnitude unfolded before her, expanding to the vast proportions of a city. The structures were growing taller and the distant sounds of life becoming clearer. She paused, detecting a faint yet undeniable shift in the atmosphere. The air itself buzzed with an unseen energy. Curious, she reached down to touch the ground, feeling a gentle, almost imperceptible tremor beneath her fingertips. This subtle vibration that hinted at secrets hidden beneath the city's surface.

With each step, Durya felt an intensifying presence of energies. She reached out, tracing the contours of an ancient stone wall, feeling a resonance of loss and yearning. These energies felt alive, almost sentient, yet shrouded in despair and regret. She imagined the entities as shadows, trapped within the confines of their own downfall.

Durya continued walking, her footsteps echoing on the cobblestone street. The feeling grew stronger, like walking through a dense fog. She paused, looking at the structures, realizing how the entities had become intertwined with the city's very foundation. The notion of being trapped by one's own shadows resonated within her, a warning against succumbing to darkness.

As she observed the city's inhabitants, she noted their respectful yet cautious demeanor. Durya brushed past a group of wanderers, sensing their diverse origins and the varied paths that had led them here, and in a moment of realization, she understood the balance Kashara offered to Isdralan. This place wasn't evil. It was a place of introspection and acceptance of the shadow self.

She continued to walk and ended up in a marketplace. This gave her the opportunity to observe the society's approach to life. Here, the atmosphere held a sense of brooding. The stalls and their wares seemed to cater more to hidden desires and forbidden wants rather than everyday necessities.

The people she observed were different, too. They moved with a heaviness, as if carrying unseen burdens. Their interactions were less about commerce and more about whispered exchanges, deals made in hushed tones that spoke of deeper, darker transactions. It was a place where many had succumbed to their darker selves, their actions and choices reflecting this surrender.

In this realm, children were scarce. Innocence and youthful joy seemed to have no place in such a setting. The few children that were present moved with a wariness uncharacteristic of their age, their eyes reflecting a premature understanding of their surroundings.

She followed the streets of the city, each turn unveiling layers of hidden history. A growing sense of urgency pulled her to an abandoned plaza. The buildings around loomed like sentinels, dark windows watching her every step.

She paused at the plaza's edge, energy surrounding her. It was here, in this forgotten part of the city, where the air hummed with a strange, almost electric tension, that she found her friend. Amidst the shadows, bound by a massive, black umbilical-like cord, was Kaci.

The sight struck Durya like a physical blow, her breath catching in her throat. Once vibrant and full of life, Kaci now appeared diminished, her vitality sapped by the dark tether.

Durya rushed forward, her heart pounding. She reached out to Kaci, who writhed in distress, her movements restricted by the bond. The scene before her mirrored the very essence of the trapped souls she sensed.

"Kaci!" Durya called out. She stood, her hands hovering, hesitant yet desperate to help. The cord pulsed as Durya's fingers touched the cord. A jolt of energy surged through her. She could feel Kaci's pain, her struggle, and the immense burden of the city's ensnared spirits, and she ripped her hand away.

Kaci's head jerked up, eyes meeting Durya's. "It's..." she gasped, pain contorting her features as she struggled against the tether's dark grip.

Durya scrutinized the cord without making contact again. It throbbed with a malevolent energy.

"We're going to get this off you," Durya declared.

"I don't know if... if you should. Cutting it might..." Kaci's voice faded.

Durya noted how a bright light surged along its length. "Then we'll find another way. I'm not leaving you like this," she said, then sighed. "Why? Why did you come here? You didn't even discuss it."

Something stirred in Durya, but she pushed it aside, focusing instead on their bond.

"I know it wasn't fair... But I was dangerous. I couldn't let the rest of you suffer the consequences of what Javina could do."

Durya placed a hand on Kaci's shoulder. "I had to face myself... I don't think we have to face these battles alone. We're stronger together."

Kaci nodded, hope crossing her face. "I know you wouldn't abandon me... I just didn't want to be a burden. If I was alone, maybe I could've figured it out." Her expression darkened, and a strange, uncharacteristic laugh escaped her lips. "But we will never be alone again, will we?"

The laugh sent a chill down Durya's spine. She tightened her grip, reminding herself this wasn't just Kaci speaking. "No, we won't be alone. And we'll find a way out of this together." She looked into Kaci's eyes, seeing both her friend and the shadow of the enemy they faced.

Durya returned her focus to the tether binding Kaci and noticed something peculiar. The light wasn't pulsating at all but was constant, its appearance changing as if the tether shifted angles, revealing different aspects like the iridescent scale of a dragon. Curious, Durya pulled a small pocketknife from her boot and pressed the blade against the cord. To her astonishment, the blade passed through it as if it were a shadow. Yet, when Durya touched the tether herself, it felt solid and unyielding.

"I came to the same conclusion," Kaci said with a shrug, her voice tired. "I tried to follow it, hoping to cut it at the source. But the closer I got, the more I despaired. Everything is so heavy."

Durya nodded, understanding Kaci's words. "It seems a wise

plan, lets keep following it." She stood up and reached out, helping Kaci to her feet. "And now, you don't have to do it alone."

They departed from the empty plaza and followed the tether that weaved through the urban landscape. Kaci halted, her eyes narrowing.

"I feel like I've seen this before," she murmured.

"Maybe you dreamt it?" Durya suggested.

It had led back near where the market place had been passing a large building resembling a temple or church. In front of it was a beggar with his cup outstretched.

"Do you live here?" Durya asked.

The man's laugh echoed with a hollow sound, devoid of amusement. "If you call this living."

"Can you help us?" she asked. "We're trying to find where this leads." She gestured toward the tether.

The beggar shook his head, his expression turning into a sneer. "I don't do handouts."

Durya's temper flared, and she was about to respond when Kaci placed a hand on her shoulder, shaking her head. "Not worth it," she whispered, her gaze shifting to a set of stairs leading into a nearby building. "Let's try in there."

After climbing the stone stairs, they encountered a man with that looked like a priest or sage. He observed them with a tranquil demeanor, his eyes widening at the tether.

"Can you help us?" Durya asked.

The man looked nervous, hesitating as if unsure how to respond. "Master Belan would know what to do," he said, then added with a sniffle, "but he is gone, gone, gone."

At the mention of Belan, Kaci's eyes widened, and Durya was taken aback. "Belan... He was there when you disappeared. In the caves."

"I know him," Kaci gasped. "You know him?"

"Not well," Durya shrugged. "I only know he showed up after you left."

The priest's face transformed into a bright smile. "He made it home! Master Belan made it home," he exclaimed, his voice infused with surprise and delight. In a spontaneous burst of joy, he performed a small, happy dance, his feet tapping on the stone floor. "No one makes it home. But Master Belan did!"

Durya's patience waned, her frustration mounting. "What are you talking about, old man? You're making no sense!"

"The Door!" the man exclaimed, bouncing from foot to foot. "It is the way out, but it never works. It was his turn, and he made it!"

Kaci, confused, asked, "What is this door?"

"It leads home," the man clarified, his movements slowing to a stop. "However, few can traverse it. It's more than a mere passage; it acts as a test, a trial of sorts."

He continued, his voice adopting a shade of melancholy. "You see, most of us here didn't choose to be in this place. We've been trapped, ensnared by our own hubris, or by our downfalls. It's a common tale among us."

"How did you end up here?" Kaci asked.

The priest settled back, his expression one of wist. "I hail from a world known as Earth, specifically New York City," he began. With a flourish of his hands, he conjured images of a bygone time. "My journey started with a dream to speak to the departed. At first, I just wanted to help people feel a sense of closure with their loss. Then it became an obsession. One night I dreamed I was in an ancient library, my fingers tracing over texts shrouded in mystery. That dream it was as tangible as the streets of New York. In this vision, I discovered a book, a tome that whispered of secrets beyond the veil. As I delved into its pages, I sought to breach the boundaries between life and death, yearning to commune with souls long departed. This quest for communion with the afterlife it consumed me, and the world I knew spiraled into an abyss. When my eyes opened again, I found myself here, in Kashara, ensnared by my longing to pierce the veil separating the living from the dead."

His gaze drifted off, lost in memories. "If I could turn back the clock, I'd tread a different path. But, you see, regret can't rewrite history. I tried to return through the Door, to no avail. Belan, though, he had faith, a conviction that it was the right path. His belief kindled a flame of hope in us all. And now, it seems he's actually achieved it!"

As he spoke, a look of realization dawned on Kaci's face. She turned to Durya. "Earth... New York. That's where Micah's from."

"That's lovely," Durya said, pressing her lips together to suppress her annoyance. His self-righteous haughtiness irked her, yet Kaci seemed enamored with the man. She reminded herself that now was not the time for petty irritations. "We can use this door to escape."

"But the tether," Kaci gestured to the dark cord binding her, "I think it's my way of ridding myself of Javina."

Durya contemplated the situation. On one hand, if Kaci and Javina were somehow intertwined, what would severing Javina's influence do to her friend? Could they both survive it? On the other hand, they had the chance to be rid of Javina once and for all. The bond between them was complex, and Durya pondered whether breaking it was the solution. But of one thing she was certain: she was ready to do whatever it took to bring Kaci back.

"What lies in the center of the city?" Durya asked the priest. This is where she felt the strongest presence of the trapped souls, and this is where the tether seemed to lead.

The priest shuddered. "No one knows for sure. It's like a prison of sorts—souls trapped far worse than ours, with a man at the center. The thing flickers in and out of existence, but lately, it's been solid and cold." He narrowed his eyes. "You aren't feeding it power, are you?" His form turned menacing, revealing great teeth.

Before Durya could react, another person entered. "Brother Al," she said. "Let's take a moment to reflect, as Brother Belan would have you do." In an instant, both figures vanished.

"This is a strange place," Durya remarked. "But now we have two places to check. Whatever is happening at the city center, and the Door. I think we should head for the door and leave this wretched place behind. What do you think?"

After a moment of hesitation, Kaci replied, "Maybe we should check the city center first. I just want this to be over." She shifted her eyes to the black rope that bound her.

Durya nodded. She would respect Kaci's choice, while keeping an escape through the door as a viable fallback plan.

As they approached the center of the city, the change in the atmosphere became clear. The air grew colder, an unnatural chill that seeped into their bones. A sense of foreboding hung heavy, like a shroud over the area. The sky above darkened, casting long, ominous shadows across their path.

Kaci's steps faltered, her expression twisting in distress. "Do you hear that?" she asked, clutching her head as if trying to block out an unbearable noise.

Durya, concerned, glanced around. "Hear what?"

"The screams... they're deafening," Kaci gasped. The tether seemed to pulse more vigorously, as if resonating with an unseen force emanating from the city's heart. "It's like before, but worse!"

"Before what?" Durya reached out to steady her friend, her eyes scanning the area for any visible threat. "I don't hear anything."

"I...I think this is where..." Kaci's voice trailed off. Something had happened on the day they vanquished the shadows in Elyndris, an event Kaci had kept to herself. Durya realized that now was not the moment to express her hurt over Kaci's reluctance to share this burden with her.

They continued. With each step they took toward the center, Kaci's demeanor grew more agitated. Her eyes darted, her breaths came in short, rapid bursts, and her hands clenched and unclenched as if grappling with an unseen tormentor. The temperature dropped further, the cold biting at their skin, frosting their breaths in the air, and the tether seemed to pulse faster now.

Suddenly, Kaci collapsed to her knees, her hands clutching her head, her body writhing in apparent agony. "It's too much, Durya! I can't... I can't bear it!" she cried out.

Durya kneeled beside her. "This was a bad idea. We need to get out of here."

"It's like ice... piercing my mind," she whispered through gritted teeth.

Without hesitation, Durya slipped one of Kaci's arms over her shoulder, hoisting her friend up. "Hold on to me," she urged.

As they distanced themselves from the city center, the grip of Kaci's suffering loosened. Her breaths became more regular, and a healthy hue returned to her pallid cheeks. In a quiet alcove, Durya allowed them a moment of respite.

"That didn't unfold as expected," Durya said. Kaci mustered a faint smile in response. "We need a deeper understanding before confronting that challenge again."

Durya realized the imperative to comprehend the tether's essence and its links to the mysterious energy and Javina. Her attention was drawn to a silent assembly of figures around an archway, their expressions blending yearning and despair. Curiosity piqued, she rose. "This looks like the door. Rest here, Kaci, while I investigate," she said.

Kaci offered a feeble nod, using a nearby pillar for support. Durya navigated through the crowd, her gaze set on the archway. As she drew closer, a vivid tableau unfolded within it. This was Elyndris, yet altered from her memories. War had plunged the land into chaos. The Aelorians, Earthborn, and humans were embroiled in a bitter struggle, their discord rending the earth. At the forefront of the human legions stood Lord Redmont, a sinister shadow encircling his head like a malevolent halo. The dark influence behind the conflict was palpable.

"How long have I been away?" Durya whispered, disbelief and urgency intermingling in her voice. The peculiar nature of time in this realm haunted her; mere hours here could mean years in her homeland. She pondered the workings of the mysterious door.

Durya cast a worried glance at Kaci, still braced against the pillar, then refocused on the archway, only to find the scene had shifted. Now she was confronted by Sharn's visage. A maelstrom of emotions surged within her — disappointment, anger, yet an undeniable bond. Realizing she might be stranded, she hoped Sharn could intervene. She yelled, "Go back, warn them! Redmont is plotting a catastrophe!"

Sharn seemed to be in the relic room, his gaze piercing through the archway to meet hers. But the divide between them muffled her pleas. He too struggled to convey his message, mouthing the words "I love you." Those words hit Durya like a wave, stirring a whirlpool of feelings and forgotten memories. There was not time to be angry and hurt. She needed to figure out how to get her message across.

Around her, others gazed into the archway, each absorbed in their own visions, lost in silent communication with people from their pasts or presents.

Durya refocused on Sharn, whose expression now bore a deep sadness. He was mouthing words she couldn't understand, his hand reaching through the archway towards her. Durya extended her hand to meet his.

Time seemed to stand still as their hands touched. Then a forceful tug pulled her towards the archway. Her heart pounded; the very fabric of the barrier between Kashara and the universe seemed to tremble at their contact.

"No! Stop!" she cried out in panic. She attempted to retract her hand, but Sharn's grip was unyielding. She was being pulled through dimensions and returning to her world, and he was crossing into hers. The ominous echo of Keres's warning — "A soul for a soul" — reverberated in her mind. What had Sharn done? Who would now protect Kaci? She felt as though she had failed them all.

Durya was engulfed in an overwhelming solitude. She was alone, utterly and completely. She stood before the mirror, her eyes searching for a glimpse of Kaci or Sharn, any sign that she could still save her friend. But the mirror offered nothing but her own reflection, staring back at her in silent isolation.

She reached out, and her fingers traced the mirror's cool, unyielding surface, clinging to the faintest hope of reopening the vanished path. But the glass offered no solace, no flicker of connection — her way back sealed. Her incantations, once potent, now fell on deaf ears, her voice escalating in frenzy and despair, yet the mirror stood impassive, a cold testament to her isolation.

Durya collapsed to the ground, a hollow shell of her former self. For the first time, she was adrift in a sea of uncertainty, directionless. The unwavering certainty and resolve that had been her compass were now just faint whispers, alien and distant. She curled in on herself, wrapping her arms around her knees, a physical barrier against the engulfing tide of desolation.

As she sat there, lost in her thoughts, Durya knew she had to muster the strength to stand up and face this new reality. Wallowing in self pity would do nothing. If she could not help Kaci, she would help Elyndris. A return home was imperative, to address the turmoil wrought by Lord Redmont and to uphold her leadership responsibilities.

Durya stood up. She might not have a plan yet, but she was stubborn, and sometimes, in the darkest of times, that was enough to light the way forward.

"I am the Baroness," she reminded herself, a title that carried weight and authority. Of all her titles, this was the most official, the most tangible.

That title was not just a name. It was a symbol of her strength, her endurance. She had survived Edward, had borne the title with dignity. Now, she would wield it as a shield and a sword, using it to protect her world from spiraling into a war that threatened to engulf everything she held dear.

Once she had stemmed the tide of war, she would return to Kashara and rescue Kaci. The image of her friend, leaning against the pillar in despair, battling her own darkness, flickered in Durya's mind. She visualized the sorrow that might engulf Kaci upon realizing Durya's absence. Would Sharn help her? Doubtful, Durya thought; he was a coward at heart.

With one last glance at the mirror, a silent vow passed from Durya to her reflection. "I will not forget about you, my friend," she whispered. She would return for Kaci, no matter the cost.

Durya scanned the room, her gaze finally settling on the arch concealed behind an ornate tapestry. Fia had entrusted her with the way back, and Durya knew there was no time to lose. As she stepped through the archway, a familiar sensation of falling enveloped her. This time, it was a choice.

In an instant, Durya found herself in the city of Ilbridge. Around her, people who had found themselves trapped in Isdralan had made lives for themselves here. These were dreamers and thinkers from various worlds, each with their unique perspectives and stories. It wasn't so different from Kashara, Durya mused, except that here, people faced their dreams and aspirations, while in Kashara, it was the hidden, darker facets of the self that were confronted. She wondered which experience forged stronger individuals.

Durya shook her head. She could not afford to be distracted. Her immediate hope was that The Golden Gull was still docked at the shore.

With quickened steps, she made her way to the hill overlooking the docks where she and Kaci had disembarked. As she crested the hill, her heart sank at the sight that greeted her—the docks lay empty, the vast expanse of open ocean stretching before her with no sign of The Golden Gull.

Despite the setback of The Golden Gull's absence, she remained determined. There had to be other ways, other paths, yet to explore. As she turned to make her way back to Ilbridge, something on the horizon caught her eye. A tiny speck, unnoticeable at first, grew larger and more distinct. Durya watched, hope reigniting within her, as the speck transformed into the familiar silhouette of The Gull. Before long, Durya could see that Captain Aanee stood at the helm, her arm raised in a wave of greeting, and the dinghy was already being lowered with First Mate Smedun aboard.

Durya hiked up her skirt and ran to meet the small boat. As Smedun rowed the dinghy to shore, Durya stepped forward to greet them. The memories of her journey, once fragmented, now formed a clear picture of the adventures and bonds she had formed. She embraced the man, the crinkly goblin's familiar presence bringing a sense of comfort.

"I never thought I'd be so glad to see this ship again," Durya said, a smile breaking through her weariness. "How did you know I would be here?"

Smedun's grin remained as she spoke. "We only just arrived back. The Earthborn sent for you. Now, what's the plan, Baroness?"

Durya, her expression turning somber, looked back one last time at the city of Ilbridge. "We must head back to Elyndris immediately," she stated. "A war is looming, one that could devastate everything we hold dear. And after we've dealt with that crisis, I need to return to Kashara. There's a friend to rescue."

Smedun's face took on a solemn look. "A hefty venture, that is. Aye, understood. Let's waste no more time then. The Golden

Gull be ready to hoist anchor on yer word."

Durya paused, a question forming in her mind. "Who among the Earthborn sent for me?" she inquired.

"Aye, that be a tale for the Captain herself," Smedun replied. "She's got a letter for ye."

As Durya and Smedun rowed toward The Golden Gull, a storm of thoughts raged in Durya's mind — strategies and worries tangling like the sea's restless waves. A motley crew of allies — the goblins, Marcus, and a strange Earthborn — they were the tools she had to work with. The war brewing in Elyndris demanded her lead, and she would rise to the challenge.

15

Convergence of Paths

The chill sea breeze smelled of brine and foreboding as Durya boarded The Golden Gull. The ship, a formidable craft with sails draped like the wings of a somber raven, swayed on the murky waters, poised for departure. Durya's heart was laden with the shadows of recent tribulations, her resolve as unyielding as the timeworn planks underfoot.

Captain Aanee, emerging like a shadow from the gang-plank's gloom, faced Durya with a presence as untamed as her windswept hair. "Welcome aboard, Baroness," Aanee said, her smile a subdued curve, her voice carrying the rich timbre of the high seas. "The Golden Gull has awaited your return."

Durya managed a small smile. "Thank you, Captain. It's good to be back."

Aanee's eyes softened. "And where's Kaci?"

Durya's smile faded. "Kaci is stuck," she said. "And Kashara... it's a complex situation. She's caught in a dark snare. I must right what's wrong in Elyndris and then go back to free her."

Aanee nodded. "Kashara, right? Traveling between worlds is

always tricky. But if there's any chance for The Golden Gull to make that journey, we'll find it."

Their conversation was abruptly interrupted as Smedun stepped up.

"Captain, we're all set," he announced.

Aanee turned back to Durya, her eyes glinting with a playful secret. "Before we embark, there's something you ought to know. We picked up a stowaway while docked."

Durya raised an eyebrow. Aanee elaborated, "A cunning little one, with a silver tongue. He's an unusual chap, but he seemed to have some deep insight. I've got a good sense for people, and I trust him. He even said that once you read his letter, you'd vouch for him."

The captain handed Durya a letter, and she took it, her expression one of skepticism. Who was this man, so bold as to assume she would vouch for him? With a careful motion, she broke the seal and unfolded the parchment, her eyes scanning the penned words.

Esteemed Baroness Durya Barclay, née Conwyn,

I extend to you my most cordial greetings. While it may be that the passages of time have clouded your recollection of our acquaintance, I assure you that our paths have intertwined in the past. I am Belan, High Priest to the venerated Order of the Celestial Veil in the esteemed Mountain Kingdom, and kin to His Majesty King Thorlyn.

Over the course of the preceding annual cycle—a span I have spent enveloped in the shadowed realms of Kashara — I have embraced my fate, as foretold by the celestial auguries at my birth. My sojourn in the darkness was a deliberate pilgrimage, seeking the wisdom hidden within its embrace.

In the depths of Kashara, I have gained profound insights and unearthed secrets of great import. It has come to my attention, through gifts akin to those of a certain companion we share, that Elyndris now stands at the precipice of dire need.

Fortune favored me with an avenue for return, an opportunity unveiled by the very decision of our mutual friend to traverse the veils of Kashara. I wish to convey to you my unwavering commitment to revisit those shadowed depths, a journey that I am certain will contribute to the illumination of her path homeward.

In the interim, I implore you to grant me the honor of your esteemed presence and to travel with me to the Mountain Kingdom. Our aim is to convene a council of like-minded allies, to deliberate upon and address the tumultuous plight befalling our beloved Elyndris.

Your wisdom and leadership are indispensable in these trying times. Together, with united purpose and resolve, we shall endeavor to restore balance and peace to our world.

I eagerly await your arrival and look forward to the privilege of standing alongside you in this crucial endeavor.

With the highest regards and in anticipation of a most auspicious reunion,

Belan,
  High Priest of the Order of the Celestial Veil,
  Brother to His Majesty King Thorlyn,

> *Guardian of the Celestial Secrets,*
> *Keeper of the Ethereal Harmony.*

Durya toyed with the idea of scrunching the letter in her grasp, then reconsidered. Belan, the Earthborn man from the relic chamber. Her memories of him hovered just out of reach, reminiscent of her recent memory lapses. But hadn't those memories returned? She clenched her jaw. The lack of mastery over her own mind was infuriating.

The letter itself was concise, yet shrouded in riddles, weaving in fragments of Belan's journey and the wisdom he had unearthed. It concluded with a veiled proposition—a journey to the Mountain Kingdom.

Durya folded the letter with care, "The Mountain Kingdom." Skepticism aside. It was a starting point. "That's our destination."

Aanee's hands met with a resonant clap. "To the Mountain Kingdom, then! A blend of adventure and mystery awaits us, Baroness."

"Where's this man now?" Durya inquired.

"In the mate's cabin. Smedun's taken to bunking with the crew," Aanee answered, gesturing the direction.

"Thanks," Durya suppressed a smile. The layout of the ship was like an old map in her mind.

Durya approached the cabin door and tapped three times.

"Enter," a voice beckoned from within.

Inside, the Earthborn, Belan, sat cross-legged on the floor, absorbed in a large marble bowl brimming with water. The scene struck a humorous chord. Earthborn were known for their reticence and not for mystical prowess. They were often brusque and unrefined, much like the orcish armies of her kin, not the human family who raised her. Yet, Belan appeared at ease with the scrying bowl.

A twinge of remorse pricked her. Kaci, too, could scry, though she loathed it. Durya recalled pleading with her friend for aid with visions, only to be told of their cryptic and misleading nature. She hadn't understood then, but her experiences in the cave, confronting various paths, had shed light on that ambiguity.

She remained silent, not wishing to disrupt his concentration, until he shuddered and exhaled.

"What did you see?" she inquired.

"Nothing promising," he answered, rising.

"Pleasure to see you again," he bowed. "Belan, High Priest of the Celestial Veil."

Durya's smile was tinged with irony. Titles and formalities usually appealed to her, but now she craved directness. "Let's skip the ceremony," she dismissed. "Call me Durya and tell me your vision."

Belan's lips twitched with amusement before he sighed. "Nothing good."

Durya was about to press for details when he added, "Your human king, ensconced in Etharion's heart, engulfed by peculiar shadows—"

"Not this again!" she cut in, but Belan gestured for patience.

"Hear me out. These shadows... they're different, like the dark reflections of one's heart. My time in Kashara makes such sights clearer. The oddity lies in his attendants—Aelorians."

Durya nodded, "That's peculiar indeed. Aelorians typically shun human contact, let alone servitude."

"There's more," Belan pressed on. "One Aelorian woman, in a vision more premonition than reality, held a dagger to the king's back."

A shiver ran through Durya, her thoughts darting to Kaci. Belan observed her concern and reassured, "It wasn't our friend. But I am curious why she's not with you."

As Durya recounted the tale of Sharn's desperate act—how he dragged her through the portal, taking her place—a tide of grief swelled within her. She spoke of her mixed feelings: her hope that Sharn would encounter Kaci and offer some solace, yet her fear that his inherent cowardice and darker nature might prevail. Belan listened, offering a reassuring hand on her shoulder at intervals. Durya couldn't fathom why confiding in him felt so natural. When she finished, Belan remained silent for a moment, absorbing her words.

"Kashara challenges those it ensnares. Yet, you stand as evidence that one can emerge stronger, more enlightened," he finally said.

Durya's cheeks flushed a deeper shade of blue, unaccustomed to such commendation. Recognition had always been a battle for her, and this unearned praise left her unsure how to react.

"We're en route to the Mountain Kingdom, as you suggested," she managed to say. "I think I need some solitude."

Belan nodded. As she moved towards the door, he called out, "Lady Durya! When we get to shore, I must remain here on the Gull." She paused, confused, and turned back to him. "But know this—when the time arises, I will stand with you, to aid Kaci and all of Isdralan."

Their eyes locked in a moment of silent understanding, and she nodded in acknowledgment.

As The Golden Gull glided over the ocean, Durya took her place next to Aanee at the helm, gazing toward the distant Elyndris. Transitioning between realms was a surreal experience. Around the ship, the air quivered like a heat haze, the water below shimmering with a supernatural light. They moved through this dreamlike space, the boundary between worlds a delicate membrane that yielded to their advance.

Intrigued by the peculiar nature of their voyage, Durya faced Captain Aanee. "What guides The Golden Gull through these otherworld passages?"

With a knowing wink, Aanee returned her focus to the distant waters. "Some mysteries are better left unsolved, Baroness," she replied. "Suffice to say, she finds her path."

Soon the waters and skies changed, signaling their arrival in Elyndris. The transition was smooth, like waking from a dream into the comforting familiarity of reality.

The Mountain Kingdom loomed in the distance, its towering peaks piercing the sky. These mountains were ancient, covered in verdant forests and snow-capped summits that glinted in the sunlight. Waterfalls cascaded down their sides, creating a symphony of sound. As they approached, the landscape unfolded in majestic grandeur. Cliffs adorned with lush greenery, crystal-clear rivers carving through the land, and quaint villages nestled in the crooks of mountains.

The Golden Gull navigated inland via a broad river that snaked through the kingdom. On either side, the land was alive with the bustling activities of the kingdom's inhabitants. The architecture was a harmonious blend of nature and craftsmanship, with stone fortresses and wooden homes built to complement the landscape.

As they disembarked, the sheer magnificence of the Mountain Kingdom struck Durya. The air was crisp and smelled like pine and earth. The sounds of wildlife, the rustle of leaves, and the distant chatter of the townsfolk created a melody that was invigorating. This was a land of strength and serenity, the earthborn as resilient as the mountains themselves.

They were met by a young Earthborn man. His simple, well-crafted attire marked him as a page or an initiate of the Mountain Kingdom. Durya noted the subtle symbols embroidered on his tunic, indicative of a society that valued tradition and secrecy. The Earthborn were shrouded in mystery, and Durya's knowledge of them was limited, based only on her brief previous visit with Micah and Kaci.

The young man greeted them with a respectful nod. "Welcome to the Mountain Kingdom," he said.

Durya nodded in return, following him as he led her and her companions through the bustling dock towards a grand fortress that loomed in the distance. They traversed the cobblestone streets, Durya taking in the sights and sounds of the kingdom—the vibrant marketplaces, the laughter of children playing, and the harmonious blend of nature and architecture that characterized the Earthborn culture.

They entered the fortress and walked through the vast stone halls. Eventually, they arrived at a familiar room—the same hall where Durya had met King Thorlyn a year ago. It was majestic, with high ceilings supported by ornate pillars and a large, round table at the center, symbolizing unity and equality.

King Thorlyn stood as they entered, his presence commanding yet welcoming. Durya noticed that his health had improved since their last meeting. His eyes were bright, and he carried himself with a renewed vigor that lent him an almost intimidating air.

Durya stood tall, her posture reflecting the strength and confidence she had honed over her recent trials. She inclined her head in a gesture of respect, acknowledging the king's authority while maintaining her own dignity.

"Baroness Durya Barclay, welcome back to the Mountain Kingdom," King Thorlyn said, his voice strong. "Your arrival is most timely."

Durya maintained direct eye contact with King Thorlyn. "Your Majesty, thank you for receiving me. I have come in response to a message from Belan, whom I understood to be your brother. He urged my swift arrival here, hoping together we might forge a path to peace for our lands."

King Thorlyn's brow furrowed in confusion. "Brother? I lost my brother in infancy," he said, old sorrow crossing his features. Then realization dawned, and he chuckled. "Ah, you must mean Marcus, your brother. Yes, he has been a loyal friend to our family for many years. Very well, let us proceed to the council. The others have already gathered."

Whatever strange magic shrouded her memories of Belan did so from his own brother as well. She took it in stride. Following the king's lead, a guard escorted Durya through the grand hall, past the throne room that doubled as a formal greeting area, and into an adjoining chamber. This room, though less imposing than the throne room, and had an air of solemnity. It was a place where matters of great importance were discussed.

The chamber was already occupied by several figures, including Marcus, Lady Elara, and Lord Hensworth. They were engaged in quiet conversation, but paused as Durya and King Thorlyn entered. The atmosphere was one of tense anticipation, each person aware of the significant decisions that lay ahead.

In the chamber, the air was tense with the urgency of the situation unfolding in Elyndris. Durya listened as the Aelorian representative, a dignified figure named Erisel, elaborated on the current state of affairs. "The Aelorian people are divided.

Half of us, led by Valeran, seek to rebuild in the aftermath of the Shadow Times and return to our ancient traditions. However, the other half, under the sway of Serathine, view the death of Arba Vitae as a harbinger of a new era."

Erisel's voice was tinged with regret. "Lady Serathine is allied with Lord Redmont, believing that this new age calls for consolidation of power, even if it means war."

"Redmont has long been plotting to seize control," Durya said, her voice low. "My public confession about Edward's death only hastened his plans. And my subsequent disappearance from Elyndris likely gave him the opportunity he needed to sway Serathine and her followers to his side."

King Thorlyn nodded. "Indeed, Baroness. Your absence created a vacuum, and Redmont was quick to exploit it. Now, both groups find themselves on the brink of a civil war, with the Aelorians fractured, Etharion hungry for power, and The Mountain Kingdom caught in the middle—"

"It is not all of Etharion," Her people were not all power hungry. "Just Lord Red—"

"I understand, Baroness" King Thorlyn's voice was gruff and menacing. A reminder she was speaking to a king.

Marcus leaned forward, his expression one of deep concern. "It's a precarious balance. The Mountain Kingdom can ill afford to take sides, yet you cannot stand idly by as conflict rages. We must unite the Aelorians and quell Redmont's ambitions."

King Thorlyn responded with a measured tone. "Marcus speaks true. The Mountain Kingdom must remain a beacon of stability amidst this turmoil. Taking sides could lead us into the very conflict we seek to avoid. However, our influence can be pivotal in brokering peace."

He paused, weighing his next words. "Our first step is to

extend an olive branch to both Aelorian factions. Lord Valeran's desire to return to the old ways aligns with our principles of harmony and balance. Meanwhile, we must also understand Lady Serathine's perspective and her followers' fears about the future."

Thorlyn's gaze then settled on Durya. "Baroness, your role in this is crucial. Your unique position and experience could help bridge the gap between these divided factions. You have seen the consequences of unchecked ambition and the devastation it brings."

Lady Elara spoke up, her voice firm. "We must also address Lord Redmont. His manipulation has exacerbated the conflict. Exposing his deceit and countering his influence will be essential in restoring peace."

"And we cannot forget those already suffering from this conflict." Hensworth's eyes flashed with anger. "We need a resolution that brings not just peace but also justice."

King Thorlyn nodded in agreement. "Indeed, the welfare of the people is paramount. Our efforts should also to heal the wounds this conflict has caused."

The room fell into a thoughtful silence, each leader contemplating the complex web of politics and power at play. A path to peace was fraught with obstacles and required a delicate balance of diplomacy, strategy, and empathy.

"We'll start by opening channels of communication with both Aelorian factions," Durya suggested. "We need to understand their motivations and fears. And we must expose Redmont's manipulations for what they are."

Marcus, aware of his unique understanding of the Aelorians, volunteered to initiate peace talks. "I'll contact both factions," he said. "Having lived among them, I can navigate their differences and hopefully bring them to a consensus."

"Your friend Kaci would have been a great asset now," murmured Lady Elara.

King Thorlyn offered his support. "The Mountain Kingdom will provide a neutral venue for these discussions. It's essential that all parties feel secure and respected in these negotiations."

Attention then shifted to the human kingdom. Durya declared her intention to travel to Etharion, the human capital named for the lands it was central too, to seek an audience with the king. She would alert him to the dangers posed by Redmont and the Aelorian conflict.

"Baroness, I would be honored to accompany you to the human court," Lor Hensworth began, his voice measured. "Given my background and position, I might aid in navigating their... well, sensibilities."

Durya, perceiving his hesitance, addressed him with a touch of humor. "Lord Hensworth, let's be candid," she said, a smirk playing on her lips. "I may be an orc, but I was raised in Marshfield by the duke himself. I'm no stranger to the intricacies of human politics."

Hensworth blushed, realizing his oversight. "Of course, Baroness, my apologies. I didn't mean to imply otherwise. It's just that, perhaps, my human heritage might be... less intimidating to the king's advisors."

Durya nodded, understanding his point. "Your appearance could indeed be an advantage in this delicate situation," she agreed. "Your human looks, coupled with my political genius, make us a well-rounded team. We'll use our combined strengths to our advantage."

Meanwhile, Lady Elara proposed a covert role. "I'll return to Westerfield," she said. "Redmont is unaware of my allegiance.

I can gather intelligence and undermine his efforts from within."

As the gathering dispersed, a heavy sense of responsibility settled on Durya's shoulders. The mission's success hinged not only on their strategic communication but also on out-maneuvering Redmont, a foe as cunning as he was ruthless. The air in the room seemed to grow denser with the unspoken acknowledgment of the danger they were about to confront.

Durya lingered a moment, her thoughts racing. Every decision, every move they made from here on out could tip the scales in this high-stakes game of chess. As she turned to leave, a sudden, ominous creak echoed through the hall—an unnerving reminder that in the shadows of their quest, treachery could lurk at any corner. With a deep breath, she stepped into the dim corridor, the echo of her footsteps merging with the haunting sound, leaving her to wonder: Were they prepared for what lay ahead?

16

Through Times Veil

Embraced by the Golden Gull, Durya felt the ship resonate with her. She stood like a statue at the helm, her eyes locked on the horizon. Its thin, distant line held her deepest fears and wildest hopes. The gilded figurehead pulsed with a song from a forgotten era, echoing tales of ancient magic and hard-earned triumphs. It stood as a guardian, its unspoken strength a comforting embrace to her tempest-tossed soul.

As she turned her back to the sea, each step Durya took toward the cabin was heavy. The growth she had fought so fiercely for did little to lighten the burden. Aanee, ever the generous soul, had given her the main cabin for their return voyage. Yet, within its walls, the air was thick with the ghost of Edward. His presence was a suffocating shroud that seemed to rob her of breath.

In this very chamber, where her choices had forever shifted the tides, her heart bled a cocktail of sorrow and steely resolve. Edward's specter, who had loathed her very being, lingered like a dark cloud, his voice casting doubt upon her every decision. Amidst the chorus of voices that could lift her—her father, her friends, Kaci, and even Micah — it was Edward's venomous whisper that haunted her, sneering at her every move.

Alone in the cabin, amidst opulence that felt undeserved, Durya grappled with the enormity of her legacy. The upcoming meeting loomed over her, a reminder of the balance she maintained between duty and heart. She longed to collect her thoughts, to forge a path forward, but the ghosts of her past clung to her, their icy fingers chaining her to memories best forgotten.

A quiet cough echoed, startling Durya. Belan, the Earthborn, sat at the ornate desk, observing her with an inscrutable gaze. Her frustration boiled over. "I thought you claimed brotherhood with the king! I appeared a fool mentioning you."

Belan's expression flickered with sadness before he met her eyes. "I am—or was—his brother. He just doesn't remember."

"I don't understand," Durya said, exasperation coloring her tone.

Belan stroked his braided beard, pondering. "I once existed in this realm, but now I do not. You and I knew each other as well. We fought the shadows together with Kaci and Micah."

Durya's skepticism faltered. The turmoil was making her memories fragmented and unreliable at best. "Fia said I regained everything. Why can't I remember you?"

Belan's smile held a melancholy edge. "The Isdralan ritual, the ancient Aelorian one, demanded a sacrifice and I offered myself. Kashara and Isdralan, they demand balance. A price must be paid."

"So, you were cast to Kashara while we went to Isdralan? But why were you erased from my memory?"

"I was removed from time itself, not just sent to another realm," Belan explained.

"Then how are you here then? And why?"

Belan's reply was simple. "I am here because my presence is necessary."

Impatience frayed the edges of Durya's composure. "That makes little sense. No more riddles. I demand to know why." A suspicion flickered in her mind. Could Belan be the forgotten ally Kaci had alluded to? Her gaze intensified. "Kaci remembered you, didn't she?"

"No, and the reason is unclear to me." Belan's sigh was heavy with regret. "I wish she hadn't. It would have spared her immense sorrow."

This revelation unraveled a myriad of questions, each clamoring for attention. The mystery of Belan's presence and his unseen sacrifices hinted at a complex intertwining in the fabric of their histories.

A subtle trace of sorrow flickered in Belan's eyes. "My gift, the vision to perceive beyond the now, showed me a destiny woven into the fabric of time. The ritual did more than use me. It erased me from our world, a sacrifice needed to bridge Isdralan and Kashara."

Durya's expression grew pensive. "If we break Kaci's bond with Javina, does that mean she will forget you?"

With a sigh, Belan responded. "Possibly. But now you see me too, after your journey to Kashara. That may have altered things."

Durya's thoughts spiraled, piecing together the puzzle. "And Captain Aanee, how is she involved?"

A knowing smile touched Belan's lips. "The Golden Gull harbors its own secrets. Some travels transcend the mere crossing of waters, venturing into realms unseen." His cryptic words suggested an even larger link between the ship and the mystical realms, a hidden history.

Unraveling the mysteries of the Golden Gull was a task better suited for a day less burdened by pressing concerns. "Since you are here, you might as well lend a hand," Durya said.

"As you wish," Belan replied.

Durya pulled an overstuffed chair across from Belan and leaned forward. "I have to convince the king that Redmont is the real threat. He could start a terrible war, but I don't have solid proof. Right now, my word isn't enough."

"You do have proof," Belan said. His smile grew as he reached into his pack and produced a small mirror, handing it to Durya.

Durya looked closely at the mirror, her frown growing. She was too proud to admit she was confused and did not understand how the it would help.

"This mirror," Belan continued, "is crafted from the same material as the one in the Relic Room, within the Caves of Chaos."

Durya's silence lingered, heavy with thought.

"That mirror from the room that led you to Kashara has a twin. It sat in Edward's bedroom for years and eventually found its way to Redmont."

Realization slowly dawned on Durya. "They are all interconnected."

Belan nodded in affirmation.

Durya's eyes widened. "Where did you find this?"

"In the Relic Room. They're stored there for their power and danger. They mustn't fall into the wrong hands."

"Of course," Durya whispered. "How does it work?"

"Just direct it," Belan advised.

Durya focused on the mirror. "Show me Redmont," she commanded.

The mist in the mirror dissolved, revealing her bedroom in Westerfield. Anger flared within her at the sight of Redmont appropriating her space. The room, though empty, bore the unmistakable, distasteful touch of Redmont's decor. Just as Durya considered discarding the mirror, Redmont appeared, speaking into his own reflection. "My lady," he murmured.

A chilling realization struck Durya. Redmont wasn't speaking to her. A sinister voice whispered, "We are not alone."

Panicked, Durya slammed the mirror down, almost shattering it.

"Was that..." Durya's voice was a hushed whisper.

"Javina," Belan confirmed, finishing her sentence.

Durya shivered, recalling the dread that had settled in her stomach. "Kaci has that woman's presence in her head? How terrible."

Regaining her composure, Durya turned to Belan. "This might suffice as evidence, if used judiciously, and if the king is convinced. But I imagine we shouldn't look through it again until the right moment."

Belan nodded in agreement. "My visibility, or lack thereof, limits my help."

Durya, understanding, then posed a question. "But, Belan, why do you still care if you no longer exist in our world?"

"Why do the gods themselves care from their distant realms? Wouldn't your heart still ache for the world you once called home?"

Her thoughts drifted to Fia's proposition of turning her into a guardian someday. The notion of becoming akin to a deity in many worlds was a daunting prospect. Would such an ascension strip her of her humanity? Would it numb her to the very emotions and connections that defined her? These questions wove a complex web in her soul, intertwining her understanding of love and duty with the mystical intricacies of countless realms.

She finally broke the silence, her voice a soft echo of deep realizations. "Perhaps the heart never truly leaves what it loves," she breathed. "Even when separated by realms, the bonds we forge and the duties we carry don't simply disappear. Your care, Belan, it seems to transcend even the boundaries of existence itself."

"The same will be true for you, Durya, as you face your own decisions," Belan said, his tone somber. "We are the sum of our experiences. In transcending, we merge with the universe's consciousness, allowing it to observe and understand itself through us." His gaze held a depth of understanding that spoke of ages and realms beyond, hinting at the interconnections of all existence.

The rest of the journey passed without incident. Upon disembarking, Durya and Hensworth were greeted with fitting fanfare. Durya cast a lingering glance back at the ship, her thoughts on Belan's presence. With a deep breath, she squared her shoulders and strode towards the castle, ready to announce their arrival.

Captain Aanee's voice called from the ship. "Baroness?" Her tone, usually firm, carried a thoughtful softness. "Few possess this, but you've earned it." The captain extended an intricately carved whistle, a knotted rope encircling it.

Durya made her way back to the gangplank and accepted the gift.

"Blow this in dire need, and the Gull will heed your call," the captain said, pausing. "When you're ready to retrieve Kaci, count on my aid."

Durya studied Aanee, acknowledging with a nod. "Thank you, Captain." There was an ineffable quality in Aanee, a spirit that sparked hope in Durya's heart. It wasn't just Aanee's resemblance to Kaci—Durya felt it was something deeper, a connection unspoken yet reassuring.

As they made their way down the road, Lady Durya strode beside Hensworth with an air of unyielding resolve toward the looming gates of the grand castle. Her orcish heritage was clear in her striking features, setting her apart in a world of men that surrounded them. When the guards caught sight of her, their eyes flickered with apprehension. Yet, there was a grace in her steps, a dignity that defied the wary looks she attracted. Hensworth, aware of the undercurrents of distrust, moved closer, his presence a vow of alliance in a realm where her kind was met with suspicion and scorn.

"We wish to request an audience," Durya announced.

The guards whispered among themselves. Durya asserted herself again, recounting her titles and her mission's urgency. She stood taller, her presence imposing.

Their unwavering presence only amplified the guards' unease. With hesitant steps, the guards ushered Durya and Hensworth into a chamber adorned with ornate splendor. Yet, amidst the grandeur, a tension lingered in the air. The castle staff, cloaked in professionalism, couldn't help but let their eyes follow the pair's every move, weaving an atmosphere of unspoken discomfort.

After what seemed like ages, an under-minister approached them. "Baroness," he began as he fumbled with his glasses, "the proper channels weren't followed for an audience with the King. Such matters usually require prior notice."

Durya clenched her fists tightly, a muscle twitching in her

jaw as she took a deep, controlled breath. "Time is a luxury we don't have," she insisted. "Etharion stands on the brink of war. This meeting can't wait."

The underminister studied her for a moment, his eyes betraying surprise. "I remember you from the shadow conflict," he said. "Your reputation precedes you. While I understand the urgency, we must still adhere to the kingdom's protocols." His voice softened. "I want to help, but we must navigate these formalities correctly."

Durya scowled, but the underminister did not see and continued drolling on. "I am here to guide you through the formalities. We'll complete the paperwork for your audience with the king. I'm quite adept at my job and can assure you an audience within a month," he stated confidently, his eyes gleaming with pride.

"Unacceptable," Durya said, familiar with such diplomatic delays. She was about to insist further when suddenly, the sharp sound of a claxon split the air. Three short bursts followed by one long, ominous wail. It reverberated through the castle, casting a shadow of urgency and alarm over their conversation.

Fear flashed across the man's face, his eyes widening as the meaning of the claxon code dawned on him. "What does that mean?" Durya pressed, sensing the severity of the situation.

"I'm not at liberty to discuss it," he began, his voice wavering. Another sound cut his words off - a distant, unmistakable blare of a war horn. Durya's heart raced. That horn—it was a call to arms. But whose?

"It's happening," Durya whispered, a realization dawning. "Just as he predicted—we may already be too late." In a sudden movement, she grasped the man's shoulders. His response was a startled squeak. "You must take me to the king now—time is of the essence." She emphasized each word with a shake, conveying the urgency.

Lord Hensworth stepped in, his voice calm but firm. "Lady, strong-arming him won't help our cause." His admonition was a gentle reminder of diplomacy, even in the face of looming war.

The man with the horn-rimmed glasses, his nerves frayed, nodded and gestured for Durya to follow, muttering about risking a hangman's noose. They were led to a room where the king, surrounded by documents, sat at a large, round oaken table. An Aelorian serving woman stood by his side.

The king, glancing up, greeted her with a royal, dismissive poise. "Ah, Lady Durya, a pleasant surprise. My condolences for your loss. Now, if you'll excuse me, I have urgent matters to attend to."

"Wait," Durya interjected, striding across the room. "Your life is in danger—there's a plot against you!"

As a guard lunged towards her, the king gestured, signaling him to stand down. "It is fine," he said, annoyance in his voice. "This is as good a time as any for a break, it seems."

"Messa, bring another goblet for our... esteemed guest," the king's voice echoed with a deceptive warmth. Messa, the Aelorian servant, glided across the room, her smile a twisted dance of cordiality and hidden spite. Lord Hensworth and the under-minister hovered near the archway, their presence a silent watch. "Please, enter," the king gestured with a grandiose wave.

Messa returned, the wine in her hands glistening like liquid rubies. She placed the goblets before the king and Durya with an air of ceremony. But as the scent of the wine reached Durya, it carried with it the unmistakable tinge of poison—the same she had used on Edward. In a swift motion, Durya knocked the king's goblet, sending it crashing to the floor, its contents spilling like blood on the stone.

The king let out a low chuckle, his amusement veiling a darker undercurrent. "My dear baroness, do you think me naïve to the ways of courtly intrigue?"

His next command was a cruel twist. He ordered Messa to drink from Durya's goblet. The servant's disdain at the thought of sharing a glass with an orc flickered across her features. A brief shadow of repulsion.

The air in the room turned frosty and the king's smile vanished, replaced by an icy glare directed at Messa. "Drink," he ordered, his voice now a sharp edge. The terror in Messa's eyes spoke volumes as she was held by the guards. Her feeble struggle and desperate glance towards the door spoke of her silent pleas for escape.

Seizing the wine glass from Durya, the king's expression grew even more ominous. "Hold her mouth open," he commanded with chilling detachment. The guard obeyed, and the king, with ruthless precision, poured the wine down Messa's throat.

Durya, no stranger to the harsh realities of their world, felt a shiver of dread. The room, once a symbol of royal splendor, had morphed into a chamber of cold judgment, the king's merciless actions casting a shadow over its grandeur.

Initially, nothing happened, and Durya questioned her instincts. But then, Messa's complexion turned ghostly white, and she collapsed, convulsing. Durya was reminded of Edward's last moments. The haunting memory of foam and blood at his mouth mirrored in Messa's plight. The king, unphased, looked towards Durya with a raised eyebrow. "Your concerns have been noted," he said dryly. "Please, take a seat." He gestured to a chair, adding, "Regrettably, without refreshments. I seem to be short a servant." With a dismissive wave, he ordered the guards to remove the body.

"You have my attention," the king began, gesturing for his under-minister and Lord Hensworth to join them. He then dismissed all but a few guards, a surprising show of trust considering the circumstances. Lady Durya steadied herself before speaking. "I believe the shadow threat never truly ceased."

The king's eyebrow arched in skepticism but remained silent.

Durya continued, "Lord Redmont, I suspect, is under the influence of a shadow entity, a woman of sorts."

The king chuckled. "A tale as fanciful as Redmont's."

Durya's surprise was evident. "You've spoken with Redmont?" she asked. The king's casual dismissal of her concerns only deepened the mystery and urgency of the situation.

"Redmont first approached me during your visit to Westerfield," the king revealed, his tone measured. "He expressed distrust towards you, citing your orc heritage as unfit for leadership, despite your human marriage." He paused, allowing his words to settle. Durya struggled to maintain her composure.

"He kept me informed of the situation, raising his suspicion that Edward was dead. I already knew this to be true," the king continued. Durya's eyes widened in shock.

"My spies in Westerfield confirmed Edward's death. Redmont, however, tried to sway my opinion against you, citing you inappropriate for leadership." He paused, gauging Durya's reaction.

Durya was taken aback. "You knew of Edward's death? How?"

"You're not the only one who can use those underestimated by society. Some of your goblin informants, for instance."

"My goblins?" Durya felt betrayed.

"Some," the king admitted, "but also serving girls and other staff members."

"Why not arrest me for treason, then?" Durya pressed, struggling to contain her shock.

"You were an effective ruler, and your noble heritage was clear. Disrupting your rule seemed unnecessary. Plus, misleading Redmont about my supposed contact with Edward was a strategic play," the king explained.

"I may have the proof you need of Redmont's treachery," Durya said, pulling the mirror from her pack and setting it on the table. The king raised an eyebrow as she invoked the mirror's magic.

The mirror's smoke cleared, revealing Redmont pacing in his room. *"Not long,"* the man muttered to himself. *"the king is probably dead by now."* A sinister laugh echoed in the background before fading. Redmont, confused, called out, *"Dark lady, here are you? I need your guidance."*

"See?" Durya urged.

"Interesting," the king mused. "But magic is too easily manipulated. It's not conclusive evidence." Durya's shoulders slumped.

"Relax, Lady Durya," the king began, reassurance in his tone. "While your magical evidence is inconclusive, I have other—"

Their conversation was interrupted by another minister, who entered and whispered something to the king. After a nod of acknowledgment, the king dismissed the man. Turning to Durya, he said with an air of surprise, "You've brought an army to my doorstep, Lady Durya?"

Durya's mind was reeling. Thorlyn and Marcus were only meant to rally the Aelorians for protection. "It was solely for your safety," she explained, her voice tinged with panic.

The king's smile broadened. "Fear not, Lady. They merely match the forces Redmont has mustered. But I must admit, you've surprised me. I've had my own plans in motion, and Redmont is quite the pawn. He's likely being arrested as we speak."

Durya's eyes widened with renewed interest. She drew the mirror closer, eager to observe every detail that might unfold within its mystical frame.

As the guards stormed into Lord Redmont's chambers, the scene in the mirror intensified. Redmont, in a state of panic, called out for Javina's aid, but his voice echoed unanswered in the opulent room. The guards, unwavering, seized him, his mystical attempts to summon Javina proving futile.

The king's lips curled into a small smile as Durya stowed the mirror away. "Magic may not be admissible, but that was a satisfying scene," he remarked. Durya chuckled in response.

Turning to Hensworth, the king inquired, "And you, are you an ally in this?" Hensworth introduced himself, stating his title. "Ah yes," the king nodded. "I am well acquainted with your father. Your loyalty shall not go unrewarded."

He then focused back on Durya. "Let's proceed with officially transferring the title to your name, separate from Edward's. And Marshfield too." Durya hesitated. Public recognition from the king was all she had ever wanted, yet now she had Kaci to consider. The king, noting her hesitation, tilted his head. "Is this not what you desire?"

"It's just..." Durya began, but the king cut her off. "Take tonight to organize your thoughts. We can discuss your decision in the morning." He then instructed the under-minister to arrange accommodations for Lord Hensworth and Lady Conwin. Durya noticed he used her maiden name, a gesture she appreciated.

As they prepared to leave, the king leaned in and whispered to Durya, "I knew Edward as a boy. Suffice to say, the world is better without him. If you repeat this, I will deny it."

In the guest room, Lady Durya lay on the plush bed, her mind a whirlwind of thoughts. The ear of the king, the recognition she craved, had always been her goal—a testament to her capability as an orc, a Conwin, to lead and excel. Yet now, these achievements paled compared to her current turmoil. Kaci was trapped in Kashara. Fia had offered further mentorship, and Sharn was gone. Elyndris felt distant now.

Bound by duty to her people, to Kaci, and even to Fia, Durya was engulfed in an ocean of sentiment. Her past, both stolen and reclaimed, whispered tales of suffering and endurance. In the realm of her orcish lineage and the human courts of Elyndris, revealing one's vulnerabilities was an unspoken taboo. Yet, in the sanctuary of solitude, the facade of invincible strength that Durya had upheld crumbled.

Her tears, no longer restrained, flowed, carving rivers of sorrow for her lost memories. She wept for Marcus' departure in her youth, for Sharn's absence, and for Kaci's uncertain fate. Each drop was a release, a surrender to her deepest emotions. This was her moment to exist not as a leader, a warrior, or a tactician, but as Durya, unguarded and profound in her sorrow.

Her hair, damp with tears, clung to her cheeks as she surren-dered to her grief. Memories fluttered about her — echoes of childhood, of laughter, and dreams left unvoiced.

She had spent her life wearing one mask after another, one

that mirrored the ragged edges of her heart, too vast for the body it lived in. Her scars, often hidden beneath layers of strength and defiance, now lay bare. In this moment, there was only room for her raw emotions and dreams, yet unfulfilled.

As Durya's initial wave of tears subsided, a new, more intense anguish erupted within her. It was a fierce tempest unleashing its fury upon her very being. This storm raged, a clash of emotions pounding against her heart, each wave a reminder of her struggles and losses. But as storms do, it waned, leaving a trail of calmness in its wake. The last tear that slid down her cheek was a symbol of this tranquility. A gentle raindrop. It marked not an end, but the dawn of her true journey towards healing and acceptance. In this moment of peace, Durya was cleansed, her spirit reborn.

17

A New Dawn

Dawn's light crept over the horizon, casting a golden hue over the city as it awoke to the day of Lord Redmont's trial. The intervening weeks had passed in a haze. In the lull, the city found its heartbeat again, thrumming with the daily affairs of its people. Marcus, King Thorlyn, Lady Elara, and Lord Hensworth took on advisory roles, navigating the complexities of governance with the king and other ministers.

As the city stirred to life beneath them, Durya knew that the day's events would be historical. The trial was not just about Lord Redmont's fate. It would show the kingdom that had weathered the siege and emerged, perhaps not unscathed, but stronger in its unity and purpose. The air was thick with anticipation, for the decisions made this day would ripple through time, affecting generations to come.

Durya found her interactions with the king enlightening. Once perceived as frivolous, she now saw a man of character and strategy, someone she might even call a friend. His ability to be cruel, calculating, yet generous when necessary was a skill she recognized in herself. When Durya expressed her wish to relinquish her leadership roles, the king showed disappointment but understanding. She wondered if he ever longed for a simpler life.

The grand judgment hall of Etharion was alive with a thrumming energy, as courtiers and commoners alike filled the chamber. High arched windows cast beams of light that danced with the dust motes, bathing the crowd in a soft, golden light.

"Lord Redmont of Westerfield," the king's voice echoed, "you are accused of treason. How do you plead?"

Redmont, a mere wisp of the man he once was, looked defeated. His voice, now a frail whisper, asserted his innocence.

The king prompted him to elaborate. Redmont, standing straighter, made his case. "I acted out of love for my people. The real traitor here is her!" he accused, pointing at Durya.

Durya remained calm, having expected this turn. In the past, such accusations would have sparked her anger, but now her mind was occupied with deeper concerns. She and the king both knew her true intentions. Despite his warnings that her stepping down might be misconstrued as guilt, Durya was indifferent. Her thoughts were already far beyond the reach of this court and its proceedings.

"Thank you for your testimony." The king's face remained unreadable, his expression unchanging as he listened to Redmont's claim. "Now present evidence of this alleged treason."

Durya felt reassured by the king's neutrality, but feared any definitive proof of Edward's murder.

As Redmont called Liana Blackwood to the stand, her dark hair was as immaculate as ever. She curtsied to the king and began her testimony with confidence.

"Your Highness, I have seen Lady Durya in the company of an Orc guard, Sharn, on several occasions." Liana detailed their visits to various establishments and their training sessions in the courtyard, painting a vivid picture of an illicit affair while Edward was bedridden.

Durya, observing Liana's performance, noted the lack of surprise. Redmont's manipulation of Liana was evident, but her testimony's flaw was clear—she spoke as if Edward were alive during these events, unaware of his true fate. This discrepancy piqued Durya's interest, revealing a crack in Redmont's otherwise meticulously crafted tale.

"An affair hardly constitutes treason, Lord Redmont," the king retorted, his voice dry but his gaze icy. "Such matters are better suited for letters, not armies."

"But I feared she had enchanted you with her sorcery!" Redmont blurted out in defense.

The king's laughter echoed in the hall, undermining Redmont's desperate claim. He motioned for Redmont to continue.

Redmont, flustered, scrambled to present further 'evidence.' He produced letters written by Durya, detailing plans against the king—documents that were forged. The king's skepticism grew with each piece of Redmont's evidence, each more desperate than the last.

After Redmont's final, feeble attempt at evidence, the king asked if he had anything more to present. Redmont, defeated, replied no. Durya, observing, couldn't help but feel a shiver of fear. She knew that if Javina's influence had prevailed, she might have been in Redmont's place.

The king's spymaster stepped forward, unveiling damning evidence against Redmont. It included communications and transactions implicating him in treacherous plots. Finally, the king highlighted the most unmistakable evidence of all—the armies Redmont had brought to the kingdom's gates. Having heard the case, the king found Redmont guilty of treason and sentenced him to death at dawn.

"This trial is now concluded," the king declared, rising from his throne. He gestured to the guards, who escorted Redmont away to his holding cell. "I will address the citizens of Elyndris at midday tomorrow," he stated, then turned and exited the hall.

As the crowd dispersed, a collective sigh filled the Judgment Hall. Durya, feeling lighter, turned toward Marcus, who gave her hand a reassuring squeeze. "I need to refresh myself before our meeting this afternoon," she said.

Marcus responded with an understanding nod. "Take the time you need," he reassured her. "I'll see you then."

Lady Durya chose not to return to her quarters, instead opting to explore the palace grounds. As she walked, the surrounding people still kept their distance, but they would offer a nod or a curtsy.

Her recent endorsement by the king had shifted perceptions, marking a pivotal moment where an orc was chosen over a human. To Durya, this minor act symbolized a significant step towards acceptance and unity within Etharion. She felt a sense of fulfillment, knowing that a future where differences were celebrated was possible. This realization made her impending departure somewhat easier.

After some time, she found herself in the grand library, reminiscent of the one she had visited before in the warrens beneath Aeloria. She felt a pang in her heart when she thought of Kaci and hoped her friend was okay. As she wandered up and down the long rows of books, she wondered if she had time to find a quiet corner to read. But before she could even choose something to read, a young attendant approached her and bobbed a curtsy. "Lady Durya, your presence is requested in the grand council."

Where had the time gone? It couldn't already be time for the council meeting. But it was, and she gave a slight nod, following the child to the great room.

The room had been redecorated with symbols of unity, representing the diverse cultures of Elyndris. A depiction of Arba Vitae to represent the Aelorians, a great mountain with wings behind for the Earthborn, even a few orcish tribal depictions (done in oil, and likely painted by a human), but she appreciated the sentiment.

In attendance, aside from the king, were Marcus; King Thorlyn of the Earthborn; Saeryn, the new Aelorian leader; along with Lady Elara and Lord Hensworth.

The meeting had already begun as Durya slipped into a seat that had been set aside for her. The king was discussing strategies for future governance, emphasizing greater inter-action with the neighboring Aelorians and Earthborn. He also proposed extending these diplomatic efforts to include orcs and goblins, fostering a more inclusive realm. When he finished his thought, he welcomed Durya.

"Welcome, my lady. I was just discussing some ideas I had for Elyndris moving forward. As Baroness of Westerfield, I would like you included in the input."

Durya blushed. The king had already known she would not accept this role, but he insisted she make the announcement in public.

Durya stood, bowing deeply, and spoke, her voice clear. "Your Highness, while I am honored by the official recognition, I must humbly decline this position. May I suggest Lady Elara Pendegras as a replacement? She is a cousin of my Lord

Edwards and would be next in line for succession."

The king inclined his head. "While we are deeply sorrowful that you decline. We welcome Lady Elara as the new Baroness of Westerfield. And, while you no longer hold the land, we welcome you to keep your title as an honorary symbol of our appreciation."

Then he continued, "On that note, Lord Marcus and I have spoken in great depth. He has abdicated from Marshfield and has been offered a newly deemed position in my court as ambassador of the lands. He will be my liaison between all the societies, cultures, and areas of Elyndris."

Marcus was glowing. He had always had a way with people, possessing a much milder temper than hers. He would never have fared well in the tribe they were born into, but he had such a deep understanding of people, not to mention his talent for magic. She couldn't have been happier for him.

However, his new role left a gap in leadership for Marshfield, the home of her childhood. Lady Evelyn and Lord Maxwell had no other living relatives. Her father had been such a wise man; his loss devastated her.

As she opened her mouth to speak, the king smiled and interrupted, "Lord Hensworth and his progeny will henceforth be known as Marshfield."

Lady Durya smiled. He had a family with children who would love playing on the grounds. Though he might appear soft on the outside, Hensworth had proven his worth tenfold. The king couldn't have chosen a better man.

The king's voice resonated through the grand council room, marking the end of their assembly. "Then this concludes our business here. I will meet with each of you individually as needed, but I expect all of you to be present tomorrow at the execution. After which, I will address the people."

His words carried a weight that filled the room with a palpable sense of gravity. The execution, a grim but necessary act in the eyes of the king, was a reminder of the stringent laws that governed Etharion. It was a somber event, yet essential in maintaining the order and peace of the realm.

As the council members rose from their seats, the atmosphere was one of contemplation. The reality of their duties, often entangled with harsh decisions, was a burden they all shared. Their presence was important at the execution. Not just as witnesses to justice being served, but also as a show of unity and strength in front of the kingdom's populace.

* * *

The next morning, the castle hummed with whispers. Instead of seeking the gossip herself, Lady Durya summoned her closest allies to her sitting room. In the company of Marcus, Elara, and Hensworth, they enjoyed a moment of camaraderie over tea.

A soft knock interrupted them. "Enter," Durya called.

Jeth, the goblin, slipped in, whispering to Durya. "Redmont has vanished. No holes, no exits, and guards were present."

Durya's face tightened. She sensed this wasn't the last they'd heard of Redmont.

Her companions speculated on the implications.

Elara raised an eyebrow. "No execution then?"

Durya nodded. "The king will have plans. We'll attend the

courtyard at midday."

Lord Hensworth reminded them it was nearing midday. As they arrived, the courtyard unfolded before them, vibrant with colors and life. The centerpiece was a grand balcony draped with regal banners, where the king stood in his royal attire. Elevated above the crowd, his majestic presence commanded attention from all present.

Below, on a lower balcony, Durya and her group were positioned in a place of honor. The king's acknowledging nod to them bridged the distance, a silent gesture of mutual respect.

As the crowd hushed in anticipation, the king addressed the assembly. His voice, clear and resonant, carried across the courtyard. He revealed Redmont had been executed in the night, a decision made to transform this gathering from a somber event into a celebration. Then continued:

"Today, as your king, I stand before you at the dawn of a new era, an era illuminated by the light of unity and strengthened by the bonds of diversity. Our kingdom, rich in history and culture, has long been a tapestry woven with many threads. It is time we embrace the beauty of each strand."

"We have faced challenges, both from within and beyond our borders. These trials have tested our resolve, but more importantly, they have opened our eyes to the strength found in our differences. Let us not forget that diversity is not a weakness; it is our greatest asset."

"I stand here to acknowledge and honor our fellow Elyndrians: the orcs, goblins, Aelorians, Earthborn, and Humans. You are not just residents of this kingdom; you are its pillars, its heart, and its soul. Each of you brings unique perspectives, skills, and traditions that enrich our land. From the industrious goblins to the wise Aelorians, the valiant orcs to the resilient

Earthborn, you all are equals in Elyndris."

"In recognition of this unity, it is my honor to introduce new leadership that reflects the diverse tapestry of our kingdom. Lord Marcus, an orc of great valor and wisdom, shall continue to serve as an advisor to the crown, symbolizing our commitment to inclusivity. He will be a bridge between cultures, will assume the role of ambassador, fostering communication and understanding among all our people."

"We stand together at the precipice of change. It is a path that requires courage, understanding, and an unwavering commitment to one another. Let us walk this path together, not as separate races or classes, but as Elyndrians, united under the banner of mutual respect and shared prosperity."

"To a future where each child can look up to the skies of Elyndris with hope and know that they, too, have a place in our great world. A future where our realm is celebrated for all its colors and patterns."

"Thank you, and may the light of unity guide us all."

As the king concluded his speech, a resounding cheer erupted from the crowd, signifying their approval and hope. Gradually, the people dispersed, resuming their daily routines. Durya, contemplating the momentous occasion, felt a deep confidence in Elyndris' path to peace and joy.

She had always preferred brief farewells and had discreetly packed her belongings the night before. The goblin Jeth had already taken them to the docks. As the nobles continued their celebrations, Durya seized the moment to slip away. She exchanged a knowing glance with Marcus, who tilted his head in understanding as she made her way out and toward the Gull.

At the docks, Aanee and Belan stood waiting for Lady Durya. The air was filled with the scent of the sea and the promise of uncharted journeys. Belan, his eyes holding centuries of wisdom, acknowledged Durya. "Every journey shapes the soul, Lady Durya. As you chase the winds of fate, may your heart find it's true north."

Captain Aanee, her back against the ship's railing, flashed a wide grin that seemed to light up her face. "Well, let's not dawdle then!" she exclaimed, with a spark in her eyes. "The sea waits for no one, and neither do legends. Kashara won't know what hit it!" Her words, full of life, sliced through the solemnity that hung in the air.

Around her, the crew moved with a sense of purpose, their actions mirroring Aanee's voice. Lady Durya stepped aboard the Gull, each footfall resonated with anticipation. As the sails unfurled, blooming like giant petals against the sky, they caught the wind and the ship began its journey towards the dark shores of Kashara.

About the Author

Beth Connor is an imaginative storyteller who has a passion for the many forms of this art. She thrives on exploring the depths of human emotion, crafting intricate characters and weaving them into compelling narratives that transport her readers and listeners to other worlds.

Beth's creative pursuits are a reflection of her life philosophy, and she is always searching for new ways to expand her knowledge and understanding of the world. She has a remarkable ability to create vivid, dynamic settings that resonate with her audience.

Beth's talent has earned her recognition as the author of several published works, including the captivating novels "Hollow City" and "Micah and the Candles of Time," as well as a contributor to "Whispers in the Mycelium." Beth is also an accomplished audiobook narrator and the host of the popular podcast, "Crossroads Cantina."

You can connect with me on:

🌐 https://www.bethconnor.com

f https://www.facebook.com/jbethconnor

Subscribe to my newsletter:

✉ http://gem.godaddy.com/signups/7b841d4930e44c349e3a8857438
join

Also by Beth Connor

Micah and the Candles of Time

An introduction to the world of Isdralan: Twelve-year-old Micah Murphy, uprooted to a dull new town and feeling abandoned by his friends, goes on an exploratory kayaking trip only to find himself lost in the mysterious world of Isdralan. As he navigates a realm where trust is as elusive as the shifting shadows, Micah must confront secrets that challenge his very future and find a way back home, or risk being trapped in Isdralan's embrace forever.

Prodigy of Flame

Follow Kaci, ostracized for her uncontrolled fiery powers, sets off on a quest through a world darkened by malevolent forces spewing from mysterious portals. Alongside a diverse trio of companions, she discovers her true potential and battles the spreading corruption, transforming her journey of survival into a quest for self-discovery and a fight to ignite the flame within.

The Golden Gull

"The Golden Gull" weaves an anthology of adventure across time and reality, from the depths of the Caves of Chaos to encounters with ancient deities and poignant romances. As Raama, the survivor of a shipwreck, explores the ship's legacy through mystical orbs, he confronts the possibility of fate's manipulation, learning that true peace lies in acceptance, not alteration. This collection invites readers on a profound journey to discover the expanse of imagination and the strength within.